Dear Readers,

This month, celebrate Mother's Day with the best kind of treat—four new love stories from Bouquet. Then again, *any* day is the right day to read romance. . . .

Marcia Evanick, veteran Silhouette and Loveswept author, starts off this month with the first in the three-book Wild Rose series, **Wife in Name Only,** in which a marriage undertaken for the sake of the children becomes a surprisingly passionate union. Next up, the talented Jacquie D'Alessandro offers **Kiss the Cook,** the charming tale of a determined caterer—and the sexy financial whiz who tempts her to turn up the heat in her kitchen.

Adam's Kiss, from another promising new author, Patricia Ellis, takes us to a Wisconsin farm, where a dispute between neighbors becomes a kiss across the fence . . . and maybe much more. Tracy Cozzens wraps up the month with her latest book for Zebra, **Seducing Alicia,** the suspenseful story of a scientist who finds herself falling for an unexpected man—without any idea that her new beau may not be exactly what he seems.

Feel the thrill of tenderness and tears, desire and delight. And when you sit back with the four breathtaking Bouquet romances this month, remember to enjoy!

Kate Duffy
Editorial Director

ROMANCE

CHEMICAL REACTION

"This isn't wise, Alicia."

"It may become infected if we don't treat it." She gently finished bandaging his hand.

"I've been trying to keep my distance from you, but this isn't helping."

Alicia fought for a decent breath. "This . . . bothers you?"

His lips twitched. *"Bothered* isn't the word I'd use."

"Oh." Understanding dawned on her, shocking and exciting her. She was actually turning him on—simply by holding his hand! Amazing. To her knowledge, she'd never had that effect on a man before. It was a revelation, giving her a surge of feminine confidence she had never felt. Danger alarms went off in her brain in a futile effort to remind her to keep her place, to stay decorous and professional. She ignored them, her fascination outweighing her uncertainty.

That look on his face . . . His emerald eyes burned with intensity, need and desire mingling—there, because of *her.* "It's really hard for you to believe, isn't it?" he said, a touch of amazement in his voice. "What makes you think you're so damned unappealing?" His thumb traced the angle of her jaw, sending spikes of delicious awareness through her. An amazing sense of freedom filled her as his lips came within a centimeter of hers. . . .

SEDUCING ALICIA

TRACY COZZENS

Zebra Books
Kensington Publishing Corp.
http://www.zebrabooks.com

ZEBRA BOOKS are published by

Kensington Publishing Corp.
850 Third Avenue
New York, NY 10022

Zebra and the Z logo Reg. U.S. Pat. & TM Off.

First Printing: May, 2000
10 9 8 7 6 5 4 3 2 1

Printed in the United States of America

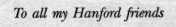

To all my Hanford friends

ONE

"Mind if I empty your wastebasket?"

Dr. Alicia Underwood came instantly alert at the sound of the unfamiliar male voice. She wasn't expecting visitors, and no one gained access to the Envirotech building without a badge.

Oh, yes. Helen had mentioned something about a new janitor. A *sexy* new janitor. Just a little curious to see if the guy could possibly live up to his reputation, Alicia paused in her mental calculations long enough to glance up from her computer.

He stood inside her office door, a warm smile on his face. Medium height, powerfully built. Classic features. Short wavy hair the color of beach sand. Flawless tan.

Instantly, all her senses went on full alert.

Alicia forced her gaze back to her computer, mentally chastising herself. Yes, it was a man. In her office. A few feet away. So what?

She knew dozens of men. So what if he was a little nicer-looking than most, a little more . . . masculine, with a body deserving of a Greek statue? One body was the same as another. They were all designed to function the same. This unusual physical response she was undergoing—shallow breathing, pounding heart, awareness of her own body—it was nothing but a basic biological reaction. Basic. That's all. A natural reaction to . . . *him*.

His image remained before her eyes, making it hard to focus on her computer monitor. No wonder her female coworkers couldn't stop talking. For once, Alicia understood why they'd been gossiping so much.

"Ma'am? I have to come around behind your desk to reach your wastebasket. I don't want to disturb you. I could come back another time. . . ." His accent was Kennedyesque New England, despite his California beach-boy looks. A fascinating contrast, especially here in a Seattle suburb.

"Go ahead. It's right here." She gestured to the wastebasket tucked near her feet. She kept it close at hand in the nest she'd created for herself—her desk facing the door, the adjacent computer table, the credenza against the wall.

Everything she needed was within reach, including her wastebasket. She'd never thought the arrangement might cause problems. Until now. The new janitor slipped behind her, his male bulk crowding her small space.

She scooted her chair against her desk to give him more room. He seemed to need every inch. There was just so *much* of him.

She gazed at him from the corner of her eye, noting details in as detached a way as her scientist's mind could manage, trying to understand her unsettling reaction to him. Thick biceps bunched below the short sleeves of his pale blue T-shirt. His back looked at least a meter across. Couldn't possibly be, but those delts—

Flashes of college anatomy loomed in her mind. He would make an excellent specimen for a course on musculature.

The janitor bent over the wastebasket, his face inches from her knees. He glanced up and his eyes clashed with hers. Alicia flushed at being caught staring.

Worse, at that angle, he could almost see up her tailored skirt. She clamped her knees together. He grinned, staying a second too long down there. Finally straightening, his eyes still on her, he dragged the plastic liner from her wastebasket and nearly emptied it on the beige carpet.

"Whoops! Almost lost it there."

His friendly remark required *some* kind of response, and Alicia automatically replied with a little laugh. Before he could attempt to engage her in small talk, she turned her pedestal chair around and hunched over her work. Work . . . What had she been working on? She could hardly remember. Why was the man lingering behind her?

She began flipping through her IN box to cover her confusion. The monthly financial report. The employee recreation newsletter, which she never read. A memo from President Fielding telling her to prepare a presentation on the alpha-gamma inversion ratio for the Board of Directors.

Of course. Results from the latest series of tests had to be analyzed ASAP.

Despite the fresh reminder of looming deadlines, Alicia couldn't help hearing every movement the janitor made. Peeking through her ebony bangs, she watched as he shook her trash into the bottom of her bag and secured it with a twist tie. The procedure finished, he settled a new liner in the wastebasket. He was much more exacting in his treatment of the trash than any janitor she'd ever seen, keeping each basket's contents in its own bag rather than dumping it all together into a pile in the janitorial cart. He must be new at this, he was being so overly careful.

Finally he slipped past her and toward the door, her trash bag secure in his hand. "Thank you, ma'am," he said before he left.

Alicia made a noncommittal sound. Keeping her eyes pinned to the president's memo, she resisted the urge to watch him go.

"Well, what did you think?" Helen entered her office before Alicia had a chance to start breathing again.

"About what?" she asked as casually as she could.

"Duh, what do you think I'm referring to, the weather?" Helen plunked her ample form in a chair across from Alicia. The other scientists on staff parceled out their casual time only to each other, but Alicia found their artificially created separation irritating and cold. In the past two years she had become good friends with Helen, a lab technician. Helen had been there for Alicia when her short-lived marriage had reached its not-so-merciful death.

In turn, Alicia was a patient listener when Helen wanted to gossip—usually about men. Helen, a bleached blonde in her mid-forties, had been around the block so often, she knew every crack in the sidewalk. She never hesitated to share her blatantly honest outlook on relationships—and men.

Right now, however, Alicia didn't have the slightest urge to talk. Not about him.

"Come on, isn't he a hunk? Did you see those arms?" Helen gave a long, low whistle. "I mean, I love Janelle and all, but as far as I'm concerned she can stay on maternity leave 'til her baby graduates college if that means we get to keep the 'Bod.' Talk about eye candy. Ooo-eee!"

Alicia sighed and neatly aligned the papers on her desk, hoping Helen would take the hint.

She didn't. Instead, she peered at Alicia as if she'd grown horns. "You do . . . notice what we're talking about, don't you? I mean, there's nothing physically wrong here, is there?"

Alicia sighed in exasperation. "No, there's nothing physically wrong with me. I just don't see what all the fuss is about. So, he goes to a gym regularly, and uses a tanning bed, by the look of it. A lot of people do. That doesn't mean I'm going to drool over him like a mindless idiot."

"Alicia! What about his *face?* Don't you think he puts Mel to shame? I love Mel, but he's married, after all, and—"

Mystified, Alicia glanced up. "Who?"

Helen stared at her like she'd lost her mind. "Mel Gibson."

At Alicia's confusion, Helen's thinly plucked eyebrows rose even higher. "The actor? From Australia? Oh, my God. You really *don't* know who he is, do you? When's the last time you went to the movies?"

"I don't know. What does it matter? Last December, I think. Leon took me to a foreign film festival." She'd done her best to be an entertaining companion as they'd sat through six hours in a dark theater. But her lack of physical responsiveness when they'd returned to her apartment had put a damper on the evening. Simply put, she was a social failure.

"Foreign film festival? Ugh!" Helen began to choke. Literally. Her hands wrapped around her own throat, she collapsed into the chair, legs flung out.

Alicia started to laugh. "The films were highly acclaimed."

Helen righted herself. "Yeah, right. I bet they all had subtitles and strange endings that didn't make sense."

"Well, some of them made sense. I think." Alicia had found more than a few utterly bewildering. Thank goodness Leon had been there to explain them—or at least his own theory behind each one.

Helen leaned forward, settling her elbows on Alicia's desk. "He's kind of young for me, and hey, I know he's got girls all over the place. Probably all skinny model types, too. But he was certainly nice to me when we chatted. His name is Jason Kirkland, and he's new to the area."

Vana's red head appeared in the doorway, and Alicia waved her in. "He lives on a sailboat! Isn't that cool?" Vana bounced on her toes, sending her mini-skirt dancing about her slender hips. "So exciting. *And* romantic."

"Vana, you, too?" Alicia said with mock exasperation. She didn't mind her coworkers' interest in the new janitor, as long as they didn't expect her to follow suit. Besides, of all of them, Vana was probably closest to this guy's type. Pretty and vivacious, interested in having fun, hanging out, whatever people in their twenties did these days.

I'm in my twenties, Alicia reminded herself with a shock. Twenty-seven. But around these two, she felt like a dorm mother.

"Yeah, me, too," Vana chirped. "Definitely me, too. Jason," she sighed. "Yum! Did you notice his *voice?* He sounds like that president, KFJ—"

"JFK," Helen supplied with a laugh. "Sure does. Definitely not from around here.

"I cornered him for a long time, and he fed me lots of interesting details," Vana continued, her expression turning dreamy. "Like the sailboat. He *lives* on one, on Lake Washington. Can you imagine having a boat rock you to sleep every night?"

"Sleep?" Helen snorted. "Who'd be sleeping, with all that nat-ur-al rhy-thm . . ." Helen's voice ended on a sultry singsong.

"Helen!" Alicia admonished, but they all laughed at her antics. Still, the idea of living on a sailboat *was* exotic. "So, how can a janitor afford a sailboat?" she asked skeptically.

Vana shrugged. "I think he said he's boat-sitting for some rich guy. He doesn't own it, but he gets to use it." She smiled perkily. "I kind of hinted that I'd be interested in a ride."

"Yeah, what kind of *ride*?" Helen asked suggestively.

"Helen!" Alicia admonished—again. It had become a game between them. Helen said the outrageous things everyone else only thought, and Alicia attempted unsuccessfully to keep Helen's mind out of the gutter. It was time for a dose of logic. She clasped her hands on her desk. "So, this guy's really just bumming off someone else, Vana. No assets of his own. Seems kind of old to be an entry-level janitor. I wouldn't get too excited about him."

"Why not?" Vana frowned at her. "I mean, I'm an administrative professional. I make good money. It's not like he'd need to earn megabucks. Not everyone has to be a workaholic like you, Alicia."

Alicia bit her lip, fighting down her irritation at the implied criticism. Yes, she worked late almost every night, and weekends. For years she had worked so hard toward her goal that it had become her entire life. She was no longer sure what the rest of the world expected of her, and she told herself it didn't matter. Nothing else mattered but preventing tragedy.

Besides, when she was absorbed in her project, she didn't feel the least bit lonely.

"Come on, Vana," Helen said. "You know she has to work hard, or your company stock options won't be worth the paper they're printed on." She rose and ushered Vana toward the door.

Alicia cast her a grateful smile. She and Helen had worked together long enough for Helen to know when Alicia was ready to retreat into her work.

"We'll catch up with you later, Doc. Vana and I are going to compare notes—and fantasies."

"Yeah. Well, don't get too wild or you'll scare the zookeepers," Alicia quipped, her mind already on the paperwork before her. She had to finish these administrative tasks—her least favorite part of the day—before she could retreat to her lab through the back door in her office, where the real work took place.

She sighed and flipped open the cover on the financial report, but she had a hard time concentrating on it. Images of the new janitor—and her coworkers' exuberant reaction to him—spun through her mind.

And just for a moment she wondered what it would feel like to worry about nothing more important than enjoying herself.

Jason Kirkland backed into the door of the utility room, pulling the janitorial cart along with him. Bottles of cleanser hung off the cart's side; paper towels, rags and brushes rested in a basket near the handle. All the tools of his new trade, close at hand.

Once inside, he palmed the light switch and shoved the cart into the corner.

The room was nothing more than a closet in the basement of the Envirotech building. The center of the cart was lined with a giant garbage bag, which contained the paper waste of two hundred office employees. A smaller bag tucked between the lining and the cloth wall of the cart contained the contents of Dr. Alicia Underwood's wastebasket.

Jason slipped out the bag and took it to a bench along one wall. There, he unscrewed the twist tie and shook the contents onto the bench's surface. He frowned. Not much. The lady doctor wasn't going to make his task easy. She was far too neat, and far too fond of her paper shredder. He'd noticed the demon machine in the corner of her office, just past her desk. He would have to defeat it.

Her recycle bin posed no problem. Every office had one. Usually the papers piled up until the box overflowed before the employees would get around to dumping them in the large recycle bags in the central work areas. He just might do the gentlemanly thing and offer to dump it for her.

Unfortunately, he'd noticed that Dr. Underwood's recycle box was remarkably empty. Either she emptied it more often than most employees, or she shredded virtually every piece of waste paper she produced.

Then, of course, there was the challenge of her computer, a typical PC-based system. He'd have to learn her password somehow, and log on when he was certain she wasn't going to be in the office. He shouldn't have any trouble. A few late-night visits and he'd have it mastered.

The laboratory itself was an entirely different matter. The fortress lay past Dr. Underwood's office, at the end of the third-floor hall. The double doors emblazoned with bright yellow-and-black radiation warning signs couldn't be breached without using a hand-geometry unit, which correlated a person's handprint with a typed-in code. He'd observed who had access. Staff scientists like Alicia, technicians like Helen and maintenance personnel.

Yet somebody cleaned the sinks and swept the floors. If not him, who?

If he couldn't find a legitimate way in, he'd have to engage in some serious breaking and entering, something he'd never attempted before.

Jason Kirkland grinned as he considered the risky task. He relished the sharp edge of awareness he attained when his safety—or his life—hung in the balance. Other men sought an adrenaline rush by racing cars, jumping from airplanes, living life too hard and too fast. He'd grown bored with all of those. The sensation never lasted; the emptiness always returned.

This time, the stakes were different. This time, he'd accomplish something worthwhile, right a serious wrong.

With a burst of irritation, he realized he was once again rationalizing his choice. It was past time for that. Instead, he focused on the day's "take." He pulled out a Nestlé wrapper and smoothed the slick paper. Nothing in Dr. Underwood's dossier mentioned that she liked chocolate.

What woman didn't? Still, the small detail was one of many that Henry's security experts had overlooked. Their report had described a hard-working genius, divorced after a two-year marriage to a college professor, now wed to her job.

Yet the report had failed miserably to prepare him for the real thing.

For instance, the washed-out mug shot of Dr. Underwood—taken for her security badge when she worked for his uncle's company—didn't begin to do her justice. He hadn't expected her to be a looker. Or so . . . *young*.

Of course, the dossier gave her age, so he knew

she was only twenty-seven, just two years younger than he was. But he'd expected a stiff woman with her hair in a bun and thick, heavy-framed glasses. He'd expected coldness, a look in her eyes or a tight set to her mouth that said *thief.*

Damn it all, she looked like Snow White.

Her short-cropped ebony pageboy framed perky features that made her seem young and guileless. And that full, slightly downturned mouth . . . Kissable. Very kissable.

Her face was only the start. When he'd been behind her desk, he'd gotten an eyeful of her sexy legs. She was a petite woman, but her legs were shaped like a model's. He could easily imagine them wrapped around a man's waist. . . .

Desire flared in his gut and he grimaced. He had to focus on his task. He found an empty box of microwavable lasagna and tossed it. Did the woman always eat at her desk? If she was that dedicated, why didn't she do her own damned research?

Dedicated didn't equal decent, he sternly reminded himself. She'd shielded the work on her desk almost as if she expected someone to steal it—just as *she* had.

He'd lingered behind her desk, trying to peer over her shoulder, doing his damnedest to learn something useful. Instead, all he'd noticed was her long, creamy neck. He'd had the crazy urge to slide his fingertips over her nape, to feel how soft her skin was. . . .

How would she have reacted to that? Probably panicked and slapped his face. A sardonic smile crossed his lips. With her all-work-and-no-play reputation, he wondered if she'd been kissed—really kissed—in a long while.

He shook his head, trying to clear away the distracting thoughts, and pulled out a yellow sticky note with six-digit numbers and Greek letters scratched on it. Scientific formulas, probably. Without any more information, the notes were useless. For the first time since graduating Princeton, Jason wished he'd paid more attention in science class.

A crumpled paper turned out to be a to-do list, the most exciting notation a reminder to pick up her dry cleaning. Jason set it with the formulas, since it included the name of the dry cleaner. It might come in handy.

If only he knew more about her . . . Perhaps he shouldn't be fighting his attraction to the woman. She'd seemed more than a little rattled by his visit to her office, and he would bet his classic Harley she wasn't immune to him, either.

Besides, getting to know Dr. Underwood better might help him uncover the information he was after.

Almost before the thought had completely formed, disgust swept through him. He'd never romanced a woman for any reason other than fun. Never intentionally used a woman. He had a few standards left, even if the lady in question was a thief.

His lips set in a grim line, he crumpled the candy bar wrapper into a wad and tossed it in the large trash bag. He knew the truth. She might look like Snow White, but Dr. Alicia Underwood was guilty as charged.

Alicia watched the clock on the wall, daring it to advance. This time she was mentally and physically prepared. Ten to nine. The janitor was due any minute.

Jason. His name is Jason and you know darned well it is. Yet she didn't want to give him a name. Didn't want to think of him as a person, instead of just an office fixture. Couldn't imagine striking up a casual friendship with this man, as she had with Janelle.

Perhaps because his mere presence was anything but casual.

She had timed him the last three days, and he always visited her office around nine. Of course, his arrival varied, depending on how long the other women in the office managed to detain him for casual conversation.

He came in at 9:13. Alicia kept her attention on her work, her back hunched as she copied her latest data sets into her log. She expected he'd get the message that she wasn't interested in chitchat. Nor was she interested in him at all. For goodness' sake, the way the women were acting around here, you'd think there'd been an accidental dose of estrogen in the water supply.

He reached behind her for her wastebasket, and an electric charge seemed to crackle in the air. His arm, peppered with golden hair, flexed as he grasped the plastic bag and pulled it out.

Realizing that her eyes were straying, she snapped them back to her logbook. As if a well-conditioned body warranted more than a casual glance! She had never been impressed with muscles. The muscle between the ears attracted her.

That was why Leon was such a valuable companion. They shared interests, enjoyed the same types of entertainment—renting documentaries, visiting museums, trading technical journals . . . Sometimes Leon seemed to want more, seemed to want to take their relationship past the platonic into the physical realm.

Once, she had hoped it might work, might finally ease the loneliness she often felt. But the few times Leon had kissed her, she'd felt so uncomfortable that it had caused a horrible awkwardness between them.

The last time he tried to embrace her, she'd given it a final chance. She'd tried to explain to him calmly and rationally that she had a problem, that she was overly sensitive—not like other women. Instead of understanding her, she had managed to cool his ardor, and they'd remained merely friends.

It didn't matter. Sex was nothing but a basic biological need, after all. She refused to worry about it, instead relying on her cerebral side, where she'd found a measure of success. She couldn't be missing much.

As Jason came out from behind her desk, he caught her eye. He stopped beside her chair and gazed down at her. At their first, unsettling meeting, she hadn't registered that his eyes were green, set off by thick, tawny lashes. Seductive eyes. Bedroom eyes.

His sculpted lips turned up in a lopsided, lady-killer smile. "Pretty busy today?"

Alicia never realized before how a man's mouth could invite intimacy, promise unspeakable delights. She mentally shook herself, angry at her involuntary reaction to his smile. Her own lips remained firmly straight. "There's nothing special about today. I'm busy every day."

"Yeah, you're the scientist, aren't you? The other girls told me about you."

"That's nice," she replied, not wanting to be rude. "But they're not *girls.*" That ought to put him in his place.

"Excuse me, ma'am," he said with persistent friendliness. "I didn't say that right. The other *women* said you're brilliant. A regular Einstein in a dress."

"That's an overstatement." Though the man had intended it as a compliment, Alicia shuddered inwardly at being compared to the wrinkled, frizzy-haired scientist. The comparison shouldn't bother

her, since her mind was all she had going for her. But it did, especially coming from this supremely physical male. She straightened a stack of papers, wishing he'd turn his potent gaze elsewhere. "They're also very good at what they do."

"Uh-huh." His eyes shifted from her face and focused over her shoulder.

Alert to the sensitivity of her project, Alicia threw her arm over her data log. "Did you want something?"

He gestured toward a gold-framed photo on her desk, a studio portrait of a three-year-old girl in ballet tights and a tutu. "Is that your daughter?"

Relief swept through her. *Calm down, Alicia. You should have known this guy wouldn't be looking at your lab notes. You're getting paranoid.* As her years of work neared fruition, Alicia found herself growing overly sensitive and possessive. But to be worried about the company *janitor*? She was losing it. He probably barely graduated high school. Maybe it *was* time for a few days off.

He propped his hands on his hips as if he meant to stay awhile, and she realized he was waiting for an answer. "No, that's my niece."

Jason swept the frame into his hand. "She's real cute. Does she live in Seattle?"

"No. Richland." He was determined to make conversation. Alicia wondered how this guy ever got his work done, considering how much he wanted to chat. And why did he bother trying to talk to her? There were plenty of other women at Envirotech dying to socialize with him. She eyed her data sets. She had critical deadlines to meet; the weight of the Wipe Clean Project grew heavier with each passing day. Still . . .

Her gaze slid sideways to his hips, less than a foot

away from her face. She had never noticed how well jeans could fit a man before. Snug in all the right places.

Her face began to heat and she forced her gaze back to the desk.

"Other side of the state, then."

"Hmm?" She yanked her gaze up to his.

"Richland. It's on the other side of the state."

"Yes." She rolled her chair hard against her desk and retrieved her pencil. "If you'll excuse me, I have work—"

"She your sister's kid?"

"Brother's."

"Do you visit often?"

"When I go on business trips I do. To Hanford, the largest nuclear cleanup project in the country. Where I hope to apply my work." She snatched the portrait from his hand and returned it to its proper spot on her desk.

"Oh, yeah. You're into cleanup, aren't you? Me, too. Guess that makes us colleagues, huh?" He chuckled, the deep sound alarmingly intimate in these business surroundings.

She sucked in a breath, fighting not to show her exasperation. "Yes, and if you'll excuse me, I really do have to get back to work."

"Hey, no problem." With his accent, it came out *prahblem*. He seemed to be waiting for her to look at him. When she finally did, he winked, gave her a cocky grin, then sauntered out of the office with her trash bag dangling from between his fingers.

He had *winked* at her. Alicia twirled her pencil in her fingers, trying to analyze why the wink should disturb her so. Certainly it bordered on sexism. She should be able to dismiss it as a meaningless distraction in an otherwise very full day. She shouldn't let it occupy her thoughts for more than a second.

Yet she was. For the first time in years, she wondered what a man saw when he looked at her.

TWO

Jason heard her voice before he passed the door of the ground-floor auditorium. He sensed the shuffle of feet and unobtrusive throat clearings that signaled an audience.

He parked his janitorial cart against the wall by the water fountain and peered inside. With the room lights out, the audience's attention centered on Dr. Underwood, illuminated by a lamp built into the podium. A projection screen behind her showed men in yellow radiation suits around fifty-five-gallon drums marked with radiation signs.

"While America was producing nuclear weapons to win the Cold War, we were also producing massive amounts of radioactive waste. Workers like these"— Alicia gestured to the screen—"are repackaging buried waste that was tossed into open pits during the mad rush to produce nuclear weapons. Unfortunately, storage is the only option where radioactive waste is concerned. Some forms, like plutonium, will continue emitting high levels of radiation for ten thousand years—longer than civilization has existed on this planet. Just one particle of plutonium ingested into a human being is fatal."

The sound of high heels tap-tapping on the tile

hall behind Jason put him on alert. He glanced around.

One of the executive secretaries hurried by with an armload of papers. He gave her a smile designed to melt feminine resistance. No go. She scowled at him, no doubt taking note of his idleness. Losing this job would really screw up his plans. In a flash, Jason pulled a bottle of cleanser from the side of the cart and began spraying the water fountain outside the auditorium door.

Pretty ironic that he was learning to clean things. He'd rarely cleaned anything before—unless he felt like it. Like washing and waxing his sleek, cherry-red race car. He'd babied that machine before he totaled it. He'd really believed it would corner the speedway doing two hundred . . .

He sighed. He shouldn't have pushed the limits, but at the time he couldn't help himself. He'd probably do the same thing today. Maybe if he'd really been smashed up, instead of crawling out of the flaming wreckage with only a few scratches and a dislocated shoulder . . .

His uncle called it living a charmed life. Considering the stunts Jason had pulled in the past few years, it was amazing he was still alive.

Yeah, he'd given Uncle Henry more than a little heartache over the years, but he would soon make it up to him. As soon as he got his hands on the research Dr. Underwood had pilfered.

The lady doctor's voice spilled into the hallway, persuasive, fervent. "Our Wipe Clean Project will make all the difference. It removes radiation from a surface, absorbing it into itself, leaving the surface free of harmful levels of radiation. Nuclear waste will be a thing of the past."

Jason continued to listen to her impassioned

speech while he wiped down the water fountain with a soft cloth. He found himself wondering if the lady doctor would be that passionate about anything else . . . like lovemaking. He shook his head, exasperated with himself He had no intention of finding out.

With a final wipe, Jason tucked the cloth into his hip pocket and wandered once again to the open doorway.

An audience member's hand shot up. He listened as Dr. Underwood fielded a technical question, and realized she was speaking to potential investors. She explained that Envirotech was in the final testing phases and about to apply for a patent.

Jason's fists clenched. While his uncle's company, Bio-Intera, went down the tubes, Dr. Underwood and this company would profit. The money meant nothing to him, but Bio-Intera was all Uncle Henry had. Dr. Underwood had worked at Bio-Intera long enough to learn about the company's amazing breakthrough. Then she'd left, taking all the data and business-sensitive findings with her. The information had paved the way for her own success.

Jason stared hard at the woman in question. There was no way in hell he would let her get away with it.

As Envirotech President Bruce Fielding began to speak, Alicia gazed out over the dozen potential investors watching their presentation. The research had proved expensive, but she had spent every penny wisely. Every cent brought her one step closer to her goal.

Movement at the back of the room drew her gaze. A wide-shouldered body in the doorway blocked the light from the hall. The new janitor. Jason.

Her mouth went dry as she stared at him. He stood with his arms folded across his expansive chest, his gaze clinging to her, his expression unreadable in the semidarkness. He actually seemed interested in the talk. But why would a janitor be—

"Doctor?"

She started, realizing someone had directed a question at her. "Excuse me?" She shifted awkwardly. "I'm afraid I missed—"

"People. Their accidental exposure to radiation doses. What about—"

"Yes, yes. I'm glad you brought that up." Alicia swallowed hard, trying to block the sudden image of her mother's jaundiced, wasted face from her mind long enough to answer the question. Yet she was eager to discuss the project closest to her heart. "I'm beginning research into engineering a strain of bacteria that would be harmless to a host, such as a human, yet absorb overdoses of radiation. Someday, I hope no one need ever experience radiation sickness. Or side effects from medical radiation treatments that harm the person they are meant to cure."

She knew her voice reflected her bitterness, and she clenched the podium, fighting to remain professional, to keep her pain from becoming apparent to the audience. They didn't have to know what drove her. No one did. "But that's in the future. Cleaning waste stored in tanks, retired reactors, or clothing worn by radiation workers—that's our immediate goal; one we've almost reached, I might add."

Amazed murmurs filled the room.

President Fielding, a heavyset man in his fifties, jumped to his feet and began his sales pitch. Alicia shifted her feet. Her ankles hurt from the high heels she'd slipped on just for this show. She'd made presentations numerous times over the years, for inves-

tors, for the Board of Directors, even on occasion for
select members of the media. She didn't enjoy public
speaking, didn't feel comfortable here, as she did in
her lab.

She glanced toward the door again. Jason was still
standing there when the lights came on. The auditorium could hold two hundred, so he was a good distance away. Yet over the heads of the investors and
the empty seats, their gazes connected. A slow smile
curled over his lips.

A strange feeling began in the pit of her stomach
as she tried to decipher the meaning of his expression. He appeared almost . . . predatory.

She swallowed hard, thankful he wasn't any closer
to her, or she might—what?

At Bruce Fielding's urging, she stepped down from
the podium and was instantly surrounded by tailor-
dressed, wealthy men, more than a few of whom were
attractive, many of them Japanese or European.

Yet her attention remained on the jeans-clad janitor, of all people. Unable to concentrate on the bar-
rage of questions thrown at her, she forced herself
to look away from him.

When she next looked toward the doorway, he was
gone.

Alicia slipped the bright orange box out of her office refrigerator. Funny how the actual contents of
the frozen meal never looked like the photo on the
box. Oh, well. At least she'd remembered to eat
lunch today. She popped the dinner into the microwave and turned it on.

This afternoon, she planned to begin the next bat-
tery of radiation tests on the bacteria. So far, all signs
were positive for the alpha and beta radiation tests.

As for intense gamma radiation, which only several feet of lead could block, there were lingering questions about potentially mutating the bacteria, which would make her discovery useless where it was most needed.

"Hey, Doc! Stick that box back in the fridge! You're going to lunch with us."

Helen stood at the door, purse in hand.

"I am?" Alicia didn't remember making a lunch date.

"You sure are. The whole group's going. Don't you remember? I mentioned it yesterday. Come on, we're all waiting on you."

Alicia automatically opened her mouth to explain that she had too much work to do, but Helen's challenging glare froze her in place.

"Not this time, Doc. No excuses. This is a special occasion."

"Right." She smiled weakly. "Sorry I forgot." She turned off the microwave and tossed out the half-baked stroganoff, then pulled her purse from her desk drawer. As usual, she was embarrassingly oblivious to the social life around her. "Um . . . What *is* the occasion? Again?" she asked as she slipped out the door behind Helen.

"Our new employee. The bio-rad department is taking him to lunch." Helen led the way down the hall toward the bank of elevators almost at a run.

"Who?" Alicia had a feeling she knew to whom Helen was referring. Mindless dread mingled with foolish anticipation in the pit of her stomach.

Sure enough, Helen's hazel eyes lit up as she shot over her shoulder, "Jason Kirkland, yummy janitor, of course."

At the elevator, Vana waited, talking animatedly with . . . him. My God, she'd have to face him, engage in conversation with him, and hope her unaccountable nervousness in his presence didn't show.

He grinned at her, his mesmerizing eyes shining. Alicia groaned inwardly. She had hoped her reaction to him would fade over time. Today was Monday, the start of a fresh work week. But the weekend had done nothing to dull his impact.

The four of them entered the elevator. Somehow she managed to be standing right beside Jason. His arm—bare from the biceps down—brushed against hers while he smiled down at her. She rewarded him with a shy smile. *He's not pursuing you, Alicia, so chill.* The guy undoubtedly had dozens of girlfriends—not that she cared. He hardly considered her potential date material, so there was no reason for her to be concerned about what he might think of her, much less to be nervous around him. Not a single logical reason.

He smells so good! A man's fragrance—a subtle musk—teased her nostrils. Many of the executives she worked with used cologne, but she had never experienced any kind of reaction to it, unless they overdid it, aggravating her olfactory glands. But on him . . . The word *pheromones* jumped to mind, scents used by animals in the wild to attract each other. Some biologists believed humans were affected by similar scents.

He bought it in a bottle, she sternly reminded herself. Yet, mingled with his own natural male scent, it was beyond delicious.

"Ladies first."

Lost in the world of scent, Alicia hadn't noticed when the elevator came to a stop. Vana and Helen were already waiting in the foyer. Jason held back, holding the doors open for her to exit.

"Oh, sorry." She stepped out, relieved to put some distance between them.

The four of them walked two blocks to a small Italian eatery and crowded around an outdoor table that usually sat two. Again, Jason ended up next to her. His shoulders were so broad, she found her own bumping into his repeatedly. She began to grow more used to touching him but soon discovered that looking him in the eye was a major mistake.

It happened when he asked her what she was ordering. Naturally she glanced at him, and found his face inches from hers. Was he leaning toward her on purpose, or just sitting at an angle? "Uh . . . spaghetti and a Caesar salad."

"That's exactly what I'm having," he said. "What a remarkable coincidence." A slow, intimate smile spread over his face, making tiny crinkles at the outer corners of his deep emerald eyes. Alicia felt his gaze clear to the toe seams of her panty hose.

She snapped her eyes away. Snatching up her iced tea, she took a hard swallow, wishing it was something much stronger—like whiskey. She rarely drank hard liquor, but in this case she'd make an exception. She felt more nervous than a cat about to be dunked in a bathtub.

"So, Jason, what's the deal? Are you married? Engaged? Dating, looking, gay, bi—what?" Helen's point-blank query drew everyone's attention, and also their laughter.

Jason took it in stride. "Single white male. Definitely hetero. I have my eye on a special someone."

Without facing him directly, Alicia knew his gaze had turned straight on her as he finished his sentence. He couldn't mean *her*.

"I *see* . . ." Helen replied, her voice laden with innuendo.

Please, Helen, don't say anything about it. Alicia sent a pleading look her way but couldn't tell if Helen noticed. If Helen turned her razor-sharp wit to suggestions about the two of them becoming some sort of couple . . . The idea was ridiculous. Perhaps if she'd been the only woman on the planet . . .

"Maybe I can show you around," Vana said, less bubbly than usual as her gaze jumped between Alicia and Jason. "Since you're new to the area."

"That'd be great."

Where *had* he come from? Funny how little anyone knew about this man—even though they were all ready to bear his children, Alicia thought. It was up to her as the levelheaded one to gather some concrete facts. "So, Jason, where were you living before you moved here?"

"The Caribbean. A small island there."

"With the sailboat?" Alicia probed. "I hear you're living on a boat someone else owns—"

Helen cut her off. "The Caribbean! So *that's* where you got your tan," she said appreciatively to Jason. "The question is, how much of you is tanned? I can just see you making use of those isolated beaches, *au naturel.*"

At Helen's outrageous remark, Vana emitted a small squeak. To his credit, Jason appeared embarrassed.

Alicia fought down the tantalizing image of Jason in the buff lying on a white-sand beach and steered the conversation to a safe topic—the weather. "You won't get much of a tan under Seattle's gray skies. Especially in the winter."

"I may not be here then."

"Aww," Vana said, her pink-stained lips drawing into a pout. "Why not?"

He shrugged and winked at her. "Depends how lucky I get."

Vana and Helen laughed at his provocative remark, but Alicia noticed how cagey he was where hard facts were concerned. She began to wonder if he was hiding something. "So, what do you do when you're not . . . janitoring?"

"Whatever strikes my pleasure." He rolled the last word off his tongue, as if it tasted delicious. "It's summer, so I water-ski, take the sailboat out, scuba dive, go rock-climbing, that sort of thing."

"Is *that* all?" Helen snorted. "No wonder you're so buff." She ran her hand over Jason's forearm where it rested on the table.

Alicia pulled in a deep steadying breath as irritation surged through her. *Nothing* embarrassed Helen, but this was going too far. Helen and Vana were treating Jason like some kind of sex god. She had no desire to become a disciple. Jason "Sexy Janitor" Kirkland was about to find out that not *all* the women of the Envirotech bio-rad department were drooling over him. Some looked for qualities in their men other than big biceps and lady-killer smiles.

"So, Jason, do you have any larger dreams?" Unconsciously, she began circling the rim of her iced-tea glass with her fingertip. She slid her wet finger into her mouth and sucked off the moisture. "I mean, other than being a janitor for Envirotech until Janelle returns."

Jason froze, every muscle in his far-too-handsome face going rigid.

She must have touched a nerve, but she wasn't about to back down. She usually lived and let live, wasn't at all inclined to belittle other people's life choices. But this man—for some reason she didn't understand, it drove her crazy that he wasn't making the most of his obvious gifts. "Well? What are your plans?"

He exhaled slowly, and his shoulder slid up in a shrug. Alicia couldn't help noticing the way his muscles moved. Fluid, like a finely honed machine. "Something will come along," he finally said. "Something always does."

Finding his answer ridiculously simplistic, she arched an eyebrow. "You mean you just let it happen?"

He turned the full power of his attention on her. "Yes. I just let life happen. Why not?"

"Well, for one thing, most people find the world a cold, harsh place. What makes you so different?"

"Maybe it's all in the attitude." This time, his smile was challenging, rather than welcoming. "Let me guess: You've planned your life out to the nth degree, with specific goals." He rested his elbows on the table and lowered his face toward hers, his eyes as hard as emeralds. "Goals you'll do anything to achieve."

Alicia swallowed, uneasy with the look in his eye. "What's wrong with that? There's nothing wrong with that."

He didn't answer. Alicia fidgeted under the intensity of his gaze. Worse, his attitude rubbed her raw. Nobody could live life that free of worries. "What about an education? Did you go to college? If so, I'm sure you could get a better job—"

Her comment fell on the group like a lead blanket. Helen and Vana stared at her like she'd just committed treason.

Jason's jaw tensed as he kept his eyes riveted on her. "Yeah," he said, his voice a tad too soft for comfort. "I went to college."

"Majoring in . . . what?"

Helen gave a stilted laugh, clearly trying to break

the tension that had escalated between them. "Probably partying. Right, Jason?"

"No." He kept his eyes pinned to Alicia. "I majored in international relations and minored in economics."

Alicia knew she looked as shocked as she felt. Before she could gather her forces and respond to his parry, Helen steered the conversation onto the hottest clubs in Seattle, and Jason finally, mercifully, turned his attention from her.

Lunch went downhill from there. Jason kept up a spirited discussion with Vana and Helen, and Alicia was left thoroughly out in the cold. *You didn't do anything that bad,* she told herself, but she knew the others thought she'd come on way too strong. And opinionated. Like a high-browed intellectual snob.

She never pretended to do well in social situations. But today, she'd really flunked out.

She attacked her spaghetti, turning it around and around on her fork. She couldn't manage to eat much of it. *So he's not dumb. You never really thought he was. What's it to you if this guy throws his life away on a low-paying, menial job? He probably earns just enough to spend his paycheck partying on the weekend.* If Helen and Vana were any indication, he had women falling all over him, a different girlfriend every week. Maybe he even bummed off them. Some women would consider it a fair trade.

She was the exception. She wasn't the least interested in him. If he ever gave her another of those lady-killer smiles, he'd learn that fact point-blank.

Besides, something about the guy just didn't add up. If he had that kind of education, opportunities would have come his way. Why hadn't he taken them? How and why had he ended up at Envirotech?

The end of lunch provided another embarrassing

moment. Helen and Vana fought—actually *fought*—to pay for Jason's lunch. To put an end to their squabbling, Alicia snatched his bill out of Helen's hand. *"I'll* pay it," she said, rising to her feet. "Welcome to the company, Jason."

Jason rose beside her and stared down into her face. "Gee, thanks, Doctor. That's damned generous of you."

She couldn't miss his thinly veiled sarcasm. "Yes, well, I'm senior member of the bio-rad department. It's my duty." With that terse statement, she spun on her heel and headed for the cash register near the front door.

And promptly landed on her face.

"Alicia!" Jason was beside her in a split second.

"Ow!" She pushed herself up on her arms, mortification flooding through her. Her knees hurt like hell and her graceless face plant had drawn the attention of all the diners in the vicinity.

"You caught your heel on your purse strap," Jason told her, turning her over and helping her sit up.

The humiliation of her pratfall onto the concrete patio equaled the pain in her nylon-clad knees, both of which were oozing blood. She hadn't scraped herself up like this since falling off her bike as a kid.

Then another, much more enjoyable sensation washed through her as Jason pulled her into his strong, warm arms. "She's okay," he called out, addressing the curiosity of the lunchtime crowd and the restaurant manager, who was running over to help. "Just a couple of scrapes. Can you walk?" he asked her, concern creasing his brow. "You hit pretty hard. Probably bruised your knees."

"Of course I can walk," she said, her words not sounding nearly as strong as she wished them to.

"Better not take any chances." With that, Jason

swept her into his arms and rose to his feet in one fluid motion.

Conscious that dozens of eyes were on them, Alicia tried to appear nonchalant about the experience of being held by Jason. Her body, however, screamed with delight. *So strong.* She felt weightless. If he wanted to, he could toss her into the air and catch her. She was certain of it. Yet he was cradling her so tightly against his chest, she knew he wasn't planning on letting her go anytime soon.

The other patrons clapped and cheered as he carried her through the restaurant toward the front door. Alicia kept her eyes on her shredded panty hose, mortified by the attention, wishing she didn't enjoy the feel of his washboard stomach against her hip.

She glanced over his shoulder to where Helen and Vana trailed behind them. Vana was frowning, but Helen's face bore the hint of a smile. Helen had retrieved Alicia's purse, and she stopped at the cashier's desk to settle the bills.

All the time Helen was paying, Jason stood patiently in the entryway, holding her. Alicia forced herself to look in his face. "Uh, I really can walk, if you want to put me down. I must be getting heavy."

"Hardly." He tossed her a little, and resettled his arms around her. "You're a small gal, Alicia."

"Yeah, well, short parents, you know."

"It's nice. Makes you easy to carry."

The other patrons had returned their attention to their own meals and conversation. Alicia still burned with embarrassment . . . and something more primal. It scared her senseless. She shoved at his rock-hard shoulders, then immediately wished she hadn't touched him. "Really, Jason, I can walk."

"Stop being so damned stubborn." At his intense

expression, her protest died in her throat. "Just let me, okay?" he said, his voice low.

Alicia looked at her lap, feeling strangely pleased that she'd lost the argument.

He studied her knees. "They're starting to swell. You'll have to keep them elevated."

"What are you, a doctor in disguise?" She tossed off the comment with a wry smile, then immediately wondered if she had somehow insulted him. His expression closed up and he looked away.

Helen came toward them and they paraded out of the restaurant. "It's four blocks to the office," Vana said. "You're not going to carry her the whole way, are you?"

Jason did just that—down the street, up in the elevator, finally arriving in her office. There, he settled her on her couch and slipped a pillow under her legs while Helen wrapped ice in a towel and placed it on her knees. Vana disappeared back to her secretarial desk down the hall, looking put out.

The ice stung, yet it felt good, too. Alicia got a better look at her knees as she lay there, and sure enough, both of them were swelling.

Helen hovered over her like a mother hen. She tried to shoo Jason out. "She needs some Betadine on those scrapes, and if you'll leave, we can peel what's left of her panty hose off her."

Jason's mouth quirked up at her comment. "Sure you don't need my help?"

"Positive." Helen showed him to the door. He seemed to drag his feet on the way out.

The door secured, Helen returned to Alicia's side. Alicia worked her panty hose below her hips, and Helen helped yank them the rest of the way off, then tossed them in the wastebasket beside the desk.

Alicia watched the disposal of her ruined hose. Tomorrow morning, Jason Kirkland would be emptying that same wastebasket, which now held her intimate apparel.

"He's very interested, Alicia."

The comment sent a forbidden thrill through Alicia, which she valiantly fought to ignore. "Yeah, he seems to be into injuries. Probably all those high-risk sports he engages in."

"That *isn't* what he's interested in. Now, girl, don't go dense on me."

"Huh?" Alicia played dumb, something she hardly ever did.

Helen rolled her eyes. "I don't believe this. I just don't believe it. You *have* been shut away in your lab too long. You're beyond redemption. Geez, girl, he couldn't keep his eyes off of you, even when you were grilling him. Man, if I was fifteen years younger—make that ten years younger—no, five—and slimmer and sexier and a looker like you, what I wouldn't do to—" She scowled down at Alicia. "Never mind. It's hopeless."

She left Alicia's side and slipped through the narrow door that connected to the next-door lab, in search of first-aid supplies.

No, it's not quite hopeless. Alicia laid her head back on a soft pillow and smiled to herself. She could still smell his marvelous scent on her own clothes, feel his arms embracing her, see the concern on his gorgeous face.

Helen returned to her and helped Alicia clean grit from her wounds and wash them with Betadine. While they worked, Helen started in again. "Just because he's a janitor doesn't mean you shouldn't date him, Alicia. For heaven's sake, girl, live a little!"

Helen's tirade had the opposite effect on Alicia. She continued talking, but Alicia tuned her out. A cold river rushed through her, dousing the warm, lingering effect of Jason's attentions. She was focused on a supremely important goal at a critical time and had no need for additional complications in her life.

She wasn't interested in dating, except for Leon. He was . . . a comfortable companion, hardly a hot date. And Jason Kirkland—despite what Helen said, Alicia didn't think he even liked her. Yes, he'd carried her, which only proved he could be a gentleman. But she was hardly his type.

The bottom line? She and Jason had nothing whatsoever in common. Nothing.

Nothing but the basic biological drive between a man and a woman . . .

She looked like a little girl. That was Jason Kirkland's first impression when he stopped by Dr. Underwood's office to check on her—and to try to get a sense of when she'd be going home. It was already after nine.

She was still on the sofa where he'd placed her after lunch, sound asleep. A laptop computer on her lap was turned on, a screen saver running. One of her hands curled next to her face, and a dreamy expression softened her features. Her black hair was tousled on the sofa's pillow, twin Band-Aids decorating her scraped knees. That's what had given him the impression of a little girl.

Until he took a second, closer look . . .

Her navy skirt had wriggled its way to the tops of her thighs, revealing the tiniest glimpse of white underpants.

Jason swallowed—hard. Heat unfurled in his gut and poured through his arteries. Yeah, she was a looker.

More than a looker. She was sexy as hell.

He cursed under his breath at his own weakness. Why now? Why her, of all people, a woman he knew he couldn't trust?

It didn't seem to matter, not when he held her in his arms. He would've carried her a mile, if he'd been so lucky. For just a few moments, she'd made him feel needed, something Jason wasn't familiar with. He'd relished the feeling, at the same time he knew how foolish it made him. Letting the woman get under his skin had never been part of his plan.

Today at lunch, his irritation at her subtle digs had made him careless. He'd leaked more than he should have about his college education. International relations and economics? They were not part of the profile Uncle Henry's people had crafted for his persona as Joe Janitor, simple guy with simple needs.

Education obviously meant so much to Alicia, he hated to let her think he was a brainless bod. Everyone else was content to think so. Not Alicia. The good doctor knew something didn't add up with him, though he doubted she really suspected him—yet.

Damn her perceptiveness. He would definitely have to keep on his toes around her, uncover her secrets before she uncovered his.

Jason carefully bent over her and tapped the space bar on the laptop to see what Alicia had been working on before drifting off to la-la land. Reading her E-mail. Specifically, a memo from President Fielding. A sentence in bold caught his eye:

"I cannot overstress the importance of completing your research in the time allotted. The future of Envirotech—and the livelihoods of 378 people and the personal fortunes of thousands of shareholders—are riding on your success."

"Bastard," Jason muttered, unsure whether he was

more offended by the man's greedy desire to profit from stolen research, or the guilt trip he was laying on Alicia.

He caught himself *No. No sympathy.* Not for her. She probably made claims she couldn't keep, even lied about her abilities. She'd made her own damned bed.

With his thumb on the mouse button, Jason swept the cursor up to the scroll bar, trying not to move the unit too much, trying damned hard not to notice the rise and fall of her breasts against her buttercup-yellow silk shell.

She fidgeted in her sleep. He jerked back. This was not a good idea. He needed to get her out of here so he could do some serious digging.

Still, he couldn't deny he liked having her here—just to look at, of course. He had no interest in her as a person. He found himself gazing at her face, and noticed her eyes moving under her lids. From the soft curve of her lips, he guessed it was a good dream.

What dreams made a woman like Dr. Alicia Underwood smile? Wealth? Fame? Why was it hard to see her yearning for those things? He knelt before her face and stared hard at her. So delicate, ethereal even. Yet there was so much brain power locked behind those pixielike features . . .

Did her conscience bother her at all? Did she ever look up from her microscope long enough to notice the world around her? The people near her?

Was she at all aware of how she affected him?

Hell. She might be a thief, but she sure as hell was a fascinating thief.

A soft sigh issued from her lips, and Jason remembered how she'd teased him at lunch, sucking on her finger. He licked his own lips.

That insistent heat was still coursing through his

bloodstream. He wasn't a guy who tread the safe side of life. Never had, probably never would. No reason to. All he risked was his own neck, and that was his to risk. Besides, living dangerously gave him such a rush.

Like now. Tasting her lips promised more excitement than leaping off the Golden Gate Bridge without a bungee cord. Slowly, carefully, Jason lowered his face to hers.

Sensing she wasn't alone, Alicia cracked her eyes open. She had to be dreaming. Jason Kirkland was right here with her, in bed, just like in her dream. Her eyes locked with his smoky emerald ones as he bent closer to her, his head angling, his mouth above hers, his lips parting. . . .

I'm not dreaming! Alicia bolted upright, nearly banging heads with him. The laptop bounced to the floor.

Jason sat back on his heels, knees spread, an all-too-knowing smile playing over his far-too-handsome face.

Indignant and feeling naked before him, Alicia yanked the sides of her skirt down. "What are you doing, here in my office? What are you doing?" Her words jerked out as she tried to gather her poise.

"I just stopped by to see how you were feeling," he said casually, crossing his brawny arms before his chest.

Alicia averted her gaze, memories of her steamy, tropical dream rushing back to her. He hadn't been wearing a shirt in them—or anything else. "I'm fine, just fine," she said, pulling in a steadying breath.

Jason handed her the laptop and she closed it with a snap.

"Knees okay?"

"Fine. A little stiff, but I'm fine. Really. Fine," she repeated, knowing she sounded as inane and off-balance as she felt. She lifted her eyes to his. He merely looked concerned. She must have imagined that he was about to kiss her. Why would a hunk like him try to seduce an egghead like her? The idea was ludicrous.

"It's getting dark out," he said. "You must have fallen asleep hours ago. Why don't I walk you to your car?"

The Envirotech building wasn't a dangerous place to be alone at night. Still, Alicia appreciated the gesture. "I thought I'd stay and finish up a few things."

"I'm sure they can wait. Don't let them work you to death." He rose and held out a hand to her. She accepted it and he pulled her to her feet.

They stood facing each other for a few, long heartbeats. Alicia was aware of nothing but the callused hand holding hers, the sound of his breath, and those incredible eyes . . .

Finally, he released her hand. She immediately missed the warmth of his touch. He stood by the door while she slipped her pumps and suit jacket back on and pulled her purse from her desk drawer.

She collected her laptop and briefcase as well, loading herself down. At the office door, she dug into her purse for her keys. Jason relieved her of her laptop, then her keys, and ushered her out. "Let me get that." He locked her office and together they left the building.

In the parking lot, dusk was closing in. Envirotech and the other businesses on the street were nestled in a small valley surrounded by evergreen-covered hills. The peaceful setting insulated the neighborhood from the noisy highway over the ridge.

She walked with a slight limp down the broad entrance walk beside Jason, breathing deeply of the pine-scented air. So fresh and rejuvenating. She sensed an imaginary path opening before her, leading her toward something special. *It must be the Wipe Clean Project. I'm so near the end. Every ending is a beginning, they say . . .*

"I take it that's your car," he said. He pronounced it *keah,* and Alicia decided she could listen to his New England lilt all day. There were only two cars in the parking lot. Hers was the sensible Toyota sedan. His had to be the beat-up Jeep, a party car if ever she saw one.

Jason walked her to the Toyota and helped her settle in, passing her the laptop. He didn't let her go right away. He rested his elbows on the driver's side window frame. "You always the last one to go home?"

She shrugged. "Sometimes. When I go home."

"Why?"

"Why what?"

He waited until she looked him in the eye, and his voice grew intense. "Why are you sacrificing yourself for this company, Alicia?"

His challenging words destroyed the sweet feeling she'd been experiencing. "I have a life beyond my work."

"That a fact?"

He sounded so damned disbelieving, Alicia grew defensive. "I go out all the time. Isn't tomorrow Saturday?"

He nodded.

"Well, I happen to have a date tomorrow."

In the dusk, she couldn't tell if he was smiling or grimacing. "What's his name?"

"That's personal." He arched an eyebrow, and Alicia knew she'd been too terse. It was hardly a secret. "Leon."

"Hot affair going?"

Now he was being nosy and rude. "That's not your concern!" She jammed the key into the ignition and turned the engine over.

Before she could put the car into reverse, he reached in and settled his hand on her forearm, his thumb lightly stroking her skin. Alicia fought the wickedly delicious sensation that crept up her arm.

"Hey. I'm sorry," he said softly. "I just . . ." He paused, a perplexed look crossing his face. Slowly, he withdrew his hand, a frown gathering between his eyebrows. "It's just that sacrifices . . . they always come with a price. Is it worth it, Alicia?"

His words hit hard, prodding an ache deep inside that she hid from everyone around her. How dared he? How dared he peer into her heart and pose such a painful question?

"Excuse me," she gritted out. With a shaky hand, she shoved the car into reverse and gunned the engine.

He stepped away from the car, then continued to stand there watching her as she backed the Toyota out of the parking space and drove from the lot.

THREE

Jason had only pretended to lock Alicia's office door. He could have picked the lock, given enough time. But getting in and out fast was the name of the game—and she'd been so trusting with her keys.

Trusting . . . Not a typical trait for a thief, even one dealing in intellectual goods.

Fighting a surge of unwelcome guilt, he settled into her high-backed office chair. Alicia had no idea he was spying on her, but this was the easiest way to reclaim the research. A lengthy court battle would solve nothing, and have the effect of opening wide the breakthrough information for any company to profit from. Henry's only recourse was to steal it back before Dr. Underwood completed her research and Envirotech took it to market.

He flicked her computer's power switch and waited while it booted up. The lady doctor was an enigma. What drove her? He didn't think she'd stolen the information for the thrill of it, or the profit. She seldom took time to play as it was.

Maybe that was the problem. Maybe if she loosened up and enjoyed life more, she wouldn't have lost sight of common decency. Wouldn't have felt pressured to take shortcuts.

Maybe, just maybe, there'd been some reason behind her theft, something he could understand, something that meshed with her guileless behavior.

He shook off the queasiness he felt. He couldn't get mired in soft emotions. Whatever her reasons, the devastating effect on Uncle Henry's company would be the same.

Bio-Intera stood on shaky ground. If something didn't happen soon, like a major patent, Henry would lose everything—his houses, his cars, his country club membership, his stock. More money even than Jason's late father had left him. For once, Jason wanted to do something for his family, contribute to the family business empire in some way. *Be more than a playboy living life on the edge.*

He was finally turning his talent for smooth talking and fast living to something that would actually *help* someone.

Hardening his resolve, he concentrated once more on her keyboard.

Finding her password might take some doing. He could find no notations in or around her desk. But then, why would a genius need to write it down?

He began to tap in a variety of passwords. It could be something—*should* be something—completely random. He'd probably have to break into Vana's desk to look for a master list for the department, which was risky, or sweet-talk the girl out of it, which went completely against the grain for him. He hadn't the slightest interest in encouraging Vana.

He tried Alicia's initials, then her full name. Her name backwards. No go.

Think, Kirkland. You've read her dossier a hundred times. What do you know about her?

A family member's name, perhaps? He tried her parents' names. They were both dead. He tried the name of her grandmother, who'd raised her since she was a teenager. She was also deceased. No husband. Alicia had divorced after a two-year marriage to a college professor, which ended about two years ago. No children.

Her brother was alive, living in Richland with that cute three-year-old whose picture sat on her desk. He didn't know the niece's name. He should've asked Alicia.

It struck him how alone in the world Alicia Underwood was. He leaned back in the chair and frowned. No wonder she buried herself in her work. In the parking lot just now, he'd almost forgotten why he'd come here to Envirotech, he'd wanted so badly to see her relax and have fun. He'd wanted to invite her out.

He rubbed the back of his neck, exasperated with himself. Any compassion he felt for her could only cause problems.

He squeezed his eyes shut to focus his thoughts, then lifted his gaze from the computer monitor to a poster hanging on the wall above. Albert Einstein, no doubt one of her idols, with the quote, "The most beautiful thing we can experience is the mysterious. It is the source of all true art and science."

Maybe . . . no, it's too obvious. He reached for the keyboard and typed in the famous physicist's name. The log-on screen vanished and the computer began launching its programs.

"Bingo."

Jason didn't waste time grazing through her files. Instead, he attached a portable disk backup system to the computer, which he'd secreted in his janitorial cart, now parked outside the door. In case anyone came around, he'd pretend to be cleaning.

He already knew the schedule of security rounds. Learning them had been his first project. A few card games with the guys had given him access to the schedule. The unambitious security staff wasn't likely to surprise him. Still, it wouldn't do to linger here.

While the backup unit did its work, he relaxed into Dr. Underwood's executive office chair. Comfy. He tugged open a desk drawer and flipped through the contents, not really expecting to find anything useful, but you never knew.

A collection of brochures caught his interest and he extracted them. The Audubon Society. Nature Conservancy. Greenpeace. The American Cancer Society. Handwritten on the top of each was a neat notation, indicating the amount of the donation or dues and the date on which it had been paid. She seemed to belong to every well-known environmental group in the country, with a few health organizations thrown in for good measure. He wondered if belonging was a requirement of her job. Considering her impassioned speech the other day about saving the planet from nuclear waste, he suspected her heart was in every one.

Confronted by yet another paradox, he returned the brochures to the drawer and slid it closed. A thief *and* a do-gooder? A Robin Hood in a dress? Did that explain Alicia Underwood?

His eyes strayed to the poster of the orca whale above her couch. What did it feel like to burn for a cause? Just once, Jason wished he could feel that passionately about something.

An hour later, he disconnected the backup unit. Now everything on her hard drive was on the slender disk in his palm. He reached over to turn her computer off, and then a thought occurred to him.

Tomorrow was Saturday. If the information Uncle Henry needed was on this disk, Jason didn't have to get close to Dr. Underwood. Still, it couldn't hurt.

He was excellent at charming women. Maybe he could dig some clues out of her that would lead straight to the research.

He fought down an unwelcome niggle of guilt accompanied by anticipation as he keyed open the computerized Envirotech directory. He did a search on the name *Leon*. Sure enough, there was only one on staff, in first-floor contracts administration. He must be one of the stuffed shirts Jason barely noticed as he made his rounds to collect the trash. Jason worked fast in almost every part of the building—to have more time in Alicia's department.

He pulled up Leon Krowinsky's company bio and frowned. So this was Alicia's Saturday hot date? Jason vaguely recalled the guy after all. He always gave Jason a cheery greeting.

Jason scowled and leaned closer. Thick black hair, pleasant features—a Tom Hanks with glasses. Seemed to have that comfortable, good-natured quality that a lot of women found attractive . . .

The thought of the sexy Alicia in this man's arms caused a primal reaction in Jason, a deep, powerful and completely unreasonable emotion. The sensation was so foreign to Jason, he almost didn't recognize it. When he worked through to its definition, he froze in the chair, striving to correlate it with his self-image—a free spirit who lived for experience, who staked no claim, who never pledged a commitment or expected one in return.

Jealousy.

Well, his foot was already in it. Too deep to back out now. Perhaps it was a risk, but hey, let the chips fall where they may. Jason keyed up her computerized appointment calendar. Saturday . . . only one listing. 12 P.M. *Aquarium. Leon.*

Jason grinned as he reached for the phone and

punched in Leon Krowinsky's home number. Someone was going to miss his hot date.

Alicia tapped her foot impatiently in front of the aquarium at Pier 59 on the Seattle waterfront. Tourists strolled past her, heading for shops, restaurants, the neighboring Imax Theater and the aquarium itself.

Leon was always punctual. It was already 12:15. What was holding him up?

"Dr. Underwood?"

Alicia's head snapped up. Jason Kirkland sauntered over to her. He wore khaki shorts, a blue cotton short-sleeved shirt and loafers. His tanned, bare legs were as firm and muscular as his arms.

He smiled down at her, his eyes sliding along her own bare legs. "I almost didn't recognize you in those shorts." His gaze danced over her scraped knees. "But I'd know those Band-Aids anywhere."

Alicia met his teasing gaze and fought down a sharp surge of pleasure. For her part, she'd recognize this man anywhere, wearing anything. Or nothing. She strived to sound casual, despite the rapid beat of her heart. "Hello, Jason. This is a surprise."

"How are you feeling?"

Feeling? Irrationally thrilled to see him. "Uh, fine."

"Knees don't bother you?"

With his accent, it sounded like *batha* you. Alicia smiled, admitting to herself that she was hooked on his voice. "No, they're much better. Thank you. So, what brings you out today?"

He glanced at the cerulean sky. "On a great day like this? Thought I'd do a little sightseeing, get to know Seattle. You going in here?"

He walked toward the aquarium entrance.

"Actually . . . yes."

"Come on." He held the door open for her. Alicia took one more look around, but Leon was nowhere in sight. She fidgeted, wondering what social protocol demanded in this situation. Should she keep waiting? For how long? Then again, the aquarium wasn't that big. Surely Leon could meet up with her inside.

At the admission booth in the foyer, Jason shoved a bill across the counter and asked for two adult tickets. Alicia fumbled for her purse. "I'm paying for myself."

Too late. The deed was done. "I've got it. You bought me lunch yesterday, remember?"

"Oh. Right." Alicia followed after him through the turnstile, trying to keep her eyes off the way his shorts snugged his tight bottom. Leon's rear end had never held any interest for her. Nor had any other man's before now.

"This is nice," Jason said as they rounded the hall toward the first exhibit, on sharks. He paused before a huge case with several small tiger sharks. "I held that kind in my hands, on a scuba trip to Micronesia."

"Really?" Alicia said, feigning an unimpressed air. "Well, I've *eaten* shark meat, in a restaurant here in Seattle."

His eyes sparkled at her playful joust. "You got one on me. I've never done that."

"Yeah, right," she laughed. "You probably catch them and eat them for breakfast."

"Only the pretty ones." He slipped his hand along her back and steered her toward the next display. *Does he consider you one of those?* she wondered. *Do you actually want him to?*

They moved through the shark exhibit to an area devoted to tidewater life. Alicia gazed in pleasure at the re-creation of a natural tide pool along one wall. Every few minutes, a man-made "tide" swept in and filled the crevices and rocks, coating the miniature life forms.

Parents, children and other visitors pressed along the sides. Jason helped her slip into a spot in front. He stood behind her and settled his hand on her shoulder. At his familiar touch, Alicia's first inclination was to bolt, but she talked herself out of it. *Cool it. He's just being friendly.* Yes, but *how* friendly?

"Guess those two are having a good time."

"Hmm?" Alicia tore her thoughts from his warm hand and followed his finger to a pair of crabs that were—well, engaged. Her face began to burn. She cleared her throat, adopting her "presentation" voice. "Actually, for crustaceans like these sand crabs, the mating ritual is purely instinctual. They don't really feel—"

"Sure they do. If they didn't *love* it, they wouldn't *do* it. And their species would die out."

"Well, I suppose on some level they do enjoy it, yes, but their nervous systems aren't capable of the higher feelings, the—"

He gave a low whistle. "Must be something in the air. Look there."

She followed his gaze to another part of the pool, to a slick rock where a pair of snails were mating. Jason stood so close behind her, she could feel the heat emanating from his body. His palm swept slowly along her shoulder and cradled her neck, branding her skin. She had never imagined that looking into a pool full of soggy invertebrates could actually be erotic. *It isn't erotic. It's just the way he makes it sound!* "They're merely responding to basic biological drives," she began to explain.

"Yeah." He spoke into her ear, his voice low. "We both know about those."

Alicia stiffened. He had to be coming on to her. *So, what are you going to do about it?* Nothing, of course. She had to remain cool and in control. She couldn't let anything distract her from finishing her project. Throwing an office romance into the mix would be a disaster at this stage.

Her project's success hinged on her own credibility, as well. The office grapevine would have a field day with this one, particularly her stuffy scientist colleagues. Dr. Underwood and the building janitor?

She shuddered. She had already been the victim of gossip and rumors run amok. It had happened two years ago, when her ex-husband dumped her for a coed at the university. She had been desperately trying to get her life back on track when the gossip of well-meaning and not-so-well-meaning people rubbed salt into amazingly sensitive wounds.

For a while, the snide comments and knowing looks directed her way had destroyed her ability to concentrate around other people. She'd finally quit Bio-Intera altogether to devote herself to private research in her home laboratory. Then Envirotech had taken an interest in her fledgling project and she'd found the strength to face the world again—more cautiously than before and, she hoped, wiser about men.

No, she couldn't allow romance to interfere again. Ever.

Alicia shrugged Jason's hand off her shoulder and hurried to the next display.

Jason watched her walk off, amazed at her overreaction to his teasing. *Or maybe she just doesn't like you, Kirkland. It would serve you right.*

With a start, he realized how badly he wanted her good opinion. Which sure as hell made no sense, considering the fact that she threatened the only family he had.

Maybe because she looked less like a threat than like someone who needed to be protected, he thought ruefully. She had stopped in front of the jellyfish display, her arms crossed, her teeth worrying her lower lip. Geez, her entire body was as tense as a coiled spring despite the relaxed surroundings. A sudden desire surged within him to alleviate some of that tension.

"Are you okay?" he asked when he reached her.

"Yes. Why wouldn't I be?"

Her eyes wouldn't meet his. She looked pale, shaken, uneasy. Her guilty conscience at work?

Guilty. Why did he keep forgetting that fact? Instead of worrying about her, he was supposed to be digging into her secrets. If he bothered to put his charm to good use, he might learn something that would help him get the research back for Uncle Henry.

He kept his voice moderate and friendly. Nonthreatening. "How about if we catch a bite? We can get our hands stamped if we want to come back. But my stomach's growling. My treat?" He smiled down at her, trying hard not to appear intimidating in any way. It would do no good to scare her off now, having gained nothing by crashing her date.

Apparently, she bought it. Her provocatively downturned mouth began to lift in a slow, almost reluctant smile. "No. Dutch treat. After all, you just started working."

"And you make a hell of a lot more than me," he acknowledged, amused by her concern over his financial situation. Thank God she had no idea . . ." Come on." This time, he was careful not to touch her as they left the aquarium.

"So, what exactly are you working on that's so important?" He watched her over the rim of his clam chowder soup spoon.

She hesitated before responding. "I thought you already knew. I saw you listening to my presentation last week."

He smiled at her. In her seat across from him at the outdoor table, the entire panorama of Puget Sound served as her backdrop. She looked like a painting. "Yeah. You're an excellent speaker."

"Thanks." She slipped her coral pink lips around the curve of her iced-tea glass and sipped. Jason fought his libidinous reaction to the innocent gesture. He'd shifted into overdrive in the past hour, just from being in her company. *Keep a clear head, buddy,* he told himself. *Keep it clean. All you need is information; then you're out of her life.*

He resumed his questioning, trying hard to make it sound like casual conversation. "I guess what I'm asking is, isn't it likely there are other firms pursuing technology along the same lines? I mean, if there's so much money to be had."

She flipped her gaze up to his, a mixture of surprise and assessment in the clear brown depths. "Yes, I'm certain some are, but it's a personal theory I've been developing for years. I haven't run across anything remotely similar in any of the literature."

"I see." Jason fought to contain his sudden anger. Uncle Henry had explained how Dr. Underwood had stolen the research from Bio-Intera's R & D department. Now she was making out that it was her very own. So much audacity in such a guileless package.

His adrenaline surged. Being around this lying woman was heady stuff. "And what happens after you're done with this project? Move on to another one?"

"There are so many ramifications with *this* one. No, the Wipe Clean Project—that's what we call it at Envirotech—should occupy me for the rest of my life."

Nothing like taking ownership when you weren't the rightful owner. He whistled low. "That's a long time. What are you . . . twenty-five or so?"

She shifted in her chair. "A little older."

"Can't be much." He smiled disarmingly. "And you've been at Envirotech since . . . you graduated college?"

"Well, no, I worked for another company while I was pursuing my doctorate. But Envirotech offered me excellent benefits and support for my project, and I couldn't turn them down."

He shoved his chowder bowl aside and leaned his elbows on the table. "It must have been exciting, to have a big breakthrough like that. When exactly did it happen?"

At his pointed query, she frowned and appeared confused. *Definitely guilty.* She was trying to think how to answer without tipping him off to the truth.

"Well," she said slowly, "I achieved the critical breakthrough about four years ago, I'd say."

She had been working at Bio-Intera up until two years ago. She'd as much as admitted she stole the research from Bio-Intera. Jason should have felt jubilant. Why did he feel such intense disappointment instead?

"Four years. Uh-huh. A long time, then," he said.

"Not really, not for science. Very fast, actually. It's been an amazing journey of discovery." Her eyes took on a luminous sheen, making her appear beautiful and flipping his heart over. Still, Jason frowned. How could anyone look so proud and excited when they had stolen from the company that had made their work possible to begin with? How could loyalty come so cheap?

Damn. Uncle Henry had discovered this woman, taken her under his wing, fostered her work, only to be robbed of it—and her—at a critical juncture. "Why did you leave Bio-Intera?" he asked suddenly, his voice sounding harsh to his own ears.

"What?" Her smile faded and her large eyes widened in surprise, giving her a deceptively innocent look.

"What makes a scientist change companies?" he asked, trying to moderate his tone.

Her gaze darted away to the sky, to the table, clearly desperate to avoid his. "Well, I—I'd rather not talk about it."

I'll bet you wouldn't. Her guilty behavior spurred a sudden fury inside Jason. And a longing to see her crack. "Was it because Bio-Intera didn't give you a big plush office and a private lab?"

"No, of course not. I don't care about those things, except that it helps my work." A frown darkened her eyes.

Despite her newly guarded look, the blood was pounding in Jason's veins and he couldn't stop his words. "Maybe because they didn't think of you as a slave, like Envirotech does?"

She gasped. "A slave!"

"I've seen your office. It's bigger than an apartment! There's even a bedroom off the lab."

"It's just a cot in a closet—"

"A perfect home-away-from-home where you can hide away from the world."

"No! That's not the way it is at all." Her eyes widened and she straightened in her seat, as if preparing to take him on. Jason hadn't seen her so alert and engaged all day, and it sent electricity to every nerve in his body.

He smiled grimly, acknowledging to himself that the thrust of his attack had changed, become personal. Become dangerous. "Isn't it that way?" he said, his voice deceptively soft. "You're there late almost every night. And Helen tells me you go in on weekends. She says this is the first day you've gotten away from work for more than four months, and only because your boyfriend insisted you go out. You eat there, sleep there—"

Alicia struck the table with her palm, rattling the ice in their glasses. Her eyes snapped with fire and soft color rose in her cheeks. "So I'm dedicated! And who are you to talk, anyway? What do you accomplish with your time that's so special?"

Though he had no defense, Jason opened his mouth to respond.

She didn't give him a chance. "You're a smart man with the charisma of a young JFK, but the only asset you use is that—that"—her gaze flicked down his chest and back up—"that sinfully brawny body of yours just to play sports and—and to drive women to distraction!"

Her forceful outburst shocked him for a moment, but then the underlying meaning of her words struck home. He didn't care about other women, but she was really saying that he drove *her* to distraction. The new possibilities for intimacy were almost too sweet to contemplate, and his blood began to race. "Alicia . . ." he began, the name almost a whisper.

She swallowed visibly, then leaned back and crossed her arms, as if to keep her distance. "You seem to know an awful lot about me, Jason Kirkland, yet you manage to share almost nothing of yourself. Why is that?"

A sick feeling filled Jason's chest. She suspected him now, and with good reason. He'd gone way too far. He'd been unable to stop at eliciting information from her. He'd let his loyalty to Henry take over, and then another emotion altogether. How in the hell had he lost control so easily? After all, what difference *did* it make to him if she holed up in her lab for eternity and never saw the light of day?

Watching her delicate skin flush, her eyes spark with passion, he realized the painful answer. *Despite her theft, despite the fact that she'd hurt his uncle, she'd gotten under his skin in a very bad way.* He sucked in a breath, determined to smooth the waters for Uncle Henry's sake, and his own. "I apologize, Alicia," he said, meaning every word. "I didn't mean to come on so strong. And you're right about me. Well . . ." He hesitated, then tried a smile on her. "Except maybe for the part about the sinful body."

She shot him a disbelieving look from under lowered lids but couldn't hide the flicker of a smile. Carefully, as if she were a wild bird he might frighten away, he reached out his hand and settled it gently atop hers. She jerked, once, pulling her hand partway from under his.

Then she stilled, allowing the intimacy. Jason took heart, and his words echoed his surprisingly intense emotions. "I haven't done much that's worthwhile in my life, I admit. I've made a career out of having a good time. Out of caring about nothing. I'm trying hard to change that."

She bit her lower lip, and his stomach tightened in response. So luscious! So unaware of her appeal . . .

He continued, "But I think maybe you've gone too far in the other direction. I hate to see you waste your youth. You're young, Alicia. Too young to be so worried all the time, so . . . pressured. Helen tells me you never break loose and have fun. You never relax. Even in the aquarium just now, I could see the tension all over you."

"Jason, I—"

"Shhh!" he commanded. "I'm talking now. Listen up."

She nodded reluctantly.

"I hate to see you work so hard that you forget to enjoy life." He squeezed her hand. "You're beautiful, smart, witty and damned sexy, but I sure as hell don't think you know it."

The color in her cheeks swept up another level as their eyes locked. He could see her internal tussle, knew on the one hand that she wanted to stalk out of the restaurant, to run away from him and his words. But on the other hand, he'd complimented her, which must not happen often because it caught her completely off guard.

She snatched her hand back and looked at her bowl. Silence weighed down on them for a full five minutes, and Jason was aware of every breath she took. He realized then that things had changed between them. They had both admitted—albeit in a backhanded way—that they were attracted to the other. Now, what would she do about it? He sure as hell knew what he wanted to do—take things to their obvious, mutually satisfactory conclusion. At the thought, warning bells jangled in his head. It would be a risk, no doubt a damned fool one. Still, the experience—

"It might grow cloudy tonight," she said in a cool, composed voice. "We get rain even in the summer here. But I don't mind. It can be refreshing." Her eyes were looking somewhere above his head, then shifted to the table. "Do you want more oyster crackers? I have an extra packet."

He tried to catch her gaze with his own, but she was avoiding him. "Alicia, even if we don't talk about this anymore, that doesn't mean I'm not right."

"Don't," she said suddenly. Then, more calmly, "I—I would prefer we pretended this conversation never took place." Her last words sounded so formal and contained, it frustrated him all the more.

Then she lifted her gaze to his, and he knew she wouldn't forget. She could pretend all she wanted, but they would both know what had passed between them. Every time they met or spoke, the attraction would be simmering under the surface, despite what they said or did. "I'll try," he finally said, knowing he wouldn't do anything of the sort.

She nodded once and resumed eating her soup.

Great way to screw up a date, Kirkland, he thought ruefully as he watched her bowed head. She had withdrawn so completely, he might as well be eating alone.

No woman had ever responded to him this way. When women weren't flirting with him, they were getting overly, unwelcomingly possessive. He couldn't recall any lady he'd been attracted to acting completely uninterested, as she was. And he knew now it was an act. *Smart, charismatic, a sinfully brawny body that drove women to distraction* . . . He fought the urge to smile. She might have said the provocative words in a fit of anger, but now Alicia was making an obvious effort to remain detached despite a strong desire to allow him close.

But why? What was she afraid of? *Don't fool yourself,*

Kirkland. She has every right not to trust you. In every way that matters.

Suddenly, he didn't care. He knew her number, and he could take care of himself. But he'd seen the depth of passion in this woman, and he intended to keep at her until she revealed it again—in *his* way.

Sitting across from Jason, Alicia trembled inside. She could hardly force the soup down, her stomach was in such a tumble.

She prayed her confusion wasn't advertised on her face for him to see. He couldn't have shocked her more if he'd stood up and claimed to be Superman. *You're beautiful, smart, witty and damned sexy* . . . He'd actually said such words to her. *Her.* And he even seemed to believe them.

He was the epitome of the social male—popular, funny, and with a body to die for. Why on earth did he care what she thought of him? Why did he care how she spent her life? Guys like Jason had never been interested in her. She'd gone through high school and college with her nose buried in books, intent on finding answers and striking back at the enemy that had killed her mother. Her studiousness had been a sure turnoff to men with fun on their minds.

Yet Jason had said those amazing words . . .

Her brain finally kicked in, reminding her of something. He'd mentioned Bio-Intera, but she hadn't. How did he know she'd worked there?

Helen must have told him. The thought didn't comfort her. It meant Jason was interested enough in her to probe for details. He was like a fiery random neutron, whizzing through the contained, balanced nucleus of her little world, wreaking havoc and sending her own electrons out of control.

Mind over matter, Alicia. That's what it's about. That's your strength. Don't set yourself up for another idiotic fall based on embarrassing emotions you can't control.

Determination swept through her. She refused to reveal herself any further to this man. An acquaintance from work—that's all he was, all he'd ever be. She'd already spent far too much valuable time thinking about him.

It was up to her to make sure he knew his place in her life.

Without realizing it, a determined smile had formed on her lips. Instantly, he grew alert, his gaze hot on her. "Done with lunch?" he asked, his brow arched with curiosity.

"Oh, yes." Reminding herself where they stood made her feel much more comfortable in his presence. She could handle this Don Juan after all. All she had to do was make sure she thwarted any attempt on his part to flirt, or charm or seduce her. Her businesslike demeanor would chill him soon enough. "I'm stuffed. Let's go back to the aquarium. I want to check out the dolphins." She sprang to her feet.

He rose more slowly. She felt his eyes on her as she led him out of the restaurant, fresh energy in her step.

Just inside the entrance, Alicia and Jason ran into Leon. He'd been wearing a hole in the paving outside the main entrance.

"Alicia! I'm sorry I'm late. The strangest thing happened . . ." Leon's voice faltered as his gaze fell on the man standing behind her. His brow furrowed. "Don't I know you? You look familiar."

"Hi, Leon." Alicia rather wished he hadn't appeared after all. She was looking forward to showing Jason Kirkland exactly how uninterested she was in him. Then again, with Leon here, Jason couldn't help but see that she was immune to his charms. "Oh, you know Jason, don't you?" she said, touching Leon's arm. "He's our janitor, at work."

Leon nodded and the two shook hands. "I thought you looked familiar. What brings you . . ."

"We ran into each other," Alicia said. "Since you were so late, we went into the aquarium together."

"Alicia, about that—" Leon said. "I received a message on my answering machine last night telling me to report to work today, that there would be instructions for a big project on my desk. Well, the person said you were involved, and that you'd be there, too, so naturally I didn't bother to call you and cancel our date. So . . . well, I drove to work, and, well . . . there was nothing on my desk. I'm more than a little confused, but I suppose there's an explanation. Perhaps I didn't get the message right, it came at me so unexpectedly—"

"Someone called you?" Understanding dawned. Alicia narrowed her eyes on the number-one suspect, who appeared to be fascinated by a case of coral in the foyer. "Was it a male someone?"

"Yes, but I didn't have a chance to get his name. Very odd, really. He sounded so terse and, well, almost rude."

"*Almost* rude. I'd say he was *exceedingly* rude." Still, deep inside she nurtured her amazement that a man would go to such lengths to be with her.

Jason turned on them, his smile full of charm and

good spirits. "Are you two going to chat all day, or are we going to look at some dolphins?"

Alicia almost told him where to stuff it, but she didn't want to fight with the office janitor in front of Leon. He might suspect . . . something. "Sure. Let's go." She slipped her arm through Leon's and followed Jason through the turnstile.

The rest of the afternoon was a nightmare. The three watched the dolphin feeding and demonstration from a dimly lit viewing area before a wide window on a blue pool. The aquarium was packed with visitors so they had to crowd onto a bench. Alicia ended up squeezed between the two men, with Jason's leg plastered against hers.

She couldn't ignore the feel of his bare skin rubbing intimately against hers every time either of them shifted. He seemed to be shifting quite a lot. Alicia tried not to move, but she felt tremendously restless, despite her best efforts to listen to the aquarium guide's talk.

At least Leon had had the decency to wear long-legged Dockers. She hardly noticed his presence beside her. He was oblivious to her distress, his glasses shining from the subdued tank lights as he watched the dolphins toss rings and balls around.

Afterward, while the three stood before a tall octopus case, Alicia watched as Jason charmed Leon, completely monopolizing his attention. The two became engaged in a lengthy discussion comparing marine wildlife in Puget Sound to the Caribbean—neatly killing half an hour.

Normally fascinated by wildlife, Alicia couldn't begin to concentrate on the wonders around her. Her silly notion of demonstrating her lack of interest in Jason—reinforced by Leon's presence—had disintegrated. Leon had forgotten she existed. He'd never ignored her like this. Was he angry that she hadn't waited, or what? Alicia felt as out of place in the complex social atmosphere as a fish out of water.

At least Jason wasn't *quite* as intent on their male bonding experience, for he kept trying to draw her into the conversation. But Alicia was too irritated at both men to bite.

The next thing she knew, Leon suggested watching the Imax movie on the Grand Canyon, and Jason took him up on his offer. While waiting in the lobby for the show to begin, the two men launched into a discussion of camping and hiking the Canyon.

"I never knew you hiked there," she said to Leon.

"Well, it was awhile back, when I was a teenager. Now, I'd be pretty out of shape for something like that." He patted his soft midriff. "Not you, though." He backhanded Jason's abdomen. "What do you do to keep in shape, anyway? I'm considering buying a NordicTrak."

Jason didn't hesitate to fill him in on his exhausting regimen of play, play and more play. Scuba diving, windsurfing, tennis, sky diving. You name it, Jason apparently did it. *When does this guy find time to earn a living?* Alicia wondered. The worst thing was how Leon ate it up. He was as bad as one of the women at work!

Alicia caught Jason's eye and scowled at him, wishing he'd just *go away*. He merely grinned at her, his lowered eyelids lending a seductive cast to his gaze.

She itched to slap him for screwing up her date with Leon. But her hands were tied until she got him alone.

Watching the Imax film was worse than viewing the dolphin feeding. She tried to break through Leon's unaccustomed reserve, slipping her hand around his and pulling it to her thigh. Jason didn't touch her at all, merely sat with his arms crossed and his attention nailed to the giant screen. What made it so bad was Alicia's realization that she wished Jason's hand were resting on her thigh, not Leon's. Only a few minutes passed before Leon pulled his hand away.

He must be deeply hurt, she thought. Guilt stabbed at her. He had done nothing to warrant this disloyalty. If only Jason hadn't appeared! Yet he had . . . And gone out of his way to be with her. She couldn't help feeling flattered, but she shoved that aside and concentrated on her anger toward Jason, stoking it to a white-hot intensity. She had every right to be furious with Jason Kirkland, a man she hardly knew, a man who passed all kinds of judgments on her personal life, who had the audacity to manipulate his way into her Saturday afternoon!

When the three of them exited the theater, Alicia couldn't remember a single frame of footage from the film.

"Well, that was fascinating," Leon said. "I love those big-screen films. Looks like next month they're showing one about space. Should be interesting, don't you think?" He addressed his question to Alicia and Jason equally.

"Definitely," Jason said dryly.

"I'm looking forward to going with you, Leon," Alicia said.

Leon shrugged. "What say we grab a bite to eat?" He looked at Jason. "I'd like to pick your brain about the best snow-ski equipment to buy, before the seasonal sales begin."

"Sure," Jason said, his tone again dry. "Sounds like a blast."

"No," Alicia said at the same instant. "I'm feeling tired, and I'm ready to call it a day. Next time, Leon." She slipped in front of him and laid her hand on his chest. "You know? We can plan something special. Just the two of us."

Leon wouldn't meet her gaze. "Great. Well, my car's this way. Where's yours?"

"I'm over there," she said, pointing in the opposite direction.

"Me, too," Jason said. They both waved good-bye to Leon and started walking toward the parking lot.

As soon as Leon was a good distance away, Alicia turned the corner of the building and yanked Jason with her. "How *dare* you cancel my date with Leon on me! What gives you the right?"

"I'm sorry. I was wrong."

Alicia wasn't ready to accept an apology. "Manipulating Leon and me, like you were God or something—"

"Alicia, I have the morals of a flukeworm. I know that."

She couldn't tell from his placid expression if he was serious, which frustrated her and fueled her anger anew. "There are rules about things like this . . . somewhere, I mean. Unwritten rules, social conventions everyone has to learn, and—"

His smiled drolly. "Rules and I have never gotten along, Alicia."

Despite his cocky words, he didn't appear smug, but actually contrite. She glared at him for good measure as she paced before him. "What makes you so special? No, don't answer that." Her anger began to dissipate in the face of his complete lack of defense. "Really, Jason, I just don't understand. Poor Leon, driving all the way to work on a Saturday. He's the one you should apologize to." She pictured that, and immediately thought better of it. "No, don't tell him. But why?" She faced him squarely, demanding an answer.

"Hey," he said reasonably, "I knew you wouldn't go out with me. What was I supposed to do?"

"Go out with you? Why would you want . . . I mean, you never asked . . ." He looked so sincere, Alicia's anger completely gave way to irrational female pleasure. He wanted to *date* her? "Why . . . I mean, why did you think I'd turn you down?"

"You're a genius scientist, Alicia. I'm a janitor. I know what you think of my . . . chosen profession. Dating a guy who cleans toilets isn't your idea of a fun time."

"That's not true." *Oh, yes it is,* she scolded herself. Since the first day. She'd been attracted to him along with every other woman in the office, but angry as well. Angry that he was merely a janitor, when it was obvious he was intelligent and charismatic and capable of so much. "Okay. Maybe a little. But it's more than that. I seriously don't think it's a good idea to encourage gossip, and office romances usually do."

He arched his tawny eyebrows and Alicia choked on her words. She was dating Leon without compunction. But no one was interested in her and Leon. She knew without a shadow of a doubt that she and Jason wouldn't receive the same bland disinterest from Envirotech employees. "I . . . um . . . I have to get home. Good-bye." She turned to leave, confused, unwilling to explain her hesitancy when he deserved some sort of explanation.

He caught her upper arm before she took a full step. "Alicia."

She turned back around and forced herself to face him. His green eyes were full of sincerity.

"I'm sorry," he murmured. "More than I can tell you. I won't pull a stunt like that again. I don't want to get in the way of your relationship with Leon. I guess I let my hormones get the best of me. So . . ."

He pulled in a deep breath. "I'll see you at work Monday. Me janitor, you scientist." He pointed at each of them, then stepped back, gave her a long look and walked away.

Jason settled into the driver's seat of his car and raked his hands through his hair. This was getting more and more complicated. He thought charming information out of the woman would be a simple matter.

But she thwarted him at every turn, growing distant the moment a spark flared between them, then gazing at him with those dewy brown eyes like she felt something for him. And he didn't want that, not from her. How could he long to get closer, knowing what a traitor she was? Where were his own ethics? He gave a self-deprecating laugh. He had none. Never had. There were better men out there, that was certain. Hardworking, job-holding straight arrows like Leon.

While a little conservative and gabby, he wasn't a bad guy. Jason even kind of liked him. He rubbed his forehead. Why was he even thinking about the good doctor's boyfriend? What did it matter? It had nothing to do with getting information from Envirotech.

Jason had a job to do, and today had accomplished nothing. In fact, he *should* have spent it back at Envirotech, searching her office, breaking into her lab, something worthwhile.

Instead he'd been chasing her skirt like he'd never been around a woman before. Like he had no control over his body's natural urges. As for that stunt switching dates on her—childish and amateurish, and likely to raise her suspicions about all his actions. What could he have been thinking?

Thing is, he'd always pulled stunts like that and rarely got in trouble he couldn't smooth-talk his way out of, even as a kid. Hot-wiring cars in high school on a lark. Stealing girlfriends from his college classmates just for the challenge of it. Being thrown in a Mexican prison because his friend had dared him to smuggle marijuana. And he never even used the stuff, hating the way it dulled his senses.

Thank God Uncle Henry had flown thousands of miles to bribe his way free. There was little money couldn't buy. Except, perhaps, self-respect.

He was an expert at getting his own way. He wasn't used to even recognizing that there *was* another way. So why now? Why did this petite ball of fire make him feel like so much slug bait with one withering glance?

Tomorrow, he'd start fresh, pretend he'd just begun work at Envirotech. No need to get personally involved with the subject of his investigation to make a success of it.

He popped the glove box and slipped out the disk that contained all of the information on her hard drive. Time to deliver it to Uncle Henry. Maybe after Henry's people uncovered the information it contained, his work would be done. He could give notice and never see Dr. Alicia Underwood again.

FOUR

Alicia peered through her office door from the short corridor leading to the lab. Any minute, Jason would be coming through the main door on his daily cleaning rounds. She needed a report from her desk but was none to keen on running into him. She'd managed to shift her schedule around and be in the lab in the mornings, enabling her to avoid conversing with him for three full weeks. Three surprisingly long weeks.

Since that disastrous date he'd barged in on, he'd kept his word, merely nodding to her as he passed her in the hall. Alicia was quite happy about that. Really.

No sign of him. Shoving open the door, she hurried to her desk, her white lab coat flapping around her hips, and rummaged through the papers piled on top. The corners were askew, and instead of a single neat stack of paper, four different piles had grown on the mahogany surface. When had she become so disorganized?

When she wasn't afraid of being in her own office, that's when!

"Morning, Doctor."

His deep voice raced along her nerve endings.

Alicia nearly jumped through the plaster ceiling. She spun to face him. "Oh. Jason. Hello."

He was leaning against the oak lintel, brawny arms crossed over his equally brawny chest. Smiling. Completely relaxed. Alicia resented his casual air, especially when she found herself wondering if she should have refreshed her lipstick or combed her hair, her feminine instincts running roughshod over her cool logic. Her reaction thoroughly irritated her, as if she was little better than a lioness strutting before the pride's leader.

He shoved away from the wall and sauntered to her desk to collect her wastebasket. He didn't seem the least disturbed being in *her* presence.

Fine. The world wasn't fair. She certainly didn't intend to linger and watch him do his work. Frantically flipping through the last stack of paper on her desk, she found her report and snatched it up. She was halfway to the connecting lab door when his alarmingly warm voice reached her. "You've been avoiding me."

She turned around, her spine stiff, her demeanor professional. "Of course I haven't. I was . . ." She forgot her words as his gaze absorbed hers, seeking something else, something more from her. She had nothing to give this man. Any man.

In the space of a heartbeat, unspoken communication spun between them.

Her mouth hardened and she lifted her chin. *Yes, I've been avoiding you.*

His eyes widened slightly. *You're afraid. Of me. That bothers me.*

He took a step toward her, and Alicia found herself waiting, wondering, anticipating—

The jarring of the ringing telephone snapped the strange connection between them. Glad for something to do, Alicia hurried to her desk and retrieved the receiver.

President Fielding, seeking a progress report. Alicia turned her back on Jason, hoping he'd get the hint that the call was private. She felt rather than saw him leave, and exhaled silently while she tried to focus on Fielding's numerous questions.

"The current protocol will work. I simply need to adjust the parameters," she told him. "It should succeed. I can't guarantee it, no." It frustrated her to no end that administrators like Bruce Fielding assumed her painstaking scientific work could be bent to fit their needs.

The hairs on the back of her neck went up, and she knew instinctively that Jason had reentered her office. Slowly, she turned around. He was carrying furniture polish and a dust cloth.

She watched out of the corner of her eye as he moved items off her bookcase and started dusting. Slowly, ever so silently, she pulled in her breath as her eyes played over his back, watched his muscles glide under his gray T-shirt as he swept the cloth in a wide arc over the mahogany surface. She knew she should be concentrating on President Fielding's voice, knew she was foolishly ogling Jason.

But she couldn't seem to focus on yet another pep talk about her work's importance to the company.

Not anymore.

Since college, Alicia had focused her energies, her ambitions, her drives like a laser beam on her goals. Nothing had ever gotten in the way. Not even her marriage. She'd dated, established a relationship, accepted Richard's marriage proposal, let her mother-in-law plan the wedding ceremony, tied the knot on a weekend and never missed a project milestone. She continued living much the same as she had when she was single, except there was a warm body in bed on the nights she made it home.

She'd imagined the right ingredients—two intellectually well-matched, mature adults—would equal a successful marriage. Richard had said he felt the same. She had respected his space, as he had hers. Far too much, it turned out.

Throughout the confusion of her marriage and the ordeal of her divorce, her work had been her anchor. She'd never lost command of her thoughts. But ever since Jason Kirkland had shown up, her mind wandered into untamed, reckless areas she'd never even considered exploring before. Areas she had thought herself immune to.

Such as . . . What would it feel like to lie naked in Jason Kirkland's strong arms? Feel every inch of his powerful body? If this was what lust felt like, no wonder it caused such trouble in the world. And if it had taken this long to come to her, would it ever come again? Or was this her one chance at experiencing unbridled, no-holds-barred, down and dirty passion with a man?

"Alicia?"

President Fielding was waiting for a response, but Alicia had no idea what he'd asked. "Yes, I understand," she lied.

Fielding seemed to accept that, and launched into another lecture, this time about the need for her to properly document every step of her process, as if she hadn't been doing that all along. She bristled for only a moment before finding herself back in fantasy land, her gaze still on Jason as he dusted her bookshelf.

As a temporary employee, Jason wouldn't be at Envirotech for long. In a matter of weeks, he'd be out of her life. Janelle had left work two weeks before her due date. Now the baby was past due. Once she had the baby, she'd be home for six weeks. And then she'd return to work and Jason would be gone.

Alicia knew there wouldn't be—couldn't possibly be—anything long-lasting between Jason and herself. She knew beyond a shadow of a doubt that her reaction was an anomaly, based purely on physical drives. She could certainly accept that. *I'm an adult. My eyes are wide open.* She wouldn't expect anything, except . . . *that.* And would it be different? Better or worse than with impatient Richard, her ex, who had accused her of being frigid and passionless? Maybe she could be normal after all, with the right man . . . Yes, that's all she wanted to know. *It's a scientific experiment,* she reasoned. *Testing the importance of physical attraction in determining the quality of sexual experience* . . . Heat flared low in her abdomen. If just looking at him was any indication—

Jason chose that moment to turn around. Alicia bit her lip and pretended her gaze had been elsewhere—out the window perhaps, or toward the couch. She knew he wasn't fooled. A slow, knowing smile slid over his lips, as sweet and sinful as syrup spreading over pancakes. Instantly, the temperature in the room shot up ten degrees. He set the spray can and cloth on the bookcase and took a step toward her.

President Fielding chose that moment to end the call. Alicia barely managed to whisper good-bye through a tight throat. The receiver all but fell from her damp palm. She suddenly knew that if she didn't distract them both, she might find herself asking Jason to help her with a little experiment, a step she wasn't ready to take. "You look like you'd be good at—"

"Yes?"

Those arched eyebrows—so suggestive! "Moving parts."

His lips parted in surprise, and she rushed to cover her embarrassment at her suggestive remark. "I mean, mechanical parts and . . . things like that." She pointed at the shredder. "My paper shredder's stuck. Maybe you could take a look?" She bit her lip and smiled hesitantly. Maintenance had promised to have the machine repaired a week ago. Meanwhile, she'd been tossing sensitive papers in her recycling box until she could take them to a working shredder.

Jason lifted his eyebrows. "Sure, I could. Since you asked so nice. Us blue-collar types are great with our hands, Alicia. Great at using them wherever they're needed." He gave her a cocky grin and headed for the door. "I have some tools in my cart. I'll see what I can do."

In a moment he was back, crouching before the machine and opening a small tool set beside him. He lifted the shredder's lid and jiggled and joggled the buttons. It looked like he knew what he was doing. But nothing happened for him, either. Alicia smiled to herself. Apparently her paper shredder had better control of its reactions around Jason Kirkland than she did. It didn't get turned on quite so easily. "It's really broken?"

"I haven't given up yet." His eyes locked on hers. She watched, entranced, as his expression began to change from casual friendliness to one charged with significance. "I'm always up for a good challenge."

Alicia fidgeted, feeling he could read her darkest desires. Getting a satisfying sexual response from her would be challenge enough for any man. "Well, thank you. I know this isn't your regular job—"

"My pleasure." That word again. *Pleasure.* He said

it like he was the king of pleasure—and she was one of his subjects.

Questions about this man gnawed at her. Maybe if she learned more about him, it would demystify him, rob him of his power over her. If she could unlock his mysteries . . . "Why are you here?" she asked suddenly.

He stiffened, his smile fading and his lips drawing tight. "To clean your office, and fix your cheap equipment." He jabbed a screwdriver into the inner workings.

"Did you get your degree? Did you graduate, I mean."

"Yes," he said slowly, no longer looking at her.

"Where'd you go to college?"

"Back East." He pulled out the screwdriver and looked over his shoulder at her. "What's up, Alicia?"

"I'm just trying to figure you out."

He shrugged and shot her a cocky grin. "I'm a simple guy, Alicia. Give me pretty girl, a cold beer, a pair of well-worn jeans, I'm happy."

Alicia arched an eyebrow at him. "I find that difficult to believe. There's something about you . . ."

He lost his smile. "I'm not a scientific project, Alicia."

Alicia stiffened defensively. "No, of course not. But you *are* an enigma."

"*Me?*" He laughed nonchalantly. "Don't read something into me that isn't really there, Alicia. I'm just a regular guy."

A regular guy! Hardly. "Then tell me, is this what you want to do for the rest of your life, Jason? Empty wastebaskets? Why the janitorial profession?"

Another casual shrug. "Why not?"

"But with a degree in international relations, you could work for a corporation—"

"I am."

"You know what I mean."

He turned back around and attacked the shredder with the screwdriver one more time. "I went to college because that was what my folks wanted me to do. Is the inquisition over yet? Damn!"

He jerked back. The screwdriver had slipped, tearing a small chunk of flesh from his palm. The blood began welling up.

"Oh, no. I'm sorry. I distracted you." Alicia ran for the first-aid kit. She came back to find Jason sucking on his palm. Kneeling before him, she pulled at his wrist. "Stop that. Thousands of germs and bacteria thrive in human saliva. You're not helping it any."

"So what?" he groused. "Sucking on it feels good."

"Here." She managed to retrieve his hand, then gently spread antibiotic lotion into the cut. She fumbled with the Band-Aid, unwrapping it and carefully placing it on his callused palm. Intent on her task—and trying to hide how his nearness affected her—it took her a moment to realize how still he'd become.

"This isn't wise, Alicia."

"It may become infected if we don't treat it." She rubbed down the sticky edges of the bandage, securing it in place.

His breath stirred her bangs. "I mean *this.*"

At his husky tone she lifted her eyes to find his inches from her own. Every sense in her body came alert.

"I've been trying to keep my distance from you, but this isn't helping."

Alicia fought for a decent breath but only half managed one. "This . . . bothers you?"

His lips twitched. "*Bothers* isn't the word I'd use."

"Oh." Understanding dawned on her, shocking and exciting her. She was actually turning him on—

simply by holding his hand! Amazing. To her knowledge, she'd never had that effect on a man before. It was a revelation, giving her a surge of feminine confidence she had never felt before. She was entering new, unexplored territory. Danger alarms went off in her brain in a futile effort to remind her to keep her place, to stay decorous and professional. She ignored them, her fascination outweighing her uncertainty.

That look on his face . . . His emerald eyes burned with intensity, need and desire mingling there, because of *her.* Cupping one hand under his, she tentatively slid her fingers up his wrist, fully aware of the smooth warmth of his skin. His surprisingly strong pulse thundered under her fingertips. "What about this contact? Does this affect you, too?"

He swore and yanked his hand from hers. "I'm not one of your lab rats."

Embarrassment swept through her. "I'm sorry. I don't—I didn't mean—I just want to understand why . . ." She gazed earnestly at him, hoping she hadn't hurt his feelings. She was so terrible at this sort of thing. Flirting was an art she'd never learned. What would another woman have done? Anything? Nothing?

"Some things can't be explained scientifically," he muttered, rubbing his wrist where she'd touched him. "Having the hots for you is one of them."

She bit her lip. He made it sound so . . . easy. But it meant the world to her. "Everything can be explained through science. I'm sure this can, too." She clasped her hands in her lap. "The thing is, Jason . . . I've never . . ." *felt this way before about a man,* she silently finished. Instead, she explained, "Men don't normally react like you just did. With me, I mean."

That got his attention. He stared at her, his brows

dipping in concern. Then he slowly raised his hand and stroked her jaw. He lifted her chin with his fingertips, bringing her mouth closer to his—almost kissing her. *He's touching me, just like I hoped he would,* Alicia realized. And she knew she'd confessed her secret to him longing for this reaction.

"It's really hard for you to believe, isn't it?" he said, a touch of amazement in his voice. His thumb traced the angle of her jaw, sending spikes of delicious awareness through her. "Why? What makes you think you're so damned unappealing?"

Despite the highly personal nature of her problem, she felt she might be able to tell this man. She knew in her heart that he wouldn't judge her harshly. She might know few facts about him, but his innate kindness was more than apparent. Unlike everyone else in her life, he expected nothing from her. An amazing sense of freedom filled her as his lips came within a centimeter of touching hers. *Yes . . .*

An intrusive female voice ended the kiss before it began. "Alicia? Oh! Hi, Jason."

Alicia and Jason jerked apart. Alicia flew to her feet, dislodging the first-aid supplies from her lap.

Vana's eyebrows furrowed with suspicion. "What are you doing on the floor?"

Jason recovered first, with such easy aplomb it amazed Alicia. As he slowly rose to his feet, not a trace of embarrassment showed on his handsome face. Was he even being real with her a moment ago? But then, why would he lead *her* on? She just couldn't get a handle on him.

He rose and gestured to the paper shredder. "Trying to fix that. I cut myself and the good doctor patched me up." He held up his bandaged hand.

"Oh. Okay." Vana looked relieved.

"I'll have to get some other tools." Jason looked

around. "Now, what were you going to shred? There's another shredder down the hall, by the copier."

Alicia gestured to the papers filling the recycle bin at the corner of her desk.

"I'll empty it for you." He swept the bin under his arm and headed for the door.

A tremor of concern shot through Alicia. Her papers . . . Her project was business sensitive. "Wait!"

He turned around, his gaze the picture of innocence. How could she suspect him? He wouldn't begin to understand what he was reading, unless he had a mysterious background in physics and biology, too! "Never mind."

He shot her a grin before he slipped out.

Jason hit the brakes and squealed into the head-on parking space in Woodland Park. He was late, and Uncle Henry was waiting for him. He grabbed the roll bar and swung out of the Jeep, then strolled over to the navy-blue Mercedes. The passenger door opened slowly. Jason looked into the dark interior and Henry gestured him inside.

Jason almost burst out laughing at the cloak-and-dagger routine. But he found himself glancing over his shoulder just the same. A couple of kids whizzed by on rollerblades. No one else was about.

He slid into the car and closed the door. Henry looked dapper as always in a tailored suit, the same gray as his thick hair. His trim features and unblemished skin made him appear to be in his forties, rather than his actual age of fifty-four. Jason wondered if Henry's older brother—his own father—would have aged as well.

In front sat Henry's discreet chauffeur, Peter, and a large man Jason didn't recognize.

"Hey, Uncle," he said.

Henry laughed jovially. He threw his arm around Jason and squeezed his shoulders. "I told you, kid, Uncle makes me sound a thousand years old. Call me Henry."

"I grew up calling you Uncle, Uncle. You expect me to change now?"

"My nephew," Henry said. Jason's chest tightened at the obvious pride in Henry's firm features. "Tyler, this kid is the most hell-raisin', wild creature ever to walk the earth. Does his best to give me heart attacks. But he's doing the right thing this time, by God. The right thing."

Henry withdrew his arm and gestured to the huge man in the front passenger seat. "Tyler, meet Jason Kirkland. My number-one, right-hand guy. He's saving my company single-handedly."

Tyler turned around slowly. His black hair glistened from an overdose of grease, and he wore a pencil-thin mustache above puffy lips. He glanced up and down Jason's body, assessing him.

As Jason did his own assessment, a tingling began at the base of his spine. Tyler's eyes were dead cold. Jason wondered why Henry had hired the guy. With his heavily muscled build, he'd look far more at home in a football jersey than an expensive Italian suit. Or as a bouncer at some sleazy nightclub.

"This is Ike Tyler. He's new to my staff."

"Tyler," Jason said, unable to contain a hint of challenge.

Tyler didn't reply, merely turned back around in the seat. But Jason noticed that Tyler kept his eyes on him in the rearview mirror, which the chauffeur had apparently allowed him to adjust to his viewing satisfaction.

Jason spoke low to Henry. "He always this friendly?"

Henry shrugged. "He does his job well. Speaking of jobs—"

"Did you find what you needed on the backup tape?" Jason asked, more than a little anxious to know if his stint with Envirotech was at an end. No more spy games. And no more Alicia.

But Henry shook his head, clearly disappointed. Jason tried not to take it personally. He refused to fail Henry. He wouldn't allow himself to be that worthless.

"Background information," Henry explained. "Old reports, that sort of thing. Good detail on how soon Envirotech will try to take our stolen technology to market. Closer than we anticipated, my researchers tell me. It's good you've gone in when you have. But the game board is already changing. It's not about documents anymore. Have you managed to get into the lab yet, where they make the actual superbug?"

Jason sucked in a breath and shook his head. "No. It's locked up like Fort Knox. I was hoping you'd get what you needed from the tape, and from the paper reports I've been feeding you."

Henry sighed. "It won't help me, Jason."

Jason's stomach knotted at the look of disappointment on his features. Though Jason had only been half serious, Henry had been ecstatic when Jason had suggested this scheme to reclaim the stolen technology. Henry had been certain all his financial problems would soon be over. Jason had tried to offer his uncle money to keep Bio-Intera afloat. But anytime he offered, Henry grew cold and unyielding. Apparently, his ego wouldn't accept that Jason—a man he thought of as a son—could be in such a position of power over him. Jason refused to hurt the only person who cared whether he lived or died.

Henry ran his hand through his silver mane. "I don't know, Jason. I supposed this might be getting too difficult for you, as inexperienced as you are. After all, you weren't trained for detective work. I *had* hoped—"

"Hold it right there." Jason knew Henry was playing on his sympathy, his guilt, his pride. Unfortunately, it was working. "I haven't given up, and I don't intend to. I've only been working there a few weeks."

Henry stared dolefully out the car window, his expression appearing suddenly haggard. "Time is running out," he said mournfully. "It's a matter of weeks, even days. The only way we can remain players is to procure a sample of the actual bacteria. We don't have the time to develop our own superbug from the research. Not anymore." His eyes glinted with intensity. "That lab, Jason—it holds something of *mine*. The most valuable thing we've ever produced. There must be some way you can get in."

"I've been trying to get past the security system. It's not easy, Uncle. After all it *is* a nuclear lab—an Omnilock, hand geometry, key cards, the whole shebang."

"Well, you're the janitor! Who cleans it? Certainly not that prissy Dr. Underwood. Envirotech must think she's made of gold from the way they treat her." His voice grew bitter, and Jason was reminded yet again that Alicia was to blame for this whole mess. The thought caused his chest to ache. "The fools. They'll learn, when she turns on them, too."

Uncle Henry's cold reference to Alicia as a thief caused a surge of disquiet in Jason's gut. She'd become a real person since he started working there, more complex than the thin-lined sketch Uncle

Henry had drawn of a calculating industrial thief. She was so damned hardworking, so dedicated to her project . . . Yet apparently she'd stolen the research the project was based on. Questions that had been simmering in the back of Jason's mind demanded to be answered. "Can you tell me, Henry, why none of your other researchers remember the formula? If she stole it from them—"

"She stole everything!" Henry slammed his fist on his thigh. "Months of painstaking work. Backup records, everything! There's no way my scientists could begin to duplicate it. Oh, they're trying, Jason. But it's so complex." He shot Jason a narrow-eyed glance. "You don't doubt my word, do you, son? Have I ever given you reason to doubt me?"

Jason ran his palms over his jeans-clad knees, feeling more uneasy than he had any of the times he'd snuck into places he didn't belong at Envirotech. Why did he feel torn over this? It made no sense. His loyalties lay with his uncle, of course, his family. He had no reason to doubt Henry's word. No reason except for Alicia herself.

He stared out his own window, the maple trees beyond blurring before his eyes as he thought of the petite doctor. Under that cool professionalism, she seemed so damned *vulnerable*.

"Jason? You will manage to get that bacteria, won't you?"

His uncle caught his attention again and he sighed. "Of course." Alicia was nothing to him, nothing. Heck, he wasn't sure *what* to think of Dr. Alicia Underwood. He only wished he didn't think of her so damned much. "They'd let me in the lab if I was a permanent employee, but I'm not. The janitor who's now on maternity leave cleaned it. Until she's back, cleaning chores have fallen to the lab techs."

"The regular janitor, what's her name again?"

Henry should know, Jason thought. Through a third party, Henry had arranged for his job interview at Envirotech just before Janelle left, the same mysterious third party who had falsified his employment record.

Over the past years, Jason had taken little interest in the business empire left him by his parents. He'd followed Uncle Henry's advice in most areas, had no real reason to question him. He'd let Henry talk him into this scheme, left the arrangements to him. But now, something in his gut rebelled at Henry's machinations. He found himself wondering who *was* this third party who could forge employment records? Why did being so underhanded suddenly feel so dirty?

Maybe it was time he grew up and found some answers.

His uncle's brow creased. "Jason? Are you with me here?"

Jason realized he'd been staring off into space for several minutes. "The regular janitor is named McKlusky. Janelle McKlusky."

"That's right. Hear that, Tyler? Janelle McKlusky." He turned to Jason. "So, if you *were* a permanent employee—"

Jason narrowed his eyes. Henry seemed to truly enjoy these machinations. His mind was hard at work on a new twist, and Jason wasn't entirely sure he was happy about it. He'd challenged himself plenty in the past weeks. It'd been exciting sneaking around, getting in where he didn't belong, hanging out in Alicia Underwood's private office after hours. But how far was Henry planning to take it? And how far would Jason be willing to go along for the ride?

"—something to consider," Henry concluded. Jason had missed what he'd said, realized belatedly that he should've been paying closer attention. With Tyler scowling at him like dead meat in the rearview mirror, he was disinclined to ask Henry to repeat himself.

"You can certainly get close to that scientist broad and learn more.

Jason stiffened at the derogatory term. Even knowing Alicia had committed a crime didn't diminish an oddly protective feeling where she was concerned. "I'm close enough." *And not nearly close enough.*

"Hey. You're the looker of the family. She's single. Get under her skin, Jason—and in her panties. Screw her eyeballs out. Women are always drooling after you." He leaned forward and slapped Tyler's shoulder. Tyler continued to sit unmoving, like a giant, greasy rock. "You should see this kid at work, Tyler. All he has to do is stand there and they come." Henry threw back his head and guffawed. "Get it? They *come!*"

"Yessir," Tyler said.

Jason noticed Tyler's lips had turned up just enough to satisfy Henry that he shared his amusement. No, he did not have a good feeling about this joker. Wherever Henry had found him—and for whatever purpose—Jason didn't care for it. When he got Henry alone, he'd find out the facts, see what he could do to determine the outcome.

Henry continued, "At the country club, all the debs flock around Jason, sweet little chicks creamin' in their silk panties, their mother hens shoving them at him, just smellin' the money. At the speedway the same thing happens, only they're white trash sluts, their boobs falling out of their little halter tops. Then there's—"

"Henry." Jason's harsh warning cut off Henry's sordid story. "Please. Let's get back to business." *I don't*

want to hear about women. Not women who smell money when they get close to me. He was dead sick of it. All of them wanting him for his money—and for the thrill of sex with a rich guy. None of them thinking twice about it. As if wanting a wealthy man was enough justification in itself for using him.

Once more, Jason found himself ruminating on society's double standard. Men who pursued wealthy women were seen as greedy scoundrels or gigolos. But if a woman scored a guy like him, she was congratulated by her fellow females for having made the catch of the century. That would hold even if he wasn't young and reasonably good-looking.

But since he was both, women fed off his attentions. *Doing* it with Jason Kirkland—casual conversation, a date, in bed—each one was worth increasingly more points on the social scale. As for the grand prize—a wedding ring—no woman would ever win it. It was a vow Jason had made when he was twenty-three, when he thought he'd been in love.

That fiasco had ended abruptly when he woke early from a night of sweet, heart-swelling romance to overhear his beloved on a private phone call. She was telling her *real* boyfriend how close they were to striking it rich.

Jason hadn't waited around to learn the extent of her plan—probably to marry him and milk him for all he was worth, keeping her lover on the side. Or to threaten a public scandal, and have Jason buy her off to get rid of her. Or simply a sham marriage filled with nothing but lies and loneliness.

The weight of his inheritance had crashed onto his shoulders when he was sixteen, the day his parents died in their private jet. He'd been close to his parents. Their only child, he'd been their golden boy. As much as possible, they'd done everything together. He'd even joined his parents on their business trips. The hollowness left by their deaths still haunted him.

Since then, he'd lived with the endless nightmares—the public spotlight and private pursuit—caused by being impossibly, disgustingly wealthy in a world full of sharks.

His solution? Enjoy himself and to hell with the rest. To hell with the women. They wanted to use him? He used them.

Thank goodness Uncle Henry had been there to step in, to act as a shield and take the heat off. Henry had managed Jason's trust until he came of age, and doubled his inheritance in the process with his smooth business practices. Been there for him. Been his family. Tried to keep him from breaking his neck in one wild escapade after another. Kept him out of jail.

Jason *owed* Henry. Or so he'd always felt. But to seduce Alicia for him . . .

"She's probably not even a challenge. Got the hots for a petri dish. Hell, maybe she's a dike."

"She's not a dike," Jason said, forcing his jaw to relax. He didn't want Uncle Henry to know he was pushing his private buttons. He loved the man, but he didn't completely trust him. Nor did he want to show any weakness when Tyler's snake eyes were pinned to him. "She likes men." *Nice guys like Leon, at least.*

"Well, there you go!" Henry said, slapping Jason's shoulder.

Using Alicia—the thought left a nasty taste in Jason's mouth. Then again, was it so much worse than all the lies he'd perpetrated so far? *Yes.* She wasn't like the other women who knew what he was. He'd never met anyone like her. "I don't need to take it that far." Jason spoke the words aloud, but he was thinking it through furiously for himself. If he and Alicia actually—*No, don't even think it.* It would be crazy, a ticket to trouble. He could never tell her what actually brought him to Envirotech, who he actually was.

Yet he wasn't looking for a lifetime commitment, by any means. A one-time thing, or a brief affair . . .

He thrust out his hand and Uncle Henry took it, clasping it warmly in both of his. "I'll get the stuff you want, but in my own way. Give me a little time."

"Okay, but don't waste any." He grasped Jason's neck in a firm, fatherly grip. "The stock dropped another five points this week, Jason. You're all I have. All the hope in the world."

FIVE

Alicia walked against the flow of foot traffic leaving the Envirotech building. While her fellow employees were going home, she was about to put in another long shift. Day and night rarely had meaning now that her company-imposed deadlines loomed ever closer.

She shivered and pulled her jacket around her. The weather had turned nasty in the past few days—wet and drizzly and depressing. She almost hadn't noticed, she'd spent so much time in the lab. After this last thirty-four-hour stretch, she finally listened to Helen's urging that she go home and relax for at least a few hours to avoid making a foolish mistake.

Stepping into the covered entryway, she looked up just in time to avoid running into a couple sharing a kiss.

The man broke the kiss and turned right toward Alicia. Their eyes locked, and both of them froze in place. Shock swept through Alicia as the truth struck. And she was the last to know, again. Dismay filled her, along with the familiar pain of betrayal.

A guilty expression swept over Leon's face. "Alicia. I . . ." He looked at the woman beside him, avoiding her gaze. "You've met Sheila, haven't you?"

Alicia's eyes met those of the slender redhead. She

vaguely recalled Leon mentioning Sheila once or twice, a new employee in his department. "Yes," she forced herself to say. "I think so. Hello." She extended her hand.

Sheila shook it and smiled tentatively, then met Leon's gaze. Wordless communication passed between them, and Sheila excused herself to go inside.

Alicia watched the glass door close behind her. She refused to let her hurt show, refused to be emotionally vulnerable. She forced her knees to appear steady and attempted a smile. "So. It looks serious."

Leon glanced toward the parking lot. "I'm sorry, Alicia. I meant to tell you. I thought we'd talk about it a couple of weeks ago, when we met at the aquarium, but then we weren't alone."

"Um-hmm."

"And since then—well, I was out of town, and you were always in your lab, and . . ." He drifted off.

You could have left me a message. But Leon had never favored confrontation, or sharing his inner feelings. At least, not with her. To be fair, she hadn't opened up either. She'd been far too afraid to risk it.

The truth settled on her like a lead blanket, overshadowing the pain of catching him with another woman. She had failed yet again to keep a man, to have a real relationship. To live like other women did. This failure was entirely her fault, and she knew it.

Leon lowered his voice, his expression tight. "You can't blame me, Alicia. I hardly ever saw you. You live in that damned lab of yours. Besides, we weren't lovers." His voice dropped to a harsh whisper. "We never even had sex."

Alicia forced her expression to remain stonelike, calm. "I know." They'd been over this ground before. There was no point rehashing it. *I know I wasn't the woman you needed me to be. I never am.*

"Maybe the mind is enough for you," Leon continued, his voice filling with righteous indignation. "But it isn't for me. I wanted more than a buddy relationship."

"I'm not blaming you, Leon." Heaven knows, the blame was entirely hers. "I'm happy you found someone. Really."

His eyes narrowing, he studied her face. Alicia remained as cool as possible under his intense scrutiny, enduring it as best she could despite the urge to escape to her car.

"This really doesn't bother you, does it?" he finally said, his tone reflecting disbelief. Her ice maiden reputation remained firmly in place.

"Leon—"

"Not even this. Geez." He shook his head once, then attempted a half-smile. "Well, I hope we can still be friends, Alicia. We had a few good times."

Alicia nodded. For a moment, wordless tension hung in the air between them, until Leon finally backed away and strode quickly into the building.

Alicia straightened her shoulders, readjusted her purse strap and walked calmly and purposefully toward her car. She even smiled and returned the greetings of a few acquaintances she passed.

Finally locked in the private world of her car, she found herself gripping the steering wheel so hard that her fingers ached. Her stomach was knotted in pain, and she could hardly swallow past the lump in her throat. A sudden swell of moisture filled her eyes. She blinked hard, but a lone tear escaped and slid down her cheek. Furious at her self-pity, she brushed it away.

Be logical. Logical. We were going nowhere. We didn't click. He was only a casual companion for you, someone to pretend to be normal with. Of course that wouldn't be

*enough for him, for any red-blooded man. Any red-blooded
man would need more.*

More than I can give.

She sucked in a breath and let it out slowly, hoping
it would help her accept the truth. Instead, she found
her thoughts drawn to Jason Kirkland.

Was it Alicia's imagination, or was Jason a more
thorough janitor than Janelle had been? Lately he
appeared in her office more than once a day, not just
emptying wastebaskets but clearing her recycle bin
for her, cleaning her countertops, washing her windows, vacuuming, dusting the blinds, even scrubbing
the floorboards.

Every time he appeared, Alicia thought over her
crazy idea of an experiment. Every time she saw him,
her gnawing hunger grew fiercer, her loneliness
more intense. With him, perhaps everything would
feel good. Perhaps she'd know for certain that she
wasn't lacking as a woman.

She was crazy to consider it. Yet she was all alone
in the world, a fact made even more clear since her
break with Leon. Who was she trying to impress with
her standoffishness? What was playing cool going to
gain her, except a lost opportunity? She'd always
heard women talk about men like Jason Kirkland, for
whom loving women was an art form, who prided
themselves on their raw sexuality. Never in her wildest
dreams had she ever imagined *experiencing* such a
man for herself.

Yet there he was, gazing at her over his shoulder
as he slowly stroked a cloth over the faucet, *caressing*
it. Jason made even tedious cleaning chores seem
somehow . . . sensual. This time, she couldn't help
smiling back.

It was all the invitation he needed. He dropped the cloth and approached her desk, sauntering like he had all the time in the world. "There's something about this office I really enjoy," he said, a smile drifting about his lips.

"Oh?" she asked, tapping a pencil on her desk as if anxious to return to work.

"Yeah."

He placed his palms on the edge of the desk and leaned toward her.

"Well, that's good," she said. "Whatever it is, I mean."

"I'd lay odds you know what it is." His voice grew husky, his magnetic gaze capturing hers.

Alicia stiffened and pressed back in her chair. "What happened to 'Me, janitor, you scientist'?"

Jason grinned sardonically. "Somehow, 'Me Tarzan, you Jane' seems to fit us better."

Alicia forced a laugh. But the image of Jason in a loincloth burned into her mind, sending wild darts of pleasure along her nerves. Tarzan and Jane . . . in the jungle, where nothing interfered with basic biology. "So, you often carry women off to your jungle lair?"

His emerald eyes gleamed. "Not women. *Woman.* Me man, *you* woman." He pointed at each of them in turn.

Alicia's blood heated at an alarming rate. She gripped the edge of her desk. "I . . . think we'd better go back to me scientist, you janitor."

Jason sat on the edge of the desk and leaned close to her. "That's going to be hard, when I keep picturing you in a skimpy loincloth—and not much else."

His words echoed her own thoughts, about him. But he couldn't possibly find her that fascinating. Still, the way he was looking at her . . . as if she was wearing almost nothing, as if he wanted to devour her . . . "Me?"

"Yeah," he said, his voice alarmingly husky. *"You."*

Alicia suddenly needed to put distance between them, to harness her wild thoughts. She jumped up and circled around him as if he were a wild animal. She stopped in the center of the room. Well, one question was answered. He *was* genuinely interested. Her experiment could proceed—if she dared. Yet she hesitated, turning away so she could concentrate without the tremendous distraction of his gaze. "This isn't exactly appropriate conversation for the professional work environment, Jason."

Jason rose and came toward her, but he stopped five feet away. "Hey, I didn't mean to make you uncomfortable. It's not easy for me to stay on my best behavior when I'm around you every day. I apologize, Doctor." Their roles once more delineated, he walked past her—too close for comfort—and returned to the sink. He sprayed it down, then began scrubbing it.

But Alicia wasn't ready to let it go. Why her? Of all the women available to a man like him . . . "I really think you're barking up the wrong skirt, Jason. Er, tree. Vana really likes you, you know."

He shrugged, turning on the faucet to rinse the sink. "Yes, I know. She's a nice lady, Alicia." He turned to face her, his expression serious. "But it's just not there. Not like—" He wagged a finger between them. "Not like what I feel with you." He lowered his voice. "It's like you said. I want to throw your adorable body over my shoulder and carry you off." Then he shook his head and laughed self-deprecatingly. "Sorry, I'm doing it again. I'm terrible at following rules, Alicia. I mean, Doctor." He turned back around and scrubbed harder at the sink.

Hold on, Alicia. Keep your sense. No need going off here. Think about it. Long and hard . . .

Trouble was, she couldn't help looking, and what she saw did nothing to cool her raging lust. Even wiping the kitchenette countertop with long, smooth strokes, he moved like an animal in the bush, all pent-up energy and power. To feel that power surrounding her, on top of her, within her—

Alicia found herself moving before she knew what she was doing. She walked in jerky strides toward the door and closed it, then clicked the lock home. A sense of destiny filled her, calming her erratic nerves. There was nothing to be confused about. If he said no, he said no. And that would be that.

Except he won't say no.

His curious gaze pinned to her, he slowly dried his hands on a towel as she crossed the miles of plush carpeting to the window. She closed the curtains, casting the room in muted shadows. Then she crossed over to him.

She stopped before him, her heart in her throat. *It's now or never, Alicia. Do it now, or regret it for the rest of your life.*

Without taking her glaze off his, she slipped her hand over his and pulled the towel from his frozen fingers. She tossed it on the counter and turned back. His eyes burned into hers, as if he could read her thoughts. She finally found her voice. "Jason. Apart from all that. All the flirting, I mean. Since you're an expert at it and I'm not, I want to set that aside. Instead, I . . . I have a proposition to make to you."

She saw him swallow, hard. "Go on."

"Well, it's a little awkward for me. I've never done this before, not like this."

"Yes?" He gazed at her so intently, she thought her knees would give way.

Stay calm. Be professional. It's what you're best at. She cleared her throat. "I was hoping you could help me with an . . . an experiment."

"An experiment."

"Yes. I'm trying to approach this scientifically. But it *is* of a personal nature, so if you refuse, I'll understand." He said nothing, merely gazed at her with those penetrating emerald eyes. Alicia rushed to explain before she completely lost her nerve. "I want you to kiss me."

SIX

To Alicia's dismay, Jason didn't reply to her request for a kiss. He continued gazing at her, his expression unreadable.

She could hardly breathe. *Perhaps I'm being too aggressive. Perhaps I'm not playing the game right. I never flirt. I don't know the rules!* Her pulse beat hard in her veins. Didn't he hear her? She had to explain before he thought she'd lost her mind.

Words clogged in her throat, then burst out in a sudden rush. "I know that sounded strange, but I assume you find me somewhat attractive, since you talked about Tarzan and Jane and that whole loin-cloth thing. And I can't help thinking along those lines, I freely admit it. But I keep wondering, though I know we have nothing in common—I keep wondering if there would be any difference, or if a kiss is just a kiss, regardless of who the guy—"

One minute she was talking, trying to outline the experiment's protocol, and the next, his mouth claimed hers. Strong arms, more exciting than she'd imagined in her wildest dreams, clasped her against his unforgiving body. Alicia reveled in it, opened her mouth to his. *Yes, yes, yes . . .* The litany filled her mind, obliterating rational thought.

He kept the kiss restrained, slow and thorough as

he explored her mouth with his own. His tongue swept past her lips, touched her own, tingled her lips with tender strokes, establishing once and for all that the desire was mutual.

He broke the kiss and stared down at her, his own look of amazement reflecting what she felt. She gasped and blinked, trying to remember how this had come about, trying to think what to do next. "I guess that answers that."

Her flip comment spurred one of his own. "So, Doctor, your experiment was a success?"

She bit her lip and smiled up at him. "Yes. But my hypothesis failed miserably."

"Failed." He slid his hands up her back to caress her shoulders. "I don't like failure. In fact, I'm unable to accept it. So you'd better explain."

She laughed self-consciously. "This is kind of hard to explain. It's so personal." She met his intimate gaze and realized how silly that observation sounded while being held in his arms. "I was attempting to prove that kissing you was less exciting than I imagined it might be."

"And it was better."

The man certainly had an ego. But she found herself nodding.

The corner of his mouth quirked up. "Funny, I wanted to know the same thing . . . about you." He traced her jaw with his thumb and Alicia arched her neck in pleasure, inviting his touch there. His voice took on a husky timbre. "And it was better."

Alicia tingled at his words, his strokes. If she'd been a kitten, she would have purred.

"So, hypothetically speaking," he said, "if we were to continue where we left off, you'd have to come up with a new hypothesis? Scientifically speaking. To make for a worthwhile experiment."

"Actually," she said slowly, amazed to find a hint of suggestiveness entering her voice, "in conducting experiments, it's best not to go with your first finding, but to repeat the test . . . to see if you achieve the same results."

He cupped her face in his callused palm. Alicia rubbed her cheek against it, sighing in contentment. "Beautiful woman, I'd like nothing more—"

"Kiss me, Jason." She was through talking. That first, powerful kiss still lingered on her lips, flowed in her blood with the promise of greater rewards. *She could do this. With this man, she could.*

"Alicia, you don't know—"

"Kiss me." Her words lacked all restraint, blatantly revealed her newly awakened need.

"Oh, hell."

Jason's resistance finally dissolved and he pulled her hard against his chest, crushing his lips against hers. This time, he was through with polite exploring. His hand imprisoning her head, he ravaged her mouth with his own.

Alicia was completely at his mercy, given up to their mutual need, awash in erotic sensations as a deep, primal need burst awake within her. *This is what they mean by animal attraction,* she thought in a daze.

She wove her fingers into his thick, tawny hair, locking his head in place so she could ravage him back. She'd never felt so hungry in her life.

Hot hands swept up her back, then down, past her waist to her bottom, cupping it and pulling her hard against his arousal. Suddenly, she was no longer on her feet. He lifted her up and placed her on the counter by the sink. Alicia spread her thighs, welcoming him between them, pressing her knees hard against his hips to keep him there. One of her pumps tumbled to the carpet, so Alicia arched her foot and let the other shoe drop.

Never breaking the kiss, Jason slipped his hands under her bottom and yanked her forward, ramming her crotch hard against his own, shocking the center of her need. Alicia groaned at the shocking, gratifying sensation, and tightened her legs around his waist.

In response, Jason growled low in his throat, his hands caressing her thighs, slipping under her skirt hem to grasp her waist. His palm flattened on her stomach and she shuddered with pleasure.

Still he didn't end his assault on her mouth. He bit and nibbled and sucked at her lips, teasing her mercilessly only to claim her mouth fully, his tongue rhythmically engaging her own. Alicia met him move for move. She closed her eyes and let her emotions carry her away, unable even to remember how she'd gotten in this position.

She felt his fingers striving to dive below the dual barriers of her tight panty hose and briefs in a desperate quest for even more intimate prey. At his obvious frustration, Alicia knew she was past caution. She was ready to peel off those inconvenient hose and underpants, ready as she'd never been for a man.

"Alicia? Are you in there?" The insistent words were accompanied by a soft tapping.

Alicia and Jason froze for an impossibly long heartbeat. He withdrew his hands from under her skirt, obviously reluctant, squeezing her bottom one last, brief moment before he let her go. He set her on her feet and tugged her skirt in place. Both fought to catch their breath.

Avoiding his gaze and fighting for composure, Alicia slipped past Jason toward the door. "Coming, Helen." She tried to sound lighthearted, but her words came out strained.

Smoothing her hair in place, she glanced at Jason. His back to her, he was bracing his fists on the countertop, shoulders hunched. *He's as shaken as I am,* Alicia realized with a delicious burst of pleasure.

With a last, calming breath, Alicia opened the door.

Helen stormed in, eyes shining with excitement. "Sorry to interrupt. I couldn't wait to tell you." Never slow on the uptake, Helen stopped, clearly sensing the tension in the air. Her gaze landed on Jason. "Oh. Hello. I didn't know you were here, too."

Jason turned to face her and lifted his hand in a polite wave. He picked up the discarded cloth and sprayer and resumed his task, cleaning the sink for the second time.

Helen continued, "I saw your cart outside, Jason, I just didn't realize . . ." She glanced from Jason to Alicia and back again. "So, what were you up to with the door locked? A quickie on the couch?"

Alicia gave her a strained smile, fighting to project a composed front. "Not quite."

"Uh-huh." Helen's eyes narrowed suspiciously, and Alicia resisted the impulse to smooth her mussed hair. "Well, I won't say anything about it, but if you aren't more careful, people will start to talk. I know how you'd hate that, Alicia, considering."

Alicia fought to change the subject. "You said you had some news?"

Helen clapped her hands. "Yes! Janelle had her baby last night."

"Wonderful! A boy or a girl?"

"A girl. Ashley Marie, seven pounds, four ounces. Mother and baby are both doing fine. We're collecting for flowers and gifts . . ."

"Here." Alicia went to her desk and retrieved her purse. Extracting a bill, she passed it to Helen.

"Thank you, Alicia. That's real generous. But that's not *all* the good news, right, Jason?"

He turned around slowly but said nothing.

Alicia looked from Helen to Jason and back again. "What? What is it?"

"Janelle's given notice. Wants to be a full-time mommy. And Jason's now our permanent janitor! Isn't that great?"

Alicia's mouth dropped open. She knew Helen was waiting for a response. "Yes, wonderful," she forced out. She faced Jason, fighting to project a calm, remote aspect so Helen wouldn't see how much her news disturbed her. "Congratulations, Jason. You do such a fine job . . ."

He smiled and spoke with just a hint of suggestiveness, "You're welcome. So do you."

Alicia felt her face heat. Suddenly, reality struck her like a slap in the face. Every day he'd be visiting her office, every single day of her working life . . . She'd have to face him every morning, remember that kiss, that searing, passionate kiss, and *try not to do it again* . . .

Helen continued to chat with Jason. "You're scheduled for rad training during the next two days. Don't forget."

"Wouldn't think of it."

"Rad training?" Alicia asked. "What does he need radiation training for?"

"So he can clean the labs, too, silly," Helen said. "We've been short-staffed since Janelle left, and frankly, I'm sick of doing double-duty."

"I see. I—" Alicia couldn't breathe, couldn't think. Now she wouldn't even have the sanctuary of her lab to retreat to. At any time, he could appear, to clean the sinks or mop the floors, or—kiss her. "I have to go . . . to . . . do something, down the hall. Now.

Right now. Please excuse me." She hurried out of the office in the direction of the restrooms.

Jason watched her confused retreat. He tossed down the cleanser and rag and sprinted past Helen toward the door.

"Jason, what's going on?"

He ignored Helen's question. Outside the door, he grabbed the janitorial cart and pushed it at a dead run down the hallway toward the restrooms. He narrowly missed Vana on her way toward her desk with a full pot of coffee. "Jason? What—"

"Forgot to do the restrooms," he tossed off.

He almost overshot his mark. He spread his feet and slid to a stop before the ladies' room door, ramming the cart hard against the wall. He fished out the magnetic CLOSED FOR CLEANING sign and slapped it on the door.

Maybe she wasn't alone in there. Maybe she hadn't even gone *in* there. Ah, well. Taking risks was nothing new to him. He shouldered his way inside, not bothering to call out first to alert any women inside.

He found Alicia sagged against a sink, pulling in deep breaths. A quick check under the stall doors assured him that she was alone.

She looked up when he entered, and her face paled. He had the urge to sweep her into his arms again, carry her away somewhere where nothing could hurt her, nothing could upset her. A crazy thought, considering her guilt. But that had nothing to do with their encounter, and he knew he was the cause of her distress. "Alicia—"

"What are you doing in here? This is the *ladies'* room!"

"They think I'm cleaning it. There's nothing in here I haven't seen."

Alicia seemed to think he was talking about her.

She tightened her arms across her chest. "I didn't know you'd be around forever, or believe me, that—that—*thing* we did—"

"Kiss," he supplied. Though it had been so much more. His groin still ached from their encounter, from his efforts to control the passion she'd unleashed. He hadn't wanted a woman so bad since . . . he couldn't recall.

"What happened in my office—it never would have happened, if I'd known."

He closed the distance between them. She backed up against the tile wall, between the towel dispenser and the sink counter. He planted his hand above her head. "I'm glad it did," he said. "And I think you are, too, if you're at all honest with yourself."

"I'm honest," she began.

Honest. A flash of pain stabbed Jason's chest at her words. She didn't know the meaning of the word. "Are you, now? Then prove it. Follow through, Alicia. With me."

"What—what's that supposed to mean?" Her gaze slipped past him, taking in the restroom. "Here?" Her eyes grew huge, as if she expected him to jump her right there and then.

He couldn't keep a smile from his face. She was unbelievable—all cool and professional until someone dared to get close; then she turned into a confused teenager. He wasn't used to such unsophisticated behavior from a woman and found that it fascinated him. The good doctor had a meaningful relationship with her microbes, yet she was completely naive about men. "Cold tiles aren't my style. I want to take you on a date."

"A . . . date."

Jason had meant to be harsh with this "thief," to demand that he take her to bed and get this attraction out of both their systems, to frighten her off so completely that he wouldn't have to struggle with his desire for her anymore. But her ingenuousness threw him completely. She seemed amazed that he would even ask her out. Which made him all the more determined to succeed, and to do it right.

"How about if I take you to dinner?"

"Dinner?"

"Dinner, food, eating—you do eat, don't you? It's one of the basic biological drives. Or does a scientist like you take some kind of high-tech pill that supplies all your body's nutritional requirements?"

"Such a pill hasn't been invented—yet. It's my next project."

He stared at her, wondering if she was serious—until he caught the sparkle in her eyes. "Until that day comes, then, you have no excuse."

She chewed her lip, drawing his gaze to her luscious mouth, and he admitted to himself that he didn't have eating on his mind. "On one condition," she finally said.

"Which is?"

"It has to be somewhere secluded. I don't want to start tongues wagging around here. Everyone at Envirotech knows somebody, and a lot of them know me, and *you*. You're all they've been talking about for weeks!"

Disconcerted, he straightened. He wasn't really a janitor, but he didn't like to think she was so narrow-minded, either. "I see. You don't have to say any more."

She touched his arm, her fingertips tingling on his bare skin, and gazed up at him with her sincere brown eyes. "I'm not ashamed of you, Jason. How could any woman be? No, it's not about you at all. If you knew what I went through when my husband ran out on me . . ."

That's right. Relief swept through Jason. It really wasn't about him. Her bastard husband had engaged in a passionate affair with a coed right under Alicia's nose. Helen had filled him in on the explicit details. Seemed everyone at the university had known about the fling, except Alicia. Until she'd come home early from a scientific conference and walked in on the lovers in her bed.

The classic scenario. But Alicia had suffered through it.

Jason knew how that felt, the betrayal of love, the slam to the self-esteem. And for Alicia, the hurtful gossip. The affair, her discovery of it, and the divorce must have provided enough juice to power the grapevine for months, both at the university and here at Envirotech.

Jason's gut burned with indignation on her behalf. He cupped her chin, his thumb stroking her cheek. "Hey, I like the idea of a secluded dinner. No one will know but you and me. It'll be our secret. If there's anything I'm good at besides cleaning bathrooms, it's keeping secrets."

He leaned over her, contemplated her marvelously sensuous lips, even now opening slightly in anticipation of his kiss. Despite the unromantic surroundings, he burned to finish what they'd started in her office. But now wasn't the time. Instead, he brushed his mouth against her forehead. "This Friday. Be ready at seven o'clock."

She nodded, speechless. He backed away from her, then forced himself to turn and leave the restroom.

"I could hardly believe it myself."

Janelle accepted her newborn from the nurse and cradled her in the crook of her arm. She smiled at

Alicia, looking incredibly vibrant despite a twelve-hour unprogressive labor that had ended in a Caesarean section. But Janelle wasn't talking about the miracle of birth.

"Two hundred and fifty thousand big ones, just like that," Janelle said in her childlike voice. "It *has* to be someone at Envirotech. Robert and me—our folks don't have that kind of money. So it has to be someone from work."

"Yes, I suppose it does."

"I guess I did a good turn for somebody. Or something." Janelle shrugged, and Alicia got the impression that she didn't want to examine the reason for the gift too closely.

Alicia worried her lip as she tried to figure it out. She'd swung by the hospital on her way home to see Janelle and her new baby, and to give her a gift. Naturally, they'd talked about her sudden decision not to return to work. Now Janelle was telling her that she'd received an anonymous gift of a quarter million dollars to start little Ashley Marie's life off on the right foot.

Janelle wasn't the least concerned about who the generous donor might be. She acted as if she'd won the lottery. "I *still* can't believe it. Maybe President Fielding appreciated me emptying his wastebasket more than I realized." She laughed gaily. "You think it might be him? I'd sure like to thank him, if it is. Now, with Robert working swing at the plant full-time, this is enough to let me stay home until my little girl here"—she traced the baby's sweet, sleepy face—"goes to school. Maybe even a private school, if the money holds out."

"Invest it, Janelle."

"Oh, yeah. That, too."

"It's odd, though," Alicia said, almost to herself.

People didn't just go around giving other people huge gifts of money anonymously. "The card gave no clue?"

Janelle shrugged. "All it said was that I could have the money so I could stay home with Ashley. Like I'd argue with that! It's right here."

She lifted the pink card from the table and passed it to Alicia. Along with a cartoon of a baby in pink booties was the straightforward "Congratulations on your new arrival" on front. Inside, a laser-printed message—impossible to trace—said what Janelle had related: "So that you can spend these precious years at home with your daughter. An anonymous friend." No actual requirement that she quit work. Still, work as the Envirotech janitor wasn't that plum of a job, and quitting now wouldn't be detrimental to Janelle if she wanted to return to work in a few years. No, it had been a sure bet that Janelle would leap at the chance to quit and stay home with her adorable newborn. Who wouldn't?

"Well, congratulations, Janelle." Trying to stifle her nagging uneasiness, Alicia smiled warmly at her as she rose to leave. "All I got you was a baby outfit. I hope it fits her. I don't know much about baby things." She gestured to the boxed gift on Janelle's lap.

Janelle patted the department-store-wrapped box. "Thank you, Alicia. All you guys have been great. I'll really miss you. But I hear my replacement is something else! I'm sorry I missed him but Robert isn't, of course."

Alicia smiled. "He's something else, all right. I'm just not sure what that something is."

On her way out of the hospital to her car, she analyzed her nagging sense that the money was somehow connected to Jason. Jason, who—now that Janelle was staying home—had her job. But why would she think Jason was involved? Why would Jason want so badly to become Envirotech's permanent janitor that he would give a stranger money? The answer was, he wouldn't. If he had a quarter million dollars to throw around, he wouldn't even *need* to work as a janitor making barely above minimum wage. No, her suspicions were groundless. So why couldn't she dispel the feeling that the mysterious gift signaled an even deeper mystery?

"You're on your own, Jason. Just don't break anything." Helen's eyes danced over Jason's body. "But you don't strike me as the clumsy type."

Jason smiled at her. "Sometimes I can tell my feet apart."

Stripping off her lab coat and tossing it in a bin, Helen stepped into the radiation monitor near the main door—a portal that checked her and her clothing for any stray exposure to radiation. A moment later, it beeped that she was clean. Before she left, she glanced back. "Oh, and don't get in Alicia's way when she's concentrating. That's rule one."

"Right." Rules. In the past two days, Jason had been dosed with enough rules to last the rest of his life. The proper procedures for working in the lab were now ingrained in his brain—and he was just there to sweep the floors and clean the tiny restroom off the main lab.

The long rectangular room looked much like any lab, except for two things. One was the series of hot cells along the far wall, where lab workers could handle small amounts of radioactive materials by wearing heavy gloves attached to portholes in the front.

The other was the huge hot cell in a back compartment. There, contained within three feet of lead, rested a two-foot-long glowing capsule of cesium-137, so radioactive it glowed blue. When a specimen needed to be irradiated, a panel slid back, exposing it to what should be lethal doses.

Jason hadn't seen this procedure—he wasn't allowed in the back room, and he didn't particularly want to go in there. Just the thought of Alicia going in there disturbed him. Radiation was so . . . elusive, so deadly. Invisible, with no smell, no feel, no way of knowing you'd been exposed if you didn't use the full-body radiation monitor. And if you *were* exposed, no way of knowing whether it would cause cancer years from now. And no way to reverse it. And he thought *he* lived a risky lifestyle.

But the most important part of the lab was a cooler against the back wall, where Alicia's bio-engineered bacteria were stored. He'd seen her remove blue-labeled petri dishes from inside. Once he made certain they contained what he suspected, he merely had to help himself and his job would be through.

The thought brought him no joy.

He glanced toward where Alicia sat on a stool, her eye pressed to the lens of a microscope. Her white lab coat made her look even more petite, and a swell of protectiveness rose in his chest.

Throughout the afternoon, while Helen had given him an on-the-job orientation in the lab, he'd kept her in his sights. Whenever their eyes met, she gave him mysterious Mona Lisa smiles, which distracted and intrigued him much more than an obvious acknowledgment would have.

Now, perhaps, he could say hello properly—and kiss that scowl of concentration off her face. That achieved, he hoped he could get past his attraction enough to learn what he needed to know about her experiments. He sauntered over to her, his gaze playing along the creamy column of her neck as she bent over the microscope.

"Think if I work real hard, they'll let me wash the beakers someday?" he joked.

He saw the flicker of her smile. Despite her outward concentration, she was definitely aware of him, he realized with pleasure. He leaned against the counter beside her. "What're you looking at?"

"Bacteriological specimen 486-G. Fifth day after exposure. Zero cell-wall damage. No radiation above background."

It took Jason a moment to realize she was speaking into a cassette recorder, not to him.

Irked by her lack of response, he scooted his hips a few inches closer along the counter. "Is that your home-brewed microbe?"

"Mitochondria intact. Remarkably healthy after a sustained dose of six rads. Jason, don't you have work to do?"

"It's done. I work fast."

Alicia shifted on the stool. Jason couldn't resist. Helen had disappeared and they were alone. He reached out a finger and traced the nape of her neck. *That* got her attention.

Alicia sat bolt upright and blinked at him. "Don't *do* that. Helen—"

Jason smiled down at her, watched her eyes grow huge as she realized they were completely alone. "She left."

"Oh."

"I told you I'd keep our date a secret, Alicia. And I promise not to make passes at you in front of anyone else. But I'd be lying if I said I wasn't counting the hours until Friday night."

"Friday . . ."

She seemed distracted, remote, which irritated Jason. All he'd been able to think about was romancing her, kissing her, making love to her. Taking their incredibly hot encounter in her office and going all out, to hell with the consequences. Today was only Wednesday, and it had already been the longest week of his life. He narrowed his eyes at her. She definitely worked too hard.

Besides, he rationalized, distracting her would delay her work, and give his uncle's firm more of a chance to catch up. He shook off the cold feeling that filled him at harboring such a calculating thought. This was about business—and a healthy dose of mutual pleasure. If he played it right and kept his cool, no one would get hurt, not even Alicia. He prided himself on his ability to handle women, to take what he wanted and give equally in return, no promises made, no hearts broken. Alicia—despite her uniqueness—was just another woman underneath.

"Enough of that." He leaned closer and slipped his hand along her cheek, then dropped his mouth on hers. He gave her a soft, warm kiss, just a little reminder of what they'd already done—what he planned to do, come Friday. She responded so completely, he had to forcibly restrain himself from taking it farther. Damn, she was sweet. He lifted his mouth and met her gaze. "Friday night."

Alicia nodded. "Yes. I—I know. I couldn't very well forget."

Jason smiled at her admission. "Good. Now that we have that settled, tell me what you're doing. In English." He propped a hand on the counter and stared down at her.

She hesitated. "You really want to know?"

"Damn straight. I want to know what occupies your mind—besides me, that is."

"You're incredibly arrogant, Jason Kirkland."

"I know. It's part of my charm. So, you've radiated these little bacteria in this dish here"—he pointed at the petri dish on the counter—"and you're analyzing a sample for the damage that's been done—is that it?"

Her eyebrows arched in surprise. "Yes, that's close. Very close."

He grinned, loving the surprise on her face, yet irritated by it at the same time. She continued to assume he was a janitor and nothing more—which he *should* be pleased with. It was, after all, the role he'd adopted, and why he was here in the first place. But he wanted Alicia to see him as he really was, all the same.

"But it's more than that, isn't it? Lots of labs do radiation experiments. But your stuff . . . It really absorbs the radiation you throw at it?"

She nodded. "Yes."

"How'd you make it? You must have started with something."

She nodded vigorously, sending her hair bouncing. "It's adapted from a strain found naturally in the Czech Republic, in the soil of a uranium mine there. The bacteria thrive despite the higher-than-usual background radiation. I began analyzing them, and saw it might be possible to take their radiation-resistant characteristics and engineer them into a bacteria that can absorb radiation from other sources." She slipped off the stool. "Would you like to see?"

"Sure." He leaned over the microscope and adjusted the focus. "Looks healthy to me. Did you say you exposed this to six rads? That would cause a human some serious damage."

"I see you were paying attention in your radiation training."

"Sometimes even *I* do what I'm told. When I'm properly motivated and rewarded."

"You make yourself sound like a lab specimen."

"Pavlov's dogs."

"Exactly."

"Not quite. I respond best when I get the experimenter to respond to me just as well." He shot a cocky grin at her, watched her begin to color just slightly as both of them recalled her own little "experiment" with him.

Alicia cleared her throat, as if anxious to get their conversation back to a professional level. "Not only can my bacteria withstand such extremes of exposure, they absorb any radiation which strikes them."

Jason turned his attention back to the microscope. It had been years since he'd fiddled with one, and he found it fascinating. "The source in the back room—where'd it come from?"

"It's a cesium capsule, on loan from the government. To them it's just waste, but it emits the gamma radiation I need to conduct my experiments."

"Nasty stuff. Doesn't it give you the creeps?"

"I'm used to it."

He lifted his eyes and met hers. "I suppose that's okay, as long as it's safe for you."

"It is." She smiled softly. "I've been doing this for years. My radiation dose is minimal. Less than if I lived in mile-high Denver or took a lot of plane flights."

"Because the higher you are above sea level, the thinner the atmosphere, and the more radiation."

She nodded. "As long as a person takes the proper precautions, it's safe. But you have to respect it for what it is, of course."

"Of course. The energy of the universe."

She nodded her head. "That's a good way to put it."

His gaze drifted along her lush lips. "Just one of the irresistible energies we have to respect." He circled her waist with his arm. She was standing so close, how could he resist?

He tugged her toward him and her initial resistance gave way. Excitement hummed along his nerves as she leaned into him and slipped her small hands up his shoulders, her passion-filled eyes boldly meeting his. Her every curve molded to his body, and he wanted badly to get lost in her. Somehow, her desire for him made him feel strong, feel worthy, because she was such an exceptional woman. And Friday was such an incredibly long time away . . .

A loud bang startled them both and they flew apart. Helen stood there, a skeptical look on her face. "Jason, aren't you done cleaning *yet?*"

He rose from the stool and strode toward the radiation monitor. It beeped clear. He winked at Helen and slipped out the door.

Helen narrowed her eyes at Alicia, her hands planted on her ample hips. "Okay, Doc. That's twice in one week I feel like I'm intruding on something extremely private. Care to 'fess up?"

"I—I was just showing him my sample," Alicia said, knowing how lame her protest sounded as soon as the words left her mouth.

"Uh-huh. So how long have you two been sampling each other?"

"We're not! Don't be silly. I mean, *really*, Helen. Is that all you think about? Men, and—and—and—"

"Sex, Alicia. You can say it. You *are* a biologist."

"Okay. Sex. Sex, sex, sex. Satisfied?"

"The question is, are you? What's going on with Jason? Has he gotten you to look up from your microscope and notice the big world around you? I imagine if anyone could, it'd be him."

Helen's perceptive yet concerned gaze crumbled Alicia's resolve to keep her date with Jason a secret. She desperately wanted to talk to someone smart about men, and knew she could trust Helen not to gossip.

"He asked me out on a date."

"Seriously?" Helen plopped onto the lab stool next to Alicia. "Where's he taking you?"

Alicia frowned. "I don't have the foggiest idea. Could be for beer and pizza for all I know. I can't imagine he can afford anything fancy. Maybe he likes to dance? Or go to the movies?" The unknown suddenly felt terribly frightening, and a swell of panic rose in her chest. "Oh, God, Helen, I don't know anything about him! What have I gotten myself into?" She buried her face in her hands.

Helen patted her shoulder. "I don't get you, girl. You obviously think he's a hunk. We all do. Half the women in this building are fantasizing about going to bed with him. He wants you, you want him—where's the problem?"

Alicia lifted her head and shook it vigorously. "No, you don't understand. Just having him *in* here . . . I'm not used to it."

"What makes you so different from the rest of us? Besides your IQ, I mean."

"Because it's not a joke to me! President Fielding expects a marketable product by October first, the start of the fiscal year. But I can't focus when Jason's around. When he shows up in my office or here in the lab, I can't take my eyes off him. My concentration is completely shot."

"It's okay to be human, Alicia," Helen said gently. "It's okay to succumb to your need for companionship, for good, healthy *sex.*" She laughed. "And he's ready to provide, I'd say. That man was *made* for lovin'."

"Helen!" Alicia felt defensive on Jason's behalf. He was more than a sex machine to her. And that was what was beginning to scare her, despite her initial idea of conducting an experiment by engaging in a wild, uninhibited, *short-term* affair. He was intelligent, witty, compassionate . . .

"You *do* know it's mutual, don't you?" Helen asked. "Hey, he spends ten times as long cleaning your office as anyone else's."

Alicia smiled softly. "I suspected that."

"Well, there ya go! If you're concerned about staying focused, there *is* a solution. And it's *not* locking yourself in your lab. Go for it. Get it out of your system. Scratch your itch! And don't worry about rumors. *I* won't tell anyone."

It was so tempting. Friday was only two days away. What sort of date did Jason have in mind? Dinner and a movie? Bar hopping? His place, her place, what? The uncertainty terrified her, but she couldn't deny a tiny burst of excitement at the mystery, as well.

She had to find out what he planned. And she had to decide just how far she was willing to go with him. And if she planned to sleep with him. That had to be decided before the evening began. Everything should be planned out logically. All the variables carefully controlled so nothing could take her by surprise. Say she engaged in one wild evening of unbridled passion. Then—

Her head shot up and she faced Helen, panic coursing through her. "And *then* what? He'd be here every day. I'd never be able to break it off, to . . . *contain* it."

"He's not a radiation sample, Alicia. Maybe you

don't *need* to contain it. If you sleep with him and you like it, then keep doing it, if it feels right. If you decide it isn't right, end it. You did that with Leon easy enough. You're both adults. I think he can handle it, if you're honest with him." She sighed in exasperation. "You may be a genius in your field, Alicia, but you're a baby when it comes to men."

Alicia traced a silken rose petal. Creamy white with soft pink edges, they were the loveliest flowers she'd ever seen. She couldn't ever remember receiving such a beautiful gift.

The fresh bouquet had been lying on her desk, tied with a pink ribbon, when she entered her office that morning. Friday morning. Only ten hours until her big date. Did Jason always treat first dates to such a magnificent gift? There were at least two dozen long-stemmed roses in the bouquet. It must have cost him a day's pay.

She glanced around, making sure she was alone, before extracting the card from the envelope nestled among the stems.

Counting the hours until tonight—JK.

She sank into her chair. Try as she might, she'd been unable to learn what he planned for their date. He seemed to think the mystery was fun. It certainly had intensified her anticipation—and her fear. The evening was completely out of her control, leaving her to imagine all sorts of scenarios. And despite her common sense and usually cautious nature, every one of them ended with a passionate seduction. Jason Kirkland—she was confident of at least this much—expected to score tonight. Score? Is that what he thought of her, as a conquest to vanquish? Probably.

No, undoubtedly.

They hardly knew each other. All they had in common was an incredible attraction that Alicia still had difficulty believing wasn't entirely one-sided. After all, as far as women went, she was pretty much a geek. No doubt he envisioned telling his bar buddies later how he'd made it with a wallflower scientist, just for kicks.

But when she was around Jason, she found it difficult to ascribe such a motive to him. Nor, in his presence, did she feel like a geek. Instead, she felt exceedingly feminine, unusually emotional and remarkably unrestrained.

Helen was right. She was a baby when it came to understanding men. She didn't know how to take this gift of flowers, what it really meant. She didn't know whether Jason wanted anything from her but sex, or whether he only saw her as an interesting challenge.

Yet he seemed so entranced by her . . .

Was it real, or was he after something else entirely? Why did she have the nagging suspicion that Jason was a complicated man who was hiding as much of himself as he was willing to reveal?

Alicia shook her head. Why was she even asking these questions? From the first, she had convinced herself that all *she* wanted from Jason was sex. She had to remember that. It had been *her* idea to seduce *him*. Somehow, he'd taken control.

She rose and took a vase from her bookcase, filled it at the sink and arranged the bouquet in it.

"Oooh, somebody likes Alicia," singsonged Vana as she came in to drop off Alicia's mail. "Who gave you the bouquet?"

"Uh . . ." Alicia stalled, staring out of the window for a moment. She turned around and smiled. "Just a friend."

Vana lifted her eyebrows. "A boyfriend, you mean. Who is it? Someone I know?"

Alicia pulled out a generous handful of the flowers. "This bouquet's huge. Would you like these for your desk?"

"Sure! Thanks, Alicia." Vana took the flowers and left.

Alicia breathed a sigh of relief. Until she realized that people would remark on Vana's flowers, and Vana would tell them exactly where she got them. Then everyone on the floor would be asking Alicia who her admirer was.

She rubbed her forehead and muttered, "Dumb, Alicia, really, really dumb."

Why did Jason have to give her such an outrageous, *obvious* gift? She thought he understood she wanted to keep this whole thing low-key.

No, she couldn't blame Jason. The gift was beautiful. It was her own fault for mixing business and pleasure. Attempting to grab the forbidden, right here in the fortress of her safe, secure working world.

What she *should* do was start thinking for a change. Big biceps and heart-melting kisses were one thing, but her reputation, her career, were the most important things in her life. She'd simply break the date before anything happened that she would regret.

She gazed at the clock. 8:57. As soon as Jason Kirkland came to empty her wastebasket, she'd tell him she couldn't make it. She'd do her best to be gracious, but she'd simply tell him the truth—she didn't want to get involved.

Chicken. Alicia tamped down the mocking voice in her head. She wasn't *afraid*, really. This was about her dream.

She stared at the clock, recalling all the years of hard work that had brought her to this point. She was almost at the pinnacle of success. Jason Kirkland didn't have any concept of what it meant to her. He was the worst sort of distraction.

8:59. No sign of Jason yet. Despite herself, her thoughts turned to their stolen kisses here in her office—and more. She pinned her gaze to the poster of the orcas above her sofa and tried to blank her mind. It didn't mean anything. Theirs was a purely animal attraction, and she was a woman of logic and thoughtfulness. She was *not* the sort to be swept away by passion.

9:03. The second hand swept around the face of her clock. She ought to get back to work, but she knew she had to remain firm in her purpose. Work would only sidetrack her.

Instantly appalled at her thought, Alicia mentally chastised herself. Already she had let her infatuation with Jason take precedence. Work was distracting her from thoughts of him!

9:07. He was bound to appear any moment. Alicia paced across her office and rearranged the roses on the bookcase. Then she paced back behind her desk. She tapped on her keyboard, checked a couple of E-mail messages, then crossed the room again to the sink. She got herself a glass of water and stared at the clock.

9:20. Restless, she returned to her desk and began sorting her reading material. She began a magazine article but read the introductory paragraph three times without having a clue what it said. Disgusted with her lack of concentration, she tossed it aside.

9:37. Still no sign of Jason. Irritated at being kept waiting, frustrated at being unable to carry through on her fresh convictions, Alicia swept up the phone.

"Janitorial." His deep New England accent echoed across the phone line.

Alicia gripped the receiver harder. She had expected he'd still be making his rounds, and she might be able to take the coward's way out and leave a message. "Jason. You're there."

"Well, hi to you, too."

Alicia fought down a surge of pleasure at the intimate warmth of his voice. "I thought you'd come by. I've been waiting for you. I wanted to talk to you, about tonight." She sucked in a breath. Time to take back control. "Perhaps tonight isn't the best idea. I have an awful lot of work to do, and President Fielding has given me a new deadline on my latest series of experiments—"

"Look in your wastebasket."

"What?"

"Look in your wastebasket."

Alicia turned her chair and glanced toward it. Not only had Jason already emptied the trash, he'd left a small gift-wrapped box inside. If she'd gotten to work instead of getting lost in thoughts of him, perhaps she would have noticed. "Oh." She pulled out the gift. It looked like a professional, department-store wrapping job, which had to mean another gift Jason could hardly afford on his salary. "Jason, you can't be doing this. It's only a first date! First the flowers, now—"

"Did you like them?"

"Yes. I *love* them." Her voice softened as she gazed at the vase on her bookcase, thoughts of control temporarily shelved. "They're beautiful. The most beautiful flowers I've ever seen. No one's ever given me . . ." She shook her head to reclaim her sense. "Anyway, thank you. But it's far too generous. They must have cost a fortune."

"As long as you like them. Open the box."

"You shouldn't be buying me gifts. We hardly know each other."

"Uh-huh." Jason sounded unconvinced. "Just open it."

Carefully, Alicia slipped a nail under the tape and loosened it, then proceeded to unfold the wrapping in her usual neat manner.

"I don't hear tearing paper, Alicia. Don't try to save the paper. Just rip into it."

"Well, okay." Alicia tore it off in two hunks. She balled up the paper and tossed it in the wastebasket. She popped open the hinged box. Nestled inside on black velvet was a classic—and probably very expensive—gold watch. "A watch."

"Not just any watch. Look at the time."

The hands were frozen at 7:00. "The time of our date?" She put her fingers on the knob to set it.

"You can try changing the time, but it won't run."

"You mean—you gave me a broken watch?"

"Wear it tonight."

"I don't understand."

"And use it."

"Oh. I see." Jason wanted her to forget about clocks, deadlines and schedules. And plans—and knowing what would come next. It was a wonderfully romantic notion. Unfortunately, she had no intention of going on their date. That was why she'd called him. Except now, as she slipped the broken watch on her wrist, the glow of anticipation returned stronger than ever, and her fears seemed silly. Would it really hurt her to give up control for one night? Her gaze fell on the report she'd been unable to focus on.

Yes, her rational mind insisted. *Don't blow this, Alicia. You're so close.* She swallowed hard and steeled herself, her fingers gripping the edge of her desk as if she feared being ripped away. "Jason, about to-

THE PUBLISHERS OF ZEBRA BOUQUET

are making this special offer to lovers of contemporary romances to introduce this exciting new line of novels. Zebra's Bouquet Romances have been praised by critics and authors alike as being of the highest quality and best written romantic fiction available today.

EACH FULL-LENGTH NOVEL

has been written by authors you know and love as well as by up and coming writers that you'll only find with Zebra Bouquet. We'll bring you the newest novels by world famous authors like Vanessa Grant, Judy Gill, Ann Josephson and award winning Suzanne Barrett and Leigh Greenwood—to name just a few. Zebra Bouquet's editors have selected only the very best and highest quality romances for up-and-coming publications under the Bouquet banner.

YOU'LL BE TREATED

to tales of star-crossed lovers in glamourous settings that are sure to captivate you. These stories will keep you enthralled to the very happy end.

4 FREE NOVELS
As a way to introduce you to these terrific romances, the publishers of Bouquet are offering Zebra Romance readers Four Free Bouquet novels. They are yours for the asking with no obligation to buy a single book. Read them at your leisure. We are sure that after you've read these introductory books you'll want more! (If you do not wish to receive any further Bouquet novels, simply write "cancel" on the invoice and return to us within 10 days.)

SAVE 20% WITH HOME DELIVERY
Each month you'll receive four just-published Bouquet romances. We'll ship them to you as soon as they are printed (you may even get them before the bookstores). You'll have 10 days to preview these exciting novels for Free. If you decide to keep them, you'll be billed the special preferred home subscription price of just $3.20 per book; a total of just $12.80 — that's a savings of 20% off the publisher's price. If for any reason you are not satisfied simply return the novels for full credit, no questions asked. You'll never have to purchase a minimum number of books and you may cancel your subscription at any time.

GET STARTED TODAY –
NO RISK AND NO OBLIGATION

To get your introductory gift of 4 Free Bouquet Romances fill out and mail the
enclosed Free Book Certificate today. We'll ship your free books as soon as we
receive this information. Remember that you are under no obligation. This is
a risk-free offer from the publishers of Zebra Bouquet Romances.

Call us TOLL FREE at 1-888-345-BOOK
Visit our website at www.kensingtonbooks.com

FREE BOOK CERTIFICATE

YES! I would like to take you up on your offer. Please send me 4 Free Bouquet Romance Novels as my
introductory gift. I understand that unless I tell you otherwise, I will then receive the 4 newest Bouquet novels
to preview each month FREE for 10 days. If I decide to keep them I'll pay the preferred home subscriber's price
of just $3.20 each (a total of only $12.80) plus $1.50 for shipping and handling. That's a 20% savings off the
publisher's price. I understand that I may return any shipment for full credit–no questions asked–and I may cancel
this subscription at any time with no obligation. Regardless of what I decide to do, the 4 Free Introductory Novels
are mine to keep as Bouquet's gift.

BN050A

Name _____

Address _____

City _____ State _____ Zip _____

Telephone ( ) _____

Signature _____
(If under 18, parent or guardian must sign.)

For your convenience you may charge your shipments automatically to a Visa or MasterCard so you'll
never have to worry about late payments and missing shipments. If you return any shipment, we'll
credit your account.

☐ Yes, charge my credit card for my "Bouquet Romance" shipments until I tell you otherwise.
☐ Visa ☐ MasterCard

Account Number _____

Expiration Date _____

Signature _____

Orders subject to acceptance by Zebra Home Subscription Service. Terms and Prices subject to change.
Order valid only in the U.S.

If this response card is missing,
call us at 1-888-345-BOOK.

Be sure to visit our website at
www.kensingtonbooks.com

BOUQUET ROMANCES
Zebra Home Subscription Service, Inc.
P.O. Box 5214
Clifton NJ 07015-5214

PLACE
STAMP
HERE

night. Why I called. The flowers are wonderful, and the watch, it's . . . priceless. But besides the work I have to do, I'm not sure it's such a good idea, with you working here permanently—Jason?"

An odd crackling sound came over the phone line. "—can't hear you—some kind of—"

"Jason?"

"Phone's not—be interference," Jason said through the crackle.

"What's going on? What's wrong with the phone? Can't you hear me?"

"Alicia? You there?—coming up." He disconnected.

Alicia stared at the receiver in her hand. That was certainly odd. Just as she'd been about to break their date, the phone line had acted up. She never remembered *that* happening before. Come to think of it, the interference had sounded an awful lot like crumpling paper.

She suddenly remembered how Jason had broken her date with Leon. When the traditional approach didn't meet his needs, he improvised. Nor was he the type of man to take no for an answer.

And he was heading up here.

SEVEN

Alicia didn't have long to wait. In a matter of minutes, Jason entered her office. He closed the door behind him and strode over to where she was sitting. He planted a hand squarely on the desk and leaned over her, narrowing the distance between them to mere inches.

"What exactly were you trying to tell me, Alicia? And don't mince words."

Now she was on the spot. Whatever she had to say would have to be to his incredibly handsome face, now staring intently at her. Alicia breathed deeply of his masculine scent and her heart raced out of control. She tried to remember what she planned to say, but all her rational arguments fled her mind.

She swallowed hard as her gaze swept over his defined chest, outlined in his tight T-shirt. Damn him! Here he was, every sexy square inch of him, in all his male glory, reminding her just by his presence why she'd envisioned pursuing a fling with him.

She lifted her gaze and he captured her eyes with his own. The emotion there startled her, reached past her rational arguments to a deeper need she tried to deny within herself. Still, she strived to fight it. "Just because you're sexy as hell doesn't mean—"

"Just because you're smart doesn't mean—"

Their nearly identical sentences were spoken at the same time. Both of them burst out laughing. "You worry too much," Jason said.

"And you don't worry enough. Everyone's going to talk about my flowers, wonder who gave them to me."

He arched an eyebrow. "And you won't tell them."

"Not yet. It's only a first date. You shouldn't even have given them to me."

"Quit questioning my gifts, Alicia. Just enjoy them. There will be more tonight. I'll pick you up at seven o'clock. Look at your watch if you forget." He tapped her watch, sending a spark through Alicia's wrist straight up her arm.

Jason was more powerful than a tornado, breaching her barriers and leaving her fears in the dust. She gave up trying to fight him. Her eyes locked on his, she realized how foolish her fears had been. Only one date. Finally, she allowed herself to succumb. He was in control of the evening's plans. With a shock, Alicia realized that she enjoyed the sensation. All that was expected of her was to sit back and enjoy herself—no deadlines, no reports, no impossibly high expectations. All she had to do was be a woman—if she could remember how. "Um . . . What do I wear?"

A slow, sensuous smile slid along his lips. "Simple. Pretend you're going to the Ritz."

Without waiting for a response, he turned and strode toward the door.

Alicia watched him go. He walked like a man in complete control of his surroundings, the king of the hill. A man who knew she wouldn't manage to break their date because he refused to let her. Where did such confidence come from? Jason's worldliness put him in command of any situation, and put her own bookish education to shame. And she'd fancied that she could control their date! Her eyes playing over his strong back, she chewed her lip, finally accepting the risk she was taking in spending time with such a magnetic man. She could do it. After all, she wouldn't be alone. For some undefined reason she trusted Jason not to hurt her.

But the Ritz . . . She didn't think there was such a restaurant in Seattle, but did he plan to take her to a fancy restaurant, on his salary? He was certainly determined to impress her—and he was succeeding. Yet what did he mean by "pretend?"

Jason stopped at the door and turned back to her. "Oh. One more thing. Don't wear panty hose."

Alicia's mouth dropped open as she remembered quite clearly how he'd fought to slide his hand down her underwear during their "kiss"—and how badly she wished he'd succeeded.

Then he winked and left her office.

Alicia outsmarted him, in her own way.

She spent hours agonizing over an appropriate dress, finally selecting a basic black cocktail dress. And she wore lacy black silk thigh-highs instead of panty hose. He'd think she'd ignored his command—at first.

She'd chosen her lingerie with equal care, selecting a rose-colored silk bra and panty set she hardly ever wore because it was so impractical.

She stared at her image in the full-length mirror in her bedroom, wondering what he would think. Basic. Nothing surprising or daring about her outfit. She hadn't wanted to exude sexiness when she bought the dress for the business functions she usually wore it to. The high heels helped, as did the fake pearl necklace and earrings. She looked fairly sophisticated. Still . . .

The idea that struck her was so outrageous, Alicia blushed just thinking about it. She'd never done anything like it.

Of course, she would be the only one who knew, unless . . . Unless the evening concluded as she hoped—feared?—it might. Still, just *knowing* for herself would give her a sense of recklessness and power. Tonight, she had a feeling she'd need every advantage.

She slipped her hands under her dress and worked her panties down her legs. The silk puddled at her feet. She stepped out of the panties and smoothed her dress back in place. Instantly she was fully aware of her nudity under her clothing. It was a decidedly wicked and delicious sensation.

Now she was ready for her date with Jason Kirkland.

The doorbell rang promptly at seven. Alicia opened the door of her small house and stared at the man on the steps.

It wasn't Jason. The man wore a navy uniform and a cap. Behind him, parked on the curb—since it would never fit in her narrow one-car driveway—was a stretch limousine.

"Dr. Underwood? I'm here on behalf of Jason Kirkland. He sent me to escort you to him."

Alicia nodded, trying to regain her composure and get over her shock. This was so far above and beyond typical first-date etiquette, she hadn't a clue what to think. "Just let me—get my purse."

She swept it off the hall table and closed the front door behind her. The chauffeur led the way to the

limo and opened the back door for her. Alicia slipped
onto the velvet seat. An identical bench faced her,
but it was empty. She had expected that Jason might
be waiting for her inside. Beside her was a minibar,
and a television was inset above the opposite bench.
Soft classical music played through stereo speakers.

The limo pulled into the street and headed onto
the highway toward—somewhere. Alicia turned her
attention from the amazing features of this room on
wheels to the window. The sun was still high in the
sky. They seemed to be heading north, toward Lake
Washington. There were several nice restaurants
around the lake. That must be where they were going.

Alicia settled back into the seat. She fought down
a mixture of anxiety and tremendous anticipation.
Was this the other "gift" Jason had mentioned, or
did he have something more planned? How could
he afford this? And why would he do it? Maybe this
was his way of ensuring that she'd be so grateful,
she'd tumble into bed with him. Maybe . . . But then,
a man like Jason wouldn't have to romance a woman
off her feet to get a little bedtime pleasure.

Would she? Would they? It was what she'd initially
planned. A brief, passionate fling. But she hadn't
imagined anything more than sex. Simple, animalistic
mating. All this—the flowers, the watch, the limousine—had the flavor of something much, much more,
something she wasn't certain she was ready for.

Worse, with romance involved, the pressure on her
increased exponentially. Would she disappoint him,
too? Would the evening end at best in an uncomfortable, embarrassing encounter she could fool him
into thinking she'd enjoyed? Or, at worst, in an argument and tears? She was afraid to anticipate any-

thing better, despite how much she longed for her secret fantasies to come true.

A billboard caught her eye as they drove past. JUST DO IT, the slogan read.

Just do it.

She could almost hear Jason saying, "You worry too much." She knew he was right. She was trying her darnedest to predict and control the world around her, analyze everything Jason did, every gift he gave her, trying to work it into a social pattern she recognized despite her limited experience.

But she had no experience with a man like Jason. She was used to getting to know a man through shared interests, through work, then gradually easing into a social relationship. Jason had stormed into her life, into her awareness, and shaken everything up— her notions of men, her ideas on relationships, her understanding of her own needs.

Lost in thought, she didn't realize at first that the limousine had turned into a long, narrow drive. They were pulling into a marina. They passed the main building, headquarters of a yacht club, and continued toward the docks.

Yachts and sailboats were moored at the docks. A few people stood or worked on the decks of some of the boats. One boat was just pulling in.

A gorgeous sailboat at the far end caught her eye, its deck softly lit with strings of paper lanterns. A man stood on deck, his gaze following the progress of the limousine toward him. *Jason.*

The limo slowed to a stop before the dock at the end. A moment later, the passenger door opened and Jason was standing there. He held out a hand to her. She took it and stepped out, unable to tear her gaze from him.

He was transformed. He wore a black double-

breasted suit—with the jacket causally open—and no
tie with his stylish collarless shirt. He wore his formal
attire in a casual way, as if he was exceedingly comfortable in it. He took both her hands in his and
squeezed them gently. "Thank God you're here. I
was about to wear a hole in the deck."

"Am I late?"

"No. I'm just anxious." He grinned, and Alicia felt
her bones melt. His appreciative gaze—slid along her
simple dress, then settled on her legs. "You followed
my instructions." His brow furrowed. "Except for the
panty hose."

She smiled secretively at him, suddenly feeling
wondrously mischievous and lighthearted, younger
than she had in years. "You said dress for the Ritz.
Aren't ties required?" She traced a playful finger
down his chest.

He grasped her hand. "I said for you to *pretend*
we're going there. And you did wonderfully. Now,
before you say anything else—before you come
aboard—you have to swear to me that you won't say
anything about how expensive it all is. Just enjoy it."

Just do it. The words echoed in Alicia's head again.
She nodded. "I promise."

He grinned.

"Even though the limousine was . . . well . . ."

He shot her a warning look.

". . . quite a surprise," she finished with a teasing
smile. "You definitely have class, Jason Kirkland."

"Come on. There's more." He held out his arm
and she took it, letting him lead her down the dock
to the side of the sailboat. The limousine drove off.

Jason stepped on deck first and helped her aboard.
Alicia looked around in amazement. The paper lan-
terns strung about cast a golden glow on the water.
A table for two stood on deck, set for fine dining,

with a white linen tablecloth and napkins edged in lace. A wine bottle waited in a stand beside the table. Soft jazz was being piped on deck from a hidden stereo system. Alicia had never been invited to such a perfect setting for a seduction. A thrill of excitement tingled in her blood and she was suddenly very glad she'd come, however the evening ended.

"Uh, do you do this for all your girlfriends?" she finally asked.

"No. Are you hungry?"

She nodded. With a hand on her back, he gently led her toward the table and pulled out a chair for her. Alicia sat down. The action reminded her she wore nothing under her dress. A shock of sensual awareness swept through her, making her feel naughty and wild and totally unlike the cool scientist she usually was. The way she was feeling, he was going to discover her secret in a matter of hours. She wondered how he'd react.

"Myrna?" Jason called into the cabin. "We're ready."

A young woman in a neat uniform strode out and placed a covered platter before each of them. A catered meal. Of course. Why not? A giddy sense of unreality flooded through Alicia.

Jason opened the wine and poured them each a glass. "I hope you like Rieslings."

"I do, yes. Thank you." Alicia sipped the wine, feeling as if she'd landed in a fantasyland. What was she doing here, with this man? Seeing Jason Kirkland out of his usual element—pushing around his janitorial cart and scrubbing countertops—completely threw her. He sniffed the wineglass in his hand, gently swirled it and finally took a sip like a regular connoisseur. "Not as good as 1994's harvest, but it'll do. Let me know if you don't like it, Alicia, and I'll send for something else."

"No, please. It's fine. But I thought you said all you needed was a cold beer, a worn pair of jeans—"

"—and a beautiful woman. Well, one out of three isn't bad."

Myrna removed the lids from the plates, revealing Caesar salads. A basket of crusty bread and an antipasto platter completed the appetizers.

"I know you like Italian food."

"How—" She stopped herself, recalling how she'd landed on her face at the small Italian eatery when their work group took Jason out. They'd both ordered spaghetti. That day seemed so long ago. But she would never forget how he'd carried her back to the office.

"We're also having chicken tortellini in white cream sauce and brisket alla Milanese. Myrna's suggestion."

The caterer returned to his side and smiled down at him. "Yes, Mr. Kirkland. I hope it meets with your approval."

"Everything set?"

"The dinners are in the oven and dessert is in the refrigerator."

Jason nodded. "Thank you. Good night."

Myrna retrieved her purse from the cabin and stepped onto the dock. Alicia watched her retreat, concern filling her. This was just too much. She was unable to simply sit back and enjoy such excess without analyzing it—and it didn't add up. She set down her wineglass. "Okay, Jason. What's going on here? How can—"

He raised his eyebrows in warning, silently reminding her of her promise.

"I know I promised not to question anything, but this—"

"What about it?"

"You know darned well what. This isn't usual for a first date."

"Says who?"

"Well, I'm not used to it."

"To being treated properly by a man?"

His words stung and she scowled. "That's unfair, and I—"

Jason hunched forward. "Your ex was a bastard, and Leon was an idiot. Yes, I'm speaking plainly, but you're worth a hell of a lot better, Alicia. Let me give it to you tonight." Alicia started at his fierce demeanor, yet found his words warming her through, as if he were a knight defending a lady. "Quit saying, quit *thinking* it's too much. It isn't. If I could give you more—Hell." He ran a hand through his hair and looked past her, toward the water.

Alicia swallowed hard, finding it difficult to keep her voice steady. "Jason."

He swung his eyes to meet hers.

"I just want to know who you are."

A flicker of something dark flashed through his eyes, then was gone. He smiled softly. "I suppose that's fair. So. What do you want to know about me?"

"Well, how about we start with family. That's fairly easy, isn't it?"

His smile seemed to stiffen, but he nodded. "Ask away."

"You grew up in New England?"

He laughed. "How'd you figure that out?"

She joined his laughter. "A wild guess. Any brothers and sisters?"

"Only child."

"Oh? I have a brother."

Jason's smile was brilliant. "See? We have a lot in common—boys in both families."

"Not a lot . . ."

"Ask me another question."

"Tell me about your parents."

He sighed. "My folks are dead. They were killed in a plane crash when I was sixteen. My uncle stepped in and saw to my welfare. Got me through college."

As she listened to his words, his matter-of-fact tone disguising a world of hurt, a wound Alicia thought long healed cracked open in her heart. "Jason, I'm sorry. It hurt like hell, didn't it?"

Jason rotated the stem of his wineglass in his fingers. "Yeah. What about you?" He lifted his eyes to hers.

Alicia swallowed. "My parents are dead, too."

For a moment, silence descended over them. So many times over the years, Alicia had tried to explain her pain, knowing the listener didn't begin to comprehend it. Until now.

Finally, Jason spoke. "You felt betrayed. Parents aren't supposed to leave their kids. Your grief was only slightly stronger than your sense of betrayal. And *that* filled you with a nasty sense of guilt. And because you'd been abandoned, you knew you could trust no one but yourself. You knew whatever you made of your life would be completely up to you."

Alicia herself could have spoken those words. Their eyes met and clung. "Yes," she said softly. He waited for her to continue and realized she longed to talk. Nothing seemed more important than sharing her deepest pain with this man, at this moment. *He understands.*

"My dad died when I was eight," she continued, "so my mom and I grew very close. She passed away when I was fifteen. She had cancer, but . . . But it looked like she was going to make it. Only a few treatments left. We were so relieved." Alicia's memories pulled her back to the worst time in her life, before she'd built a carefully guarded wall around her deepest emotions.

"Then she began to get even sicker. Her hair fell out again, her skin turned yellow. She couldn't keep anything down. That's when we learned there was a problem with her treatment. An accident. They gave her an overdose of a radiological isotope that was supposed to kill the cancer cells. Instead, it killed *her*. My grandmother got a lawyer, and he got us a malpractice settlement." She couldn't keep the bitterness from her voice. "The money put me through college, but not before my grandma died, too."

"No wonder you're trying to find a cure for radiation. You think you owe it to your mom."

"I want to keep the same thing from ever happening to anyone again!" Alicia gripped her wineglass. "The frustration of knowing she'd been irradiated, and knowing there was no way to cure it, no way to take it back. I never want anyone to go through that again."

Admiration shone in his eyes, warming her through. "So you've dedicated your life to finding a fix."

She nodded, overwhelmed with the memories, with how good it felt to share herself, her vulnerability with this man, a man who understood because he'd also suffered.

He tossed his napkin on the table. "You're tremendously admirable," he said dryly. "All I've succeeded in doing since my parents died is screw off."

"Jason!"

"I mean it. You'd be sick if you knew what I've done. I sure haven't done a damn thing to make airplanes safer."

"No, you don't understand." Without thinking

twice, she clasped his hand where it rested on the table. Immediately, his gaze riveted on her. Her words spilled out before she realized what she was going to say. But the truth couldn't be denied. "You know how to live life. I barely see what's around me. People stopped mattering to me. I knew I couldn't rely on anyone else to be there for me, so I gave up on them." Her self-realization startled her at the same time that it freed her. "I'm not sure, suddenly, right now, whether I'm doing what my mom would have wanted. I'm so obsessive about it. I know it's not healthy. I *know* it."

He opened his mouth to interrupt, but she pushed ahead. "Until now, my work is all I've had. Even getting married didn't broaden my horizons, though I'm sure I thought it would. I thought it would be an easy way to make sure I was . . . normal."

Her confession finished, she leaned back, feeling amazingly relaxed and aware of herself as she hadn't been in a long time. She breathed in, pulling the clean outdoor air into her lungs and absorbing the scents and sounds around her, around them. She'd forgotten how good it felt to relax, outside in the night air.

She released his hand, but he clasped hers before she could withdraw it. He settled his elbows on the table and leaned closer.

"You're *not* normal, Alicia," he said, his voice low, his emerald eyes capturing hers. "You're much, much better. You're special. I knew it the first moment I laid eyes on you. I've known a lot of people, Alicia, but I've never met a woman like you."

Her doubt must have shown on her face, because he smiled and reassured her, "Trust me, that's a very good thing."

Alicia blinked, emotion lifting her heart, her spirit.

She hadn't felt so close to another person since her mother's death. She had never imagined her date with Jason would turn out this way. Casual conversation, perhaps even sex, but this total baring of her innermost self . . . ? "I didn't expect . . . I never thought—I mean, I wasn't prepared for—I imagined you would take me bowling, Jason."

Jason chuckled and squeezed her hand once before releasing it. He relaxed back into his chair. The tremendously intense mood that had surrounded them began to lift. "You know, of all the sports I've tried—and I've tried just about everything—I've never been bowling."

"I've only done it a few times myself, but it's an enjoyable exercise."

"It gives you a workout?"

"I meant mental exercise—determining the correct angle for the ball to roll to knock over the pins."

He chuckled. "Somehow I'm not surprised you approach it that way."

"I'm boring, Jason."

"You're unique. Myself, I have a preference for sports with an element of risk. The more likely I am to break my neck, the more exciting it is." He chuckled and speared a lettuce leaf. "Unlike your way, it's a very stupid way to enjoy a sport."

"Why do you do that, risk your neck?" Alicia asked, not willing to let it slide by as a joke.

His eyes darkened. "I suppose, when my parents died, I stopped caring. Sixteen isn't a good time for such a blow. All those unspent hormones, adolescent mood swings, confusion about who you are."

She nodded.

"I started out by teasing death, seeing if it would grab me, too. Came close a few times, too. After a while, I became addicted to the adrenaline rush. I have to admit, the older I get, the less satisfying it is." He sighed. "Maybe I've just been trying to fill a void with . . . something. I don't know." His gaze connected with hers, deep and steady. "Or maybe it's just that I'm starting to see there are much better ways to get satisfaction."

His gaze awakened a deep hunger in Alicia, and she realized how long it had been since she'd been completely, thoroughly satisfied. In her work, sometimes. With a good meal like tonight's dinner, now and then. With a man, never.

"The riskiest thing I've done is jaywalk," she finally said, conscious of his silence as he gazed at her.

"No, Alicia Underwood," he said, his eyes sparkling. "The riskiest thing you've ever done is date me."

His words sent an alarming surge of heat through her. She shifted on her chair and realized that she had already made a choice, when she elected to leave behind her underpants. She already knew what was coming. And she was ready to take the risk, even knowing she might disappoint him. Nor did she feel afraid. Not anymore. Jason was a person, just as she was, with his own feelings and needs. She was able now to look beyond herself to reach out. And she so longed to connect with another human being. *But not just any human. This man in particular.*

During the rest of dinner, conversation flowed effortlessly along the contours of their lives, from where they were borne through funny moments as kids to her failed marriage. Alicia found herself sharing the pain of her divorce, and he told her of his own broken engagement. She knew in her heart that he understood the sense of betrayal she had felt, the disillusionment. For he had felt it, too.

As the evening deepened, the lanterns seemed to

grow brighter, keeping the night at bay and surrounding them in an enchanted world. Moonlight sparkled off the calm surface of the lake, painting a golden path across its surface. Alicia stopped worrying about the cost of the magnificent catered dinner, stopped thinking about what might happen tomorrow, or Monday when they both returned to work. All that existed was this man, reminding her just how much of a woman she really was.

He finally presented her with dessert—chocolate mousse.

Alicia's eyes grew wide. "I *love* chocolate. How did you know?"

"Lucky guess." Jason smiled down at her, thinking of the Nestlé wrappers he'd found in her trash. If she had any idea . . .

But she didn't. She fully believed he was the company janitor, and only that. She'd been too nervous about this date to suspect him.

His pretty, brainy thief had been difficult to woo here tonight, but he had done it. She had tantalized and teased him long enough, confusing him with her innocent demeanor at the same time she made him burn for her.

In the wake of her ridiculous kissing experiment, he'd given up trying to fight his passion for her. Why fight it? He was used to living passionately, dangerously. He could justify making love with Alicia, despite the fact that her past sins threatened his uncle's future welfare. In fact, his knowledge of her secret would add a dash of spice to their encounter. He'd done a lot of things in his life, but making love to a woman he was spying on was new even to him.

If she hadn't been guilty, he'd have been tempted to feel guilty himself for his dishonesty. He reminded himself for the hundredth time that she would get exactly what she wanted from him—a night of hot and heavy sex. Despite her reserve—or perhaps because of it—he knew she desperately craved a passionate sexual encounter. He would make the experience memorable for her, wonderful in every way. Teach her, even. Show her what her sensuous body was capable of.

And he—he would get her out of his system and, soon enough, out of his life for good.

He shoved down a twinge of regret at the thought, reminding himself of his live-for-today philosophy.

She won't be hurt, he repeated to himself. She would never learn the truth, if he managed it right. The theft of the bacteria would go undetected for months—maybe forever.

He sat across from her and watched as she ate, enjoying the way her lips curled around her spoon. A bolt of desire swept through his body. He'd been looking forward to tonight ever since he met her, he suddenly realized. He finally had her to himself, without the distraction of her project—or his own secret goal. "Dance with me."

"Hmm?" The spoon still in her mouth, she looked up, her brown eyes wide.

Jason removed the spoon from her fingers and tugged her to her feet. He pulled her against him, holding one of her hands and anchoring his arm around her waist. "You do know how to dance, don't you?"

"Not really, no."

She looked almost afraid as she said the words, as if she'd made an unforgivable social gaffe. "It's easy. Just sway to the music. Like this." He moved her in a gentle circle.

At first, she was alarmingly stiff in his arms. "I told you I couldn't."

"Relax. Close your eyes and feel the music."

"Okay, I'll try."

He ran his hand up and down her back, coaxing her to relax. "That's it." Gradually, she softened against him, and he pulled her closer, tucking her head against his shoulder. She tightened her arms around him in response. An aching pleasure filled Jason, a mixture of satisfaction and need that he refused to consider too closely. "See? You're an excellent dancer."

She made a dissenting noise. "It's all you, and you know it."

"No, it takes two to dance."

For long moments, he led her in a gentle circle, their slow movements on the swaying deck hypnotic, lulling, yet increasingly sensuous. He marveled at the feel of her in his arms. Her sleek curves, tiny waist and tantalizing fresh scent kindled a burst of desire sharper than any he'd felt in years of easy living.

She resettled her arms around him, pressing her sweetly rounded chest against his. His desire sharpened to an almost painful ache. Nothing mattered tonight but loving her. He was used to risk, thrived on it. For once, the risk itself didn't entice him, but the precious, forbidden treasure he held in his arms.

She was the first to break the silence, her voice almost a whisper. "Jason."

"Hmm?"

"I have a gift for you, too."

"More than just being here? That's enough of a gift for me."

"It's related to that, definitely."

He leaned back and looked at her face. She bit her lip, smiling one of her Mona Lisa smiles. "You've got me curious. What is it?"

"I can't say."

"Oh?"

"I want you to find out."

"How?"

"Move your hands lower."

"Lower?" He was already cradling her lower back. Never one to hesitate, he stroked his hands downward until he was cupping her soft, round bottom. He knew he couldn't keep his excitement from his voice. "Like this?"

"Lower."

"Lower. Yes, ma'am." He ran his hands under her bottom, down her thighs. Soon, her dress gave way and he was holding her silk-clad legs. "Like this?"

"Now move your hands higher."

Jason swallowed. Did she have any idea how erotic she was being? When he first met her, she hadn't struck him as a sexually adventuresome woman, yet she exuded a repressed passion that he'd wanted more than anything to tap. Apparently she didn't hesitate to go after what she wanted, and that something was him. Making it even sweeter was the fact that she had no idea how filthy rich he was. She didn't want his money—she wanted *him*.

He slipped his hands up her silk stockings, learning with a burst of satisfaction that she had indeed followed his instruction about not wearing panty hose. The heat of her bare skin burned into his palms. He tightened his grip on her thighs and she sighed softly.

"Like this?"

She quivered against his chest, her answer barely a whisper. "Higher."

As slowly as he could without going crazy, Jason smoothed his hands up her thighs. To his shock and delight, he encountered the exquisitely soft, bare skin of her bottom and hips. "Oh, God," he groaned as his fingers sank into her naked flesh. All the time they'd been eating dinner, she'd been sitting there, bare-assed.

She leaned back and gazed at him, her Mona Lisa smile growing into a larger one of immense satisfaction. "Do you like my gift?"

There was only one answer to that.

EIGHT

Without losing the tantalizing hold he had on Alicia's bottom, Jason ran his lips along the arch of her neck. His hot breath burned in her ear, and her entire body ached with need.

"Alicia, in case you couldn't tell, I want you. Badly."

Alicia wrapped her arms around his neck and nibbled his earlobe. She'd never felt more open with a man, more herself. "Jason, don't expect too much. Please."

She could tell he hadn't really heard her. His hands left the relative safety of her bottom and slipped toward her stomach, the tips of his fingers grazing her thatch of hair and sending alarming tingles through her. "You're a marvel. People think you're a prim scientist, but you're an extremely passionate woman."

"No, I'm really not."

"Yes, you are. You just don't know it yet."

Alicia squeezed her eyes shut, knowing she had to set him straight. But she was too caught up in the wickedly delicious sensations he was causing. She slowly, carefully rose up on her toes, causing his fingers to slide over her femininity. Darts of pure pleasure shot through her body and she hugged Jason tighter. Quickly, before she lost her sense of purpose, she burst out, "My husband thought I was frigid."

"What?" Clearly shocked, Jason jerked back and looked at her. "You're kidding."

She exhaled, realizing she wanted to share even this dark secret with Jason. "No, I'm not. To tell you the truth, I don't know that he isn't right. I tried—I tried with Leon."

The corners of his lips twitched. "I sense a 'but' coming."

"It was a disaster. We were half undressed, and I—I froze up. As much as my mind wanted me to be normal, be casual about—sex, my body . . . I couldn't let him."

Jason seemed unperturbed by her revelation. If anything, his eyes glinted even brighter. "Maybe Leon wasn't what you needed."

"And you are."

"Maybe. At least in this. Wasn't that the purpose of your experiment?"

This time he smiled fully, and she found her tense muscles relaxing, her own smile growing. "Are you always so confident, Jason Kirkland?" On impulse, she began tenderly stroking his jaw.

He chuckled. "It's not just me, sweetheart." He gently squeezed her shoulders, catching her full attention, his gaze taking hold of hers. "Alicia, I do discriminate. In fact, I've become very selective in my old age. Do you have any idea how sexy you are? Do you even begin to comprehend how hot you make me?"

"Well, I . . ."

"Remember that little scene in your office?"

She felt heat rising in her cheeks. She nodded. "Of course. That's why we're here tonight. But nothing's ever as easy as it appears. I've been disappointed before. So when I started feeling—attracted—to you, I thought perhaps with you, I would—"

Jason kissed her, effectively shutting her up. This time keeping his hands where only a gentleman would put them, he held her close, making love to her mouth, slowly and thoroughly. Alicia closed her eyes and melted into the embrace.

A ship's horn blasted through her awareness. Jason broke the kiss. A yacht was pulling into the opposite berth. Darkness had descended, and their boat was lit up like a Christmas tree. Anyone looking could see them clearly.

Jason took her hand and led her belowdecks. No longer held in his heated embrace, Alicia's mind kicked in and her knees started to tremble with anxiety. Or was it anticipation? Inhaling a last breath of the cool night air, she followed Jason down a short ladder and through a passage to a narrow door on the right. Jason pulled her through it. She caught a glimpse of a double bed, a pile of men's clothing, a dresser, a low wood ceiling, an overhead electric light. Before she could fully process her surroundings, he pulled her into his arms again.

When his lips slid to her jaw, Alicia asked, "You live here?"

"Um-hmm." He pressed his lips to her neck, grazing her skin and making her arch her body seeking more. "I love your neck."

Her gaze landed on the mirror over his dressing table. The sight of Jason ravishing her added an extra thrill to his seduction. Even her own face—she looked totally unlike herself, or rather, her image of herself. Things were moving so fast, and she had precious little control of her reactions to Jason. Her thoughts—she squeezed her eyes and fought to focus, to keep from being swept completely away. What had she been thinking about? The cabin—"This is a nice room."

"Tight." She heard the smile in his words as his hands slipped once more to her bottom, now strangely familiar yet entirely exciting. "But tight can be good. Very, very good."

His tongue teased her earlobe, dove inside. Alicia sighed as heat consumed her from the inside out. Like a chemical reaction in the laboratory. Volatile. Explosive. Her gaze shifted to the bed behind him. Soon . . . An image sprang to her mind of Jason, naked and hot, rising above her as he buried himself deep inside her. The vision triggered heated moisture between her thighs. *Hungry.* She was suddenly so hungry for Jason, she could barely remain on her feet. Her gaze on the bed, she murmured, "At least it seems big enough."

"Definitely big enough." Alicia's face grew warm as he slipped her hand over his rock-hard erection, demonstrating quite clearly how ready she had made him. Now that they were out of the public eye, his restraint had vanished. And so did hers. Alicia squeezed and stroked him, but before she could pursue that course of action, he dropped to his knees.

She stood as still as a statue as he lifted the hem of her dress, revealing her nakedness. As he gazed at her, a powerful, knee-weakening blast of desire shook her. He pressed his lips on her mound, giving her a sweet, liquid kiss.

Alicia stiffened. If he touched her *there* with his tongue, she wouldn't be able to stand it. Despite her sensitivity, Richard always insisted on touching her there, saying that her discomfort was all in her mind. After all, other women loved to be touched.

Jason lifted his face. "Sensitive?"

She nodded, ashamed once again by her inadequacy. Now he would realize how poor a lover she really was. "Yes." The confirmation came out on a strangled breath.

"Doesn't matter. I can work . . . around it." He smiled and rose to his feet, his hands caressing her back. When he saw her dismayed expression, he sobered. "Is that what this is about? Guys being rough with you?"

"Rough? No, Richard wasn't rough. It was all me. I didn't—react like he wanted me to."

"And you think that was *your* fault?" He sounded incredulous.

Alicia opened her mouth to respond, but he cut her off.

"Hell, Alicia, it doesn't take a rocket scientist to know not to do something that actually hurts. Some women like to be touched there, some don't. Probably means you have more nerve endings there than the average woman, Alicia. That's a good thing."

She nodded, tears suddenly in her eyes. He understood. And he didn't think she was a freak. Logically, she knew she was physically okay, but when Richard had been so frustrated when she'd clenched her legs and asked him to stop, it had damaged her self-esteem worse than she'd realized.

Jason cradled her face in his hands and kissed her forehead, then her cheeks and, finally, her lips. "If I do anything that makes you the least uncomfortable, just tell me and I'll—"

"Stop?" And their lovemaking would end just that quick.

"Stop doing whatever bothers you. I'll do something different."

"Oh." Relieved, she leaned against him, her head resting against his chest. She heard the pull of a zipper, felt air on her naked back. Jason peeled the fabric from her shoulders and her safe little black dress landed on the floor. Her bra soon followed. Now she wore only her stockings.

Jason set her away from him and gazed at her, then cupped her naked breasts. He rasped his palms over her aching nipples. "You're gorgeous," he murmured. "I knew you'd be incredible, but—oh, God." He closed his eyes and pressed his forehead to her shoulder. Alicia stroked his hair, wondering at his sudden emotion. He lifted his head then, and without another word swept her up and laid her on the bed.

She watched as he stripped off his jacket and began unbuttoning his shirt. She caught a glimpse of tanned chest as he worked down the buttons and her pulse raced. He was all hers. This was real, and she knew without a doubt that this experience would surpass her fantasies. She knelt on the bed and tugged him to sit beside her, so she could undress him herself. As she freed each button, she touched the skin she bared, as smooth and golden as in her dreams. "You should hear how the women at work talk about you."

He cocked an amused eyebrow. "Is that why you want to sleep with me? Because they imagine I'm good in bed?"

"Well, partly." She chewed her lip, hoping he wouldn't think she only wanted him for his beautiful body. She finished unbuttoning his shirt and slid her hands over his tanned chest, every bit as broad and muscular as she had imagined it would be. "But I also want you because—" She stopped, suddenly aware that her initial plan of a wild, purely physical affair had dissolved in the wake of new, strong emotions. She wanted him because she cared for him. He was sensitive, smart, funny and sweet, not to mention strong and sexy. She lifted her face to his. "Because . . . it seems right."

He ran his fingers through her hair, his eyes filling with emotion. "That's not a very scientific thing to say."

"This isn't about science. It isn't even about biology, though I keep telling myself it is." She smiled at him. "You understand. I know you do."

Jason suddenly pulled back, his eyes clouding. "What am I doing?"

"Jason?" Alarmed, Alicia pulled closer to him, leaning into him so her breasts brushed his chest. She slipped her hands along his cheeks and turned his face to hers. "What is it?"

"Alicia, I don't know where this is going. I don't generally care when I'm with a woman. But this is different."

"Oh, Jason." She began to wrap her arms around his neck, but he grasped her shoulders and made her face him.

"I can't—I can't make any promises. We're doing this for your experiment, remember?"

Alicia's spirits sagged at his words, but she fought valiantly to project nonchalance, pretend a sophistication she completely lacked. "Of course we are. You know how important science is to me. That's why I picked you to be my subject, because you're so good at living in the moment. I certainly never expected—"

His shoulders relaxed. "That's all I needed to hear." He was suddenly through with talking. He pressed her hard against him, his hands sweeping across her bare back. He stretched back on the bed and pulled her on top of him. Lifting her, he swept an erect nipple into his mouth, grazing it in torturous circles with his teeth and tongue. Alicia moaned at the fire that shot through her.

He rolled her over, caressed her breasts, her stomach, her hips. His mouth and hands seemed to be everywhere at once. Alicia grasped his hair, ran her hands along the amazing width of his shoulders, reveled in his powerful masculinity. Just as she was certain he would strip off his pants and take her, he surprised her yet again. He slipped out of her grasp to the foot of the bed and lifted one of her legs into his lap. Gradually, as if unwrapping a wonderful present, he rolled down her stocking, kissing and nuzzling her bare skin as it was revealed to him.

Alicia watched in delight as he flung the stocking away. Caressing her foot, he began to lick and suck each of her toes. She gasped as exquisite curls of pleasure danced up her legs. His knowing gaze met hers as he worked his magic.

"Jason, that's—phenomenal." She gasped and wriggled on the bed, the ticklish pleasure almost too much to bear.

He smiled as he set down one tingling foot and retrieved the other one. "You've been neglected too long. I don't want to overlook anything."

Alicia swallowed and nodded, unable to believe how wonderfully the evening was turning out. She knew she'd never forget tonight, no matter how long she lived or how many other men she slept with. A forbidden image popped into her mind of them together, like this, for countless nights to come. She immediately squelched it. Tonight existed out of time. She knew that was how he wanted it. She wouldn't think of anything but the moment, and Jason.

Finally, her legs liquid and tingling, he returned to her empty arms. She moaned at the feel of his hard chest pressed to hers, explored the shape and feel of his hard, sinewy body, the very essence of masculinity. And he was hers.

He caressed her in turn, setting fire to every inch of her skin. "You're so sweet, so sweet," he said, his breath hot on her skin. "I can't get enough of you."

Alicia whimpered as he ran his hands up the insides of her thighs, danced so near her femininity yet resisted touching her. His agonizing teasing transformed her sweet desire into a fierce, wanton hunger. For the first time she understood the essence of being female, the deep-seated urge to mate that blotted out all other concerns.

"Please," she cried, her fingers digging into his shoulders. "Please, Jason. Oh, God, please." She spread her legs, arched her hips, wanted more, and yet more. She had never been so hungry for a man, for . . . something else—release perhaps—that ecstasy that drove people to mate but that she had never achieved.

He sensed her need and responded to it. His callused fingers danced over her femininity like a song, never hurting that tender nub of pleasure, never demanding more than she was ready to give. He played her like an instrument, making sweet music spin through her entire body. She shuddered, her legs tensing and relaxing as the waves of pleasure built into a raging storm. She brushed against the threshold, knowing what was beyond, certain it wouldn't happen. She had never—

Opening her eyes, she met his gaze, read the command there: "Submit."

Yes. Finally, Alicia relinquished control. Instantly, violent waves of pleasure slammed her through the threshold and beyond, into realms of inexpressible glory. Her body shook as she completely gave herself over to the feelings, to him. The pleasure was almost too intense to stand, wave after wave of it, crashing into her, threatening to take her into oblivion. "Jason," she gasped. "I can't stand—"

"Darling, *yes,*" he cried in her ear, his breath a warm caress beside her and within her.

"Don't stop. Never stop."

"I won't."

Another wave of pleasure swept over her, rocking her. She had never experienced anything as strong. The waves came quickly then, one after the other, each one taking her to new, more intense heights of pleasure. As one wave faded, she managed to cry, "Jason, please, I can't take it anymore."

She heard him laugh, as if from a long way off, but he didn't let up—not yet. Not until she was completely wrung out.

He smiled down at her sweat-sheened face, his fingers stroking her slowly, promising—threatening—more. "Enough?"

She grinned wickedly. She'd never experienced such pleasure, but she was ready to test her limits. Ready to trust. "Almost."

His fingers drifted over her still-tingling flesh. "More?"

"No. I want you." She tugged at his still-clothed buttocks. "Inside me. *Now.*"

His eyes grew bright at her command and she knew he liked her newfound confidence. She had nothing to be ashamed of, nothing to hide from. She was a woman—a sexy, aware woman making love to a man who truly desired her. She had never felt so free.

Jason rose and stripped out of his pants in a matter of seconds. Still dazed from the aftershocks of pleasure, Alicia merely lay there and enjoyed the sight.

He was even more magnificent completely naked

than she'd imagined—muscular thighs, narrow hips and the broadest chest she'd ever seen. Even before he finished pulling off his socks, Alicia had spread her legs, inviting him, craving the long, hard shaft of him inside her. He didn't disappoint her.

But he did tease her mercilessly. He knelt between her legs, his hands planted on either side of her head, his eyes locked with hers. Then he slid inside her only an inch, before withdrawing, giving her just a taste of the satisfaction he could provide.

Alicia arched her hips toward him, desperate for his fullness inside of her. "What do you think you're—"

"More?"

"More!"

He slid in several inches, then withdrew again. "I'm testing a theory."

"How to kill me with wanting you?"

His voice took on the tone of a newscaster's. "Preliminary findings show that Alicia isn't satisfied with two inches."

"That's an accurate assessment. Now give me more."

He slid in deeper this time, nearly all the way. Again he began to withdraw. This time Alicia locked her legs around him, so he didn't get far. "You're determined to drive me out of my mind, aren't you?"

"Yes," he breathed. "I'm going to torture you until you admit you're not frigid. Tell me you're not and I'll give you what you want."

"You're blackmailing me."

"Damn straight." He shoved in a few inches, then withdrew almost all the way.

"Jason!" She dug her heels into his back, tried to make him return, but he resisted mightily. She could see his effort to restrain himself on his face, in his bunched biceps. It served him right.

"Say it, Alicia." He shoved halfway in, then withdrew with agonizing slowness.

"It," she gasped.

"Very funny."

A swift stroke of punishment. Alicia moaned.

"Say you're not frigid."

Still she resisted, the game exciting and fascinating her. "You're not frigid."

Another punishing stroke, slamming hard against her and withdrawing almost all the way. The sharp pang of pleasure brought tears to her eyes. "Please, I'm begging—"

"Say it."

"All right, you win! I'm not frigid!"

"Damn straight." All barriers were finally gone. He thrust hard into her, over and over, slamming into the center of her, sending her spiraling out of control, and then, unbelievably, once more over the edge.

She sank her fingers into his tense back as he swept over the peak himself, her name on his lips.

Gradually, Alicia came back to herself. He collapsed on top of her, spent, and she held him close. She stroked his back with a sudden, fierce possessiveness, as an animal might feel for its mate. The feeling wasn't entirely welcome. They'd made no promises; their relationship was still too new for such intense feelings—but longing filled her heart just the same.

The only truly surprising thing was that she'd ever wondered whether Jason and she would end up like this, in bed, their sweat-slicked legs wrapped together, his lips tracing her hairline, his hands stroking the tangled hair from her face. Nothing had ever felt so inevitable, so *right*.

He hoisted himself on his elbows and gazed down at her. "Making love with you is such a rush. I could lie with you like this for the next few years and be perfectly happy."

His words, his sensuous tone warmed her. She tried to keep it light, not wanting him to see how deeply he had touched her heart. "Oh, I think you'd get bored, considering all the wild things you usually do."

"Nope. Being with you is more exciting than jumping out of an airplane at ten thousand feet."

Being with you. Perhaps it was more than sex for him, too. "Is that all?"

"More exciting than helicopter skiing in the Alps in perfect, virgin powder."

"I'm not nearly as cold, at any rate. And in case you didn't notice, I wasn't a virgin."

He chuckled. "Virgins don't interest me. You do. Making love with you is more exciting than diving the Great Barrier Reef."

"Not as wet."

His hand coasted around her hip to tease her femininity. "I don't know about that," he said with a wicked grin.

She sighed and pressed her head back into the pillow. "You've done so many interesting things. All I've done is be a drone for Envirotech. I can't remember the last time I learned something new, or even took a vacation."

He traced her eyebrows, one at a time. "That's sad. Tell me what you want to do, and I'll make it happen."

She smiled at his earnest expression. He'd already blown his entire paycheck on her, she was certain. "What are you, some kind of magician?"

"Yes. Tell me what you want, Alicia. What do you want that you haven't had a chance to enjoy?"

She bit her lip and turned her head away. "I don't know. Lots of things. Nothing I can't do without."

"Tell me." He pulled her face toward his. "You like to travel? Where would you like to go?"

She shrugged. "I've always wanted to go to Egypt and see the pyramids."

"And?"

"Well, Italy, to see the great masters, the architecture. And Venice."

"And?"

"I'd like to go Down Under. I have a thing for koalas. That Great Barrier Reef you mentioned—I saw it in a movie, at the Imax—"

"—on a date with Leon?" he asked dryly.

Alicia decided to ignore *that* particular comment, but she relished this small sign of his jealousy. "I'd like to see it like that, from under the water. I'd love to learn to scuba dive." He opened his mouth to speak and she laid a finger on his lips. "But right now, I want something much . . . closer at hand." Her fingers drifted over his shaft, which immediately began to thicken.

His eyes turned smoky. "Exactly how do you want it?"

"Lie on your back and I'll show you."

"Yes, doctor." He complied and she knelt over him, her mouth dancing down his chest, his abdomen, and settling on his erection. Feeling deliciously sensuous, she began to pleasure him, wanting to give him as much ecstasy as he'd given her.

Jason sank his hands into her hair, his moans of pleasure filling her with joy and a sublime sense of power. To have such a brawny man under her control—it was a heady sensation, the stuff of fantasies.

When he neared his peak, Alicia stopped. She slipped away from him to the foot of the bed and shot him a wicked look.

He cried out in frustration and longing. "What are you—"

"Did you like my gift?"

"Alicia," he groaned, stretching his arms toward her. "Alicia, get back here. You're torturing me. Just *look* at me."

"Oh, I'm looking." My God, he was a masterwork of virility. His obvious desire only added to an already perfect body, all hard lines and angles and incredible, unstoppable sexuality. She gazed at him, amazed that *she*—eggheaded, introverted Alicia Underwood—had such a masculine piece of work to relish, to enjoy, to . . . torment.

"Alicia, what are you up to?" he asked, his eyes narrowing. "If you're not back here in a couple of seconds, I'll—"

"Patience," she chided. "The first lesson a scientist learns. You have to wait for your rewards." She stroked the sole of his foot and he started. Smiling, she pulled his foot into her lap and began giving him the same toe treatment he'd given her.

He groaned. "That's good, darling. Very, very good. But I was on the verge of—"

She glanced up. "I know. Very well, being the kind-hearted soul I am"—she slipped off the bed and strode around to his side—"I won't make you suffer quite as badly as you made me." She straddled his thighs and gazed at his erection. "Then again," she said, her fingers drifting over his shaft, "I like seeing you like this. Gives you a taste of what you've been putting me through ever since you showed up at Envirotech, with those tight T-shirts you wear, and your incredibly wide back, and those marvelous buns squeezed into skin-tight jeans—"

"Damn it, woman, quit talking." Jason sat up and grabbed her, hard, lifting her onto his erection. He collapsed back in satisfaction, certain he'd achieved his objective, his hands locked on her thighs.

Alicia fought down the incredible surge of pleasure he'd caused. She lifted herself almost all the way off and slid down gradually, with exquisite slowness, torturing him as he had her. Meeting his frustrated gaze with a teasing grin, she lifted once more, even more slowly this time.

But he didn't let it continue. He grasped her hips and impaled her fully, shocking her with delight. *"That's* where you belong, and don't ever forget it," he rasped out.

Then he took control of the situation, rocking her hips against his, forcing her rapidly to the brink. Alicia leaned forward, clinging to him as he clung to her, their mutual passion obliterating their game as he took her fast, furious, once more over the edge.

Afterward, Alicia lay cradled in his embrace, her chest pressed to his. With a sudden burst of happiness, she lifted her head and gave him a sound kiss. "You're wonderful, Jason. I hope you know that." She kissed him again, hard and deep and slow.

When she broke the kiss, she found a look of boyish wonder on his face. It filled her heart with gladness. "That's for being the best lover I've ever had."

"Yeah. You, too." His look of wonder faded, his eyes growing distant. He sat up and swung his legs over the edge of the bed.

"Jason, is something wrong?" Concern washed through Alicia. "Did I say something wrong? I'm not good at this, you know. I'm sorry, but I haven't had many lovers. I don't know how to be casual." Feeling suddenly vulnerable, she gave his shoulder a tentative touch.

Jason grasped her hand and pressed it to his mouth. "I'm just trying to convince myself that's what this is, but I'm having a hard time doing it."

His words filled Alicia with joy. She wasn't alone in feeling this deepening connection with him. He felt it, too. So why did it seem to disturb him? "There's no hurry, Jason. I'm not demanding anything. We already discussed that."

He tugged on her arm, bringing her to sit near him, then yanked her onto his lap. The feeling of being enfolded in his arms, both of them completely naked, filled her with renewed longing. Incredible, after all their lovemaking. More than she'd enjoyed during most of her marriage, all in a single night.

"Did you make any plans for the weekend?" he asked. "And I don't mean washing your hair. Anything important?"

"Other than this? Well, I was planning to go to the lab tomorrow, and probably Sunday, too, to complete the final series of exposure tests—"

"No, you're not." He resettled her on his lap, his hands wrapped possessively around her waist. "I'm kidnapping you."

"What?" She stared at his sparkling gaze. A hint of a smile teased his lips.

"You heard me. I'm kidnapping you. This weekend, you're mine."

Alicia woke to the sound of the shower. While this was a large sailing yacht, the living quarters were still cramped. With the bathroom backing up against the bedroom wall, the shower sounded thunderous.

Alicia rubbed the sleep out of her eyes. She had

spent the entire night on his boat, only the last few hours asleep. Bright sunlight poured through the porthole above her head. She stretched luxuriantly. She felt like doing absolutely nothing—except, perhaps, staying in bed. She couldn't recall the last time she'd felt so relaxed. Her project, President Fielding's demands, the upcoming deadlines, all of it seemed so distant. Because of Jason. He had done what even marriage had failed to accomplish—remind her that there were other things in life than work.

Wondrous, marvelous other things.

Alicia was considering joining Jason in the shower when a ringing startled her. Her gaze followed the sound to the cellular phone on the dresser. She reached out and grabbed it.

"Hello? Jason Kirkland's residence."

"Why, hello. I didn't realize Jase had company," said a jovial man's voice. "Who is this?"

"A friend of Jason's. And you are . . . ?"

The man chuckled. "A friend. Give the phone to him, sweetheart."

His condescending tone rubbed Alicia the wrong way. She tried to sound coolly professional. "He's unavailable at the moment. If you tell me who this is, I'll tell him you called."

The man's polite veneer vanished and his voice took on a rough edge. "Busy? If he's not working for me, he's not doing anything worthwhile. Get him. Now."

Alicia was sorely tempted to slam down the phone. Was this the type of person Jason usually associated with? It didn't seem at all like someone he'd choose to spend time with, the man was so rude. And what did he mean, that Jason worked for him? Jason was an Envirotech employee. Alicia wasn't about to let the man intimidate her. "Jason is occupied, as I've explained. If you'll leave your name and number—"

"What are you, his personal sex-etary?" The man broke out in a braying laugh. "Let me guess. He picked you up at the office, wasting his time on women instead of working! Damn!"

Alicia gripped the sheet about her, embarrassment warring with her fury. "I don't have to listen to this! Whoever you are, you're insulting and—"

"Hey, I call it like I see it, babe. You're a short-timer, if you don't realize it. They all are. Jase hates committing to women. Just watch and see. Unless— wait a minute." The man's voice turned silken and sophisticated once again. His quick change sparked a sense of familiarity in Alicia. "There is this . . . scientist woman Jase has been talking about. Maybe you're her?"

"I'm—" Why did this man's voice sound so familiar? A niggle of concern rose in her chest as she fought to place the man's voice.

NINE

Alicia's upset voice carried to Jason in the bathroom. Grabbing a towel, he stepped out to find her sitting on the bed, the phone to her ear, her face set in concentration.

Only one person would be calling him here, someone Alicia shouldn't be talking to. He jumped toward her and snatched the phone from her fingers. "Who is it?" he asked the caller harshly. He flashed her an apologetic look, then turned away, tightening the towel around his hips.

Henry sounded furious. "What in the hell do you think you're doing screwing around? I specifically told you this weekend was *critical.* You're supposed to be breaking into that lab!"

Irritation surged through Jason. God knew what Henry had said to Alicia, not knowing it was her. "Henry! This isn't the time. Call me back later."

"Later! Go get me a sample, Jason. You're right *in* there now. I've seen to it. Don't waste any more time."

Jason's voice turned steely. "Don't push me, Henry."

Henry said nothing for a moment, perhaps sensing that he'd gone too far. Sure enough, he changed tactics, adopting a fatherly tone. The man had the most mercurial moods of anyone Jason had ever known, which he used to get what he wanted. "So you're calling me Henry, now? What happened to 'Uncle'? Hey, I'm sorry, kid. You know I believe in you. I *rely* on you, son."

Jason shoved his hand in his hair, conscious of Alicia sitting on the bed an arm's length away. "It's all right. I just can't talk now, okay?"

Henry's voice dropped to a conspiratorial murmur. "This girl you have—is it Underwood? Her voice sounded sort of familiar. Did you take me up on my suggestion?"

He turned back to Alicia. She sat quietly, absorbing every word of the conversation.

When he didn't reply, Henry guessed the truth. "You did, didn't you? You've got her in your bed! Excellent work, Jason. I sincerely apologize for my complaints. Now you can get her to tell you *all* her secrets. So, when will I have it?"

"Soon. In a few days. Just don't call me again, not this weekend, okay?" An agony of guilt slashed through Jason. Their lovemaking hadn't been motivated by deception, not at all. But he wasn't about to explain their complicated bond to Henry.

"Of course I won't call again. I wouldn't think of interrupting a master at his work. I honestly didn't think she'd be dumb enough to fall for you, Jason, a brainiac like her. But hey, this is great! Kid, you're the best."

The line went dead. Jason gently set the phone on the dresser. He forced a cheerful, nonchalant tone, but his gut churned sickeningly at having to deceive her yet again. From the day he'd met her, he'd told her nothing but lies—except for how much he desired her. Their physical connection—that alone was the truth. "My uncle can . . . get a little crude. I hope he didn't say anything insulting to you."

Alicia flashed him a proud gaze. "I'd be lying if I said he didn't. He also implied that you frequently have women in your bed."

Jason knew she was trying to hide how much this bothered her. "Hey." He sat next to her on the bed. "Henry lives in a fantasy world. He thinks I'm some kind of playboy. He's more interested in my sex life than I am—that is, until I met you." He grinned boyishly and traced her cheek with his finger.

He could tell she didn't buy it. "Uh-huh. What kind of job are you doing for him?"

"Job?" Jason thought furiously. What had Henry leaked to her? Damn him for calling. During their passionate interlude, Jason had blissfully forgotten how he'd met Alicia, what he did during the week while posing as an Envirotech employee. He had reveled in showing Alicia how responsive she really was, and found himself opening up as he never had with a woman. For a few precious hours, the shadow of loneliness that had hovered over him for years had finally receded. He'd looked into her eyes as she lay beneath him, cradling his body, and his heart had expanded, making him feel like he could conquer the world.

Now Henry had invaded his private fantasy and given him a nasty dose of reality.

"He said if you weren't working for him, you weren't doing anything of value," Alicia prodded.

Jason shrugged. "Sometimes I run errands for him. Small side jobs. Couriering papers to his clients, checking out construction sites, that sort of thing."

She tucked her legs under her, making her look even smaller, even more vulnerable. But he knew her sharp mind was going a mile a minute. "Does he own a business?"

"Yes, but I really don't want to waste time with you talking about Henry." He pulled her close and began unwrapping her sheet while nuzzling her neck.

Unfortunately, Alicia was too smart and too curious to fall for his ploy. "So why doesn't he hire you full-time? Why did you take the job at Envirotech?"

Jason sagged and nested his forehead on her shoulder. He knew he couldn't get out of this if he didn't lie through his teeth. But the thought of doing so, now, after the wonderful intimacy they'd shared, made him physically ill.

He pulled back and gazed at her. He would share with her as much as he could. "Things are complicated with Uncle Henry. I owe him, Alicia. He took me under his wing when my parents were killed. But now . . . I don't completely trust him." As soon as he said the words, he realized how true they were. After all these years, why was he doubting Henry now?

He already knew the answer. Because of the woman in his arms. He wanted to doubt him, doubt what he said about Alicia. He traced her soft cheek with his fingers, wanting so badly to believe in her that his chest ached.

His emotions in turmoil, he tried to sound much more relaxed than he felt. "You got an earful from him, I'm sure. But he's not usually that bad. He's been good to me, never denied me anything. He can be a very thoughtful, funny guy. A great guy, when he wants to be."

"So why aren't you working for him? I mean, you are, but instead of at Envirotech?"

He crumpled the edges of the sheet in his hands, determined to be truthful though it would undoubtedly mean losing her respect. "Because I haven't felt like working, Alicia. I've been playing instead."

She nodded. "You mean all those sports and things. I've always wondered . . . How can you afford them all? None of them are cheap. Certainly on a janitor's salary—" Suddenly she gasped. "Is it—oh, my God, Jason, I'm sorry."

Confused by her reaction, Jason's stomach clenched in concern.

She pressed her hand to her mouth, looking mortified. "It's insurance money, isn't it? A trust fund for you. I'm such an idiot, sticking my nose in where it doesn't belong."

Relief flooded him. An explanation, and she'd supplied it herself. He'd be a fool not to take advantage of it. *The way you've taken advantage of her,* an internal voice taunted.

In defense, he wrapped his arms around her and tucked her close. "You're right to wonder about a guy who's nearly thirty and has absolutely nothing to show for himself. Completely right. When I think of all you've done with your life—and you're younger than I am. . . ." *And without my financial resources . . .* "It shames me, Alicia. I'm not used to feeling this way, but I'm beginning to think it's high time I did." He kissed her lips gently, and she responded so sweetly, he had to give her another kiss, a deeper one.

Soon they were engaged in an emotion-filled embrace, the passion escalating anew. He broke the kiss and pressed his forehead to hers. Desperation filled him. Time was running out. "Let me love you again, Alicia. Right now. This weekend. As much as I can."

She nodded, her dark eyes filled with emotion. "Yes." She spoke the word on a breath.

Jason laid her back on the bed. He began covering her face, her body with kisses and caresses, suddenly terrified of the void he would feel after he lost her. But he knew better than to fool himself. There was no future for them. Not after he completed his task.

Alicia dug her fingers into his shoulders as he worked his way down her chest, his tongue encircling an already erect nipple. Sweet, so sweet. And so responsive to his every touch, as he responded to hers.

He sucked one dusky, tender peak into his mouth and heard her satisfied moan. Gently, he parted her thighs, slipped his fingers over her femininity. She was already wet and ready for him. He slid a finger inside and she tightened around him. He lifted his gaze to hers. "Alicia, I want to kiss you, there. I want to love all of you, in every way."

She cradled his face in her hands. "Anything, Jason. I trust you not to hurt me."

He knew she was thinking of her clumsy ex-husband, but the words painfully reminded him how little she should be trusting him. He couldn't give her the truth, but he could give her a taste of pleasure. Gradually, he worked his way down her stomach, teasing her navel, the inside of her thighs, making the anticipation last for both of them as he neared the apex of her need.

As he kissed her mound, he felt her tense. But he kept it gentle, and soon she relaxed under him. He grazed her folds with his teeth and she quivered in pleasure.

"That's good, Jason. That doesn't hurt."

He did it again, and again. Soon she was moaning for more. He thrust his tongue inside her, nestled it between her folds, tasted her wetness, her sweetness. "Jason," she panted, her hands entwined in his hair. "I've never felt anything—Oh, my."

His mouth occupied, he couldn't respond. He could only love her. Of all the women he'd slept with—from sophisticated society women to good-time party girls—none responded to him as Alicia did. She held nothing back from him, and he reveled in it. She made him feel more a man, more worthy, than he ever had.

He swept his hands up her flat stomach, up her rib cage, to cup her full breasts. He brushed his fingertips across her nipples, timing his feather-light strokes with his intimate nips and tastes. He wanted to do it right this time, not to hurry, not to treat her as casually as lovers of his past. He wanted her to feel exquisite pleasure as long as possible. And he wanted to be the one to make her feel that way.

She thrashed on the bed, and he knew she was almost out of control. "Jason, please, yes."

He increased his pace, higher and harder, higher still, and she approached the threshold. Her thighs tensed on his shoulders. She cried out his name, and Jason suddenly wanted, needed, to be part of her, to worship her with his entire body.

He brought himself up and thrust full into her, groaning aloud at the awesome sensation of joining with her. She bucked against him, pulling him deeper into herself. He held her close as he loved her with smooth, long strokes, promising himself that he would make it up to her, some way, somehow.

She cried out a final time, her eyes meeting his just before she lost control. "Ah, Jason, I love you!"

The words echoed over and over in his mind like a litany as he pounded the last few times into her, before being swept away with her to a far-off, glorious place the two of them could share. *I love you.*

He collapsed beside her, began to think beyond the haze of his desire. Love? My God, how *could* she? She wasn't supposed to love him. She didn't mean it. She wouldn't if she knew the truth about him.

"Jason."

At her soft touch on his face, Jason stopped breathing.

"I meant what I said. I know it's soon, but I've never felt this way before."

"Hey, it's okay," he said, striving for a light tone. He didn't quite manage it, his words coming out as a croak. He had to put distance between them.

He pulled away and stood up. He glanced at her, saw confusion and hurt on her sweet features. He forced a casual smile to his face, not wanting to hurt her, only wanting her to understand that love didn't belong here. Not with him.

She was far too honest for her own good. He should have seen this coming. She'd been an innocent, despite having been married. How could he have fooled himself into believing that their lovemaking would mean nothing but sex to her? He knew women and their needs. Deep down, perhaps he had known better. But he hadn't wanted to face the truth. He'd been too obsessed with wanting her.

Now he was going to hurt her. If he played it right, if he was careful, she'd never know he was behind the theft of her bacteria, or even that a theft had occurred. But there was no way he could hide his desertion of her.

She was too damned good for him. The thought was absurd and he knew it, considering her history. She'd had her reasons for stealing—a desire to prevent human suffering, the noblest of reasons. And with him—with him, he knew her reactions had been completely honest. Simply put, she lacked the sophistication to fake it.

Avoiding her gaze, he grabbed a pair of shorts and a sweater and slipped them on. "I'm going on deck. There's plenty of women's clothing in the bottom drawer. I'm sure something will fit you. Join me when you're ready."

He forced himself to appear nonchalant as he strode through the door.

TEN

Alicia bit her lip and blinked back a sudden surge of tears. She was such a fool! She was incredibly naive about men and relationships, she knew that. So why did she open herself up for hurt?

She knew Jason didn't love her. He was far too worldly to fall in love with her in the space of a day. She was one in a series of flings, and he knew all the rules. He was probably just going through the motions.

No. No, he felt something for her. Perhaps he wasn't ready to admit his feelings, whatever they were. But he did care for her, on some level. She was certain of it.

So, she had blundered in confessing her feelings, when they'd both agreed to keep it casual. It wasn't the end of the world. She would do exactly as he did, and pretend she hadn't said the words. Perhaps they could get this weekend back on track.

Then again . . . She rose and pulled open the bottom drawer. Sure enough, there were stacks of women's shorts and shirts, just waiting for guests of Jason Kirkland's. A surge of anger and jealousy coursed through her. This only verified what she already knew, that he was a womanizer. Still, it hurt to see the evidence of it. Somehow, she found it hard to reconcile the man she had grown so quickly to love with her image of a man who loved women as a hobby. There had been nothing casual in how he'd treated her.

Yet she couldn't deny the evidence, or the way he'd stiffened up a few minutes earlier.

She shook her head as a new thought occurred to her. She was being ridiculous. Jason was living here, but he didn't own this boat. The clothes probably belonged to the owner's wife.

After freshening up, she pulled out a pair of white shorts and a red sweatshirt and slipped them on. If she was one of Jason Kirkland's "women," then that's what she had expected to be all along. She forced herself to remember her initial plan: to experience a wild fling and leave it at that.

She left the bedroom and entered the galley. Jason looked up from frying bacon and smiled at her, his eyes sweeping appreciatively over her bare legs. "I see you found something that fits."

Alicia spread her sweatshirt-clad arms. "Yes, I did. Can you tell me whose clothes these are, or is that an off-limits question?"

"It's not off-limits. They come with the boat."

She nodded, understanding him to mean that the boat's owner left them there.

"We're eating breakfast outside. Someone thoughtfully left a table and chairs on deck." He winked.

Alicia met his warm gaze and her heart expanded. He was gracefully overlooking her gaffe in admitting her love for him. She stepped up the short ladder to the deck and looked around. Brilliant sunlight shone off brass fixtures and the glossy hardwood deck.

"This is a beautiful boat, Jason," Alicia called down to him.

"Thanks. I mean, I'm glad you like it," he called back. "Breakfast is almost ready."

"Can I help?" She began to descend the ladder.

Jason was there in an instant, blocking her way. "Absolutely not. Get back on deck."

"Aye, aye, Captain." She turned, and he took the prime opportunity to push her up by her fanny.

Alicia walked around the deck, hugging her sweatshirt to her. She glanced at the other boats moored at the dock. Some were small schooners, some powerboats. A handful were yachts about the same size as this one.

Jason appeared with a plate of food and set it on the table. He pulled out a chair for her, just as he had last night, and she sat down. "Cooking's not my strong suit," he said with a laugh. "I hope this is edible."

"It smells wonderful, and it looks even better."

"Spoken like a well-trained first mate." He kissed the top of her head before vanishing back down the stairs. He returned with his own plate and a pot of coffee.

While they ate, Alicia asked about the boat, her curiosity nagging at her. "I didn't get a good look at this boat last night, since it was dark, and we were . . . busy." She met his smile over scrambled eggs and bacon. She knew in an instant that in the bright light of day, doing something as mundane as eating breakfast, her feelings for him remained just as strong. "But this is about the nicest boat at the docks. Whose did you say it was?"

"Ah . . . Dr. Benson's," Jason said, not meeting her eyes. "Gerald Benson."

"Is he a medical doctor?"

"Who?" He appeared fascinated with buttering his toast. "Oh, Dr. Benson?"

"Yes. What's his specialty? Maybe I've heard of him. He must be a high-paid specialist to afford this boat."

"Uh, he's not a medical doctor."

"Oh, so he's a doctor like *I'm* a doctor."

Jason nodded. "That's right. Some kind of . . . mathematician, I believe."

"Wow. They must pay mathematicians a lot these days. Is he associated with the university? I don't recognize his name."

"He's on sabbatical. That's why his boat's available. Now eat. You're breakfast is getting cold."

She smiled. "You must think I'm terribly nosy."

"Not at all. You're just interested in me. I can't complain about that." He gave her a warm smile over the rim of his coffee mug.

Alicia sighed inwardly and tried to put her curiosity on hold. Jason was usually so congenial, so willing to share. Except when she asked the wrong questions; then he closed up like a clam. She wondered what he was hiding from her—and why. Was it because he didn't know her well enough? What she knew of him reminded her of a crazy quilt. Clarity here and there, with massive holes that persistently remained unfilled. One thing was certain—he kept her intrigued.

After breakfast, she insisted on helping with the dishes, though she found it terribly distracting to share such a tiny space with him. He kept brushing against her on his way from the sink to the cupboards. He would slip his arm around her and give her a small, familiar squeeze, warming her heart. Or run his hand along her bottom, as if he could hardly keep his hands off her.

Their conversation was easy and casual, about nothing and everything. And not about work. Neither of them mentioned Envirotech. Alicia didn't even want to think about work, and she definitely didn't want to imagine what life would be like once they both returned to their jobs on Monday. Would he even ask her for another date, or was this a one-time thing? And what did she expect it to be? She only knew she wanted to be with him as much as possible. Dating him was like drinking a magic elixir, and she was hooked.

Alicia was so engrossed in her thoughts, she dropped a handful of clean silverware. Knives and forks scattered across the hardwood floor. "Darn!"

She and Jason dropped to their knees at the same time and smacked heads. "Ouch!"

Jason sat back, rubbing his head and laughing. "Let me."

"Don't be silly. I'll get them." Alicia had already picked up most of them. Jason rose to his feet with a fork and a knife. Alicia started to rise, until she caught a glimpse of a fork under the built-in table. She crawled under to retrieve it.

"Can't say that I mind the view, to be perfectly honest," Jason said.

Alicia bit her lip and smiled to herself. She snagged the fork and began to wiggle back out. Then her eyes caught a silver plaque on the wall under the table. It was a rectangle only three-inches wide. She wouldn't even have noticed it, except for a particular name which stuck out like a red flag. The plaque recorded the manufacture date of the boat, five years ago, and the company: KIRKLAND ENTERPRISES, PROVIDENCE, RHODE ISLAND.

Kirkland, as in Jason Kirkland? That was a coincidence. And it had been built in New England, where Jason had grown up. Jason Kirkland. The name—it sounded vaguely familiar now, or was she just imagining that she'd heard it before?

"If you stay down there any longer, I'm going to join you."

Alicia's pulse surged in her ears. She almost didn't register Jason's suggestive comment. She blinked, read the plaque again and swallowed hard. Just a coincidence. Of course. It had to be. Even if Jason happened to own the boat—she finally considered that outrageous possibility—it didn't mean he'd *built* it.

But if he *did* own this incredible boat, what was he doing emptying wastebaskets at Envirotech? What was he doing in her life?

Unease swelled in her chest. She had the frightening notion that she had stumbled into something terrible. But what?

Strong hands wrapped around her waist and began sliding Alicia out from under the table. A moment later, she was on her feet, Jason's arms wrapped around her. He plucked the fork from her hand and tossed it in the sink. "I'd do it with you anywhere, Alicia, but under the kitchen table isn't my first choice." His voice grew seductive as he ran his hands over her back and bottom. "Then again, watching your cute fanny bouncing around made for a great after-breakfast treat." He nuzzled her neck, sending alarming thrills through Alicia's body. "God, I love your body, your *neck.*"

Alicia forced herself not to succumb to his charms. Her body reveled in his touch the way a starving man craved food. But she had subjugated her intellect to her body's sensual needs long enough. She had to surface, to *think.* She shoved at his chest, leaning back until she could look him in the eye. "Jason, I—I can't stay after all."

"What?" His smile began to fade. "We're going to take the boat out, go for a sail. I want to show you so much."

"I have work to do." Taking advantage of his surprise, she freed herself from his grasp. She turned and headed for his bedroom—*his* bedroom? On *his* boat? She no longer knew. She knew nothing anymore, about herself and her needs least of all. She only knew that she hated feeling this way, longed for the closeness they had experienced last night, before she'd seen that plaque.

Jason followed her. "Alicia, what's wrong?"

Alicia grabbed her purse and her wrinkled cocktail dress. She plucked at the sweatshirt. "If you don't mind, I'll wash and return these clothes to you later. I'd rather not wear this dress in public at this time of day." She scooped up her pumps and headed for the door.

Jason blocked it with a brawny arm. "Stop right there. You can't leave, not without telling me what I did."

Her gaze clashed with his, read the frustration there. "I don't know, Jason. I wish I did. You're far too sophisticated to be a janitor, that's all I really know. This boat—it's incredible. But you don't want to tell me how you happen to be living on it."

"I *did* tell you. Dr. Benson—"

"Right. Then tell me: What's Henry's last name?"

"Henry? My uncle? Why?"

"Just tell me, Jason. Tell me the truth. *Who are you?*"

Alicia held her breath, her eyes on his, exploring, trying to see the truth beneath. Finally, he broke the gaze, his eyes dropping to the floor. "You know the truth, Alicia. I'm the company janitor."

Alicia stared at his handsome profile, disappointment crushing her. He still wasn't being straight with her. He hadn't lied, but he hadn't told her a thing. By the way he tried to deflect her questions, it was clear he was hiding something. Something big.

She stepped closer to him, forcing his gaze to meet hers. "Is that how you decide what the truth is?" she said, her voice laced with pain. "By what you can get me to swallow? You may be able to fool all your other women, Jason, but that isn't good enough for me." She clutched her crumpled dress and pumps to her chest and edged out the door past him. "I can't stay here right now." Her voice shook, and she couldn't stop it. "I need room to think."

His steps followed her down the gangway. "Alicia, you can't walk home from here."

"I'll call a cab from the yacht club."

"Don't be silly. I'll drive you."

She ignored him and kept walking. She stumbled on the ladder leading out of the hatch. Jason caught her in his arms and forced her to face him, pressing her fast against him. She hated herself for craving his touch, even now, when she knew he was lying to her.

His eyes burned like twin emeralds. "Alicia, whatever you think of me, I haven't lied about how I feel—what we've done together. I meant every bit of it."

Alicia wriggled in his grasp. "Just let me go. *Now.*"

"I'm not ready to." He dipped his head and buried his mouth on hers. To her utter mortification, she found herself responding as if nothing had ruined it. After all, she still knew nothing. Nothing. Except that she loved him. And that summed up her problem perfectly.

His tongue swept inside her mouth, possessed hers with silken caresses. Alicia forced herself to stiffen and pull back. Calling on all her inner strength, she managed to tear free of his arms and climb out on deck. Her knees threatened to give way beneath her as she made her way onto the dock and toward the yacht club, an impossibly far distance away.

This time, Jason didn't try to stop her.

ELEVEN

Checking the truth of the few facts Jason had told her turned out to be depressingly easy. At home, curled on the couch with the Seattle phone book in her lap, Alicia scanned the pages, desperately seeking answers.

She found two Gerald Bensons listed. She called each of them, pretending to be the Lake Washington Yacht Club. Both said they didn't own a boat, nor had they ever owned a boat.

Acting on the assumption that Dr. Benson had an unlisted number, Alicia contacted the mathematics departments at the University of Washington, University of Puget Sound, Pacific Lutheran University, virtually all the colleges in the area. Only one had a Dr. Gerald Benson on staff, in the fine arts department.

A spark of hope rose in Alicia when the switchboard operator put her through to Dr. Benson's office. Chances were he wouldn't be there on a Sunday, anyway.

Then a deep voice answered, "Hello?"

"Dr. Benson? Dr. Gerald Benson?"

"Yes, may I help you?"

"This is going to sound like a strange question, but do you own a sailboat?"

"A sailboat? No, but I'd like to. Are you perhaps giving one away?"

"So you don't own one. Have you ever owned one?"

"Who are you, miss? A private eye?"

"I'm just trying to find a particular man with your name. Do you know a man named Jason Kirkland?"

"Who?"

"It sounds like I have the wrong Dr. Benson." *Probably because he doesn't exist.*

"Yes, I'd say you do."

She forced a laugh, trying to find some humor in the situation. "Besides, my Dr. Gerald Benson is a mathematician."

"Then I'm definitely not your man. I can barely balance my checkbook. Sorry."

She thanked him and hung up, her confusion growing into a tight knot of burning disappointment. Why had Jason lied to her? Or had she merely assumed Dr. Benson lived in Seattle? Maybe Dr. Benson didn't live in the area. It was possible Jason had moved the boat—so he could work as a janitor at Envirotech? Why?

At least she had a few more facts to check out, from the paltry handful Jason had given her.

She pulled on her coat and left the house, then drove downtown to the Seattle Public Library. On the way there, she tried to convince herself that it would all become clear, that there was nothing to worry about. There had to be a rational explanation for Jason's not telling her the truth. It could be something completely mundane.

Perhaps it *was* his boat—but he was embarrassed to admit it. Why? Because the only job he could get was as a janitor? No, that made no sense. Okay, suppose he had *stolen* the boat. She hated to even imagine such a thing, but considering how cagey he was being, it wasn't beyond the realm of possibility. Then again, it was registered to *somebody*, or the owner wouldn't be allowed to moor it at the yacht club. When the club opened on Monday, perhaps she could nose around there. She wasn't anxious to return to the area, though, and she doubted the club would provide a total stranger with facts about one of its clients.

Maybe she could use the boat's license number to learn the name of the owner. But how? Would the DMV give her the owner's name? She doubted it. Her research skills hadn't prepared her for the kind of street digging she wanted to engage in. But if there were any answers in the library, she knew how to dig them up.

She pushed through the door and headed straight for the reference desk. She had to wait fifteen minutes while the young man in front of her argued with the librarian about why they'd changed the policy on magazine checkouts.

Finally, it was her turn. "I hope you can help me. My question might seem rather . . . obscure, but maybe you have some reference book or other . . ."

"What are you looking for?" The woman arched her eyebrows over her glasses, pen poised above a piece of scratch paper.

Alicia almost hesitated to say it. Her search for Dr. Benson proved nothing. If she learned the answers she was seeking, she would know one way or another whether Jason had lied to her. And that thought threatened to break her heart.

"I need to know about a company named Kirkland Enterprises. I believe it's based in Providence, Rhode Island, and is engaged in shipbuilding. And the family—anything you have about the family."

"Is that all?" The librarian tapped a few keys on her computer terminal and checked the call number of a reference book. She jotted the number on the notepad, then tore off the sheet and handed it to Alicia. "Start there. It's a listing of American businesses, broken down by type. From there, try"—she jotted down another number—"this reference, which lists firms doing business in Rhode Island. We don't have as much on East Coast businesses as we do those on the West Coast, but it should give you a starting point. And if you're interested in the family, once you have the owners' names, try the periodicals catalogue. It's on microfiche around the corner there. If they're anybody, an article or two will have been written about them."

Alicia nodded and thanked her. She searched out the reference book and found Kirkland Enterprises with very little effort. Immediately she was struck by the size of the family-owned corporation. Not only did the company build ships, it owned lumber mills, mines, off-shore drilling operations in Alaska, computer firms, overseas investments—all at an unrevealed value. As a family-owned corporation, it didn't have to reveal the value of its assets to the public.

Alicia moved her finger down the list, looking for the name of the actual owners.

The name stuck out as if in sharp relief *Jason Kirkland Sondheim.* Alicia's legs gave out and she sat down, hard, at the nearest table, dragging the heavy reference book with her. Jason? Her Jason Kirkland?

It had to be him. It had to be.

Furious, Alicia slammed the book closed so hard, nearby patrons turned and stared at her. *Calm down,* she counseled herself. *It's not that uncommon a name. You don't know for a fact . . .*

But everything began to click. His overabundance

of confidence, the expensive sports he engaged in, the gifts he'd given her . . . The way he'd treated her, like she meant something to him.

What about that, Alicia?

It didn't matter. She couldn't trust a thing that had happened between them, because she couldn't trust *him*.

She blinked back a rush of bitter tears.

After what seemed ages, she finally had the energy to continue her pursuit of the truth.

Once on her feet, she feared her leaden legs wouldn't support her. She managed to make it to the microfiche index. Supposedly his parents had died tragically when he was sixteen—about thirteen years ago or so. Assuming he was twenty-nine, as he'd said he was approaching thirty. She wasn't certain what his actual age was. He hadn't told her. Just one of those little personal details he'd never gotten around to sharing.

There was more than one entry under Jason Kirkland Sondheim, which lead her to James and Donna Sondheim, his parents. For the next two hours, she sat glued to the microfiche reader. Sickened and fascinated, she read account after account of his parents' deaths. In this one thing, he hadn't been lying. He just hadn't mentioned that they'd died in their personal Lear jet, returning from a business trip to Alaska.

And Jason—left all alone, his family obliterated in one instant. Compassion tightened her chest, but she fought it valiantly. She didn't even *know* this man anymore. And she shouldn't be sparing him any sympathy. She needed to focus. Then maybe she could begin to understand *why*.

She moved on to more recent news stories. After a period of years when he'd dropped out of sight,

Jason Sondheim resurfaced. Alicia hit the forward button on the reader, looking for a particular mention of him in the *New York Post*. She slowed the machine but overshot the article. Slowly, she rewound, until Jason Sondheim was smiling out at her. A photo with this one. She blinked hard, looked at the lady on his arm. A tall, gorgeous blonde.

She read the copy: "Kirta Vandermeer will snag one of Rhode Island's most eligible bachelors next month, Jason Sondheim, owner of Kirkland Enterprises. Ms. Vandermeer is the daughter of New York scion David Vandermeer, whose business holdings were shaken by the S&L debacle. Kirkland Enterprises should put his daughter on much firmer ground. Founded by Jason's enterprising grandfather during the World War II heyday of shipbuilding on the East Coast, Jason's father expanded the business into a variety of rock-solid ventures, ranging from mining to computers and communications. Jason, a Princeton graduate, is known to have a taste for recreation, often leaving his company in the hands of a board of directors headed by former CM CEO Donald McEady. Net worth of Kirkland Enterprises is estimated at $7.2 billion; Jason's personal financial portfolio is rumored to be $520 million, a sizable nest egg for the bride-to-be to set up housekeeping. The wedding is set for May 2."

In the entire article, Alicia found only one fact he'd shared with her—that he'd once been engaged.

After that, the tone of the articles went decidedly downhill. Jason was pictured with his arm around one society deb after another, and a few women of more questionable character. The copy portrayed him as a playboy living the high life. Some of the women appeared sophisticated, some Hollywood brassy, some foreign-born exotic. Every one was gorgeous.

Tears filled Alicia's eyes. What had he ever seen in her? She shook her head and tried to shove her personal feelings aside. The more important issue was what this man was up to. Why was he posing as a janitor? For kicks? It couldn't be. Something was up.

There were no articles about Jason for the past four years, as if he'd dropped out of sight. Yet his life had been reported on enough. Why had no one at Envirotech recognized him? Alicia was familiar with the phenomenon of hiding something in plain sight. No one expected the janitor to be a wealthy man in disguise, therefore no one had made the connection. She certainly hadn't, not that she ever paid attention to society news.

She only had one more reference to check, an article from six months ago. Jason wasn't even mentioned. It was about Bio-Intera, her former employer, a subsidiary of Sondheim-Pendrell. She knew that. What she hadn't remembered was that Sondheim-Pendrell was owned in turn by Kirkland Enterprises.

Alicia swallowed a knot that had formed in her throat. Bio-Intera . . . where she used to work. The firm competed with Envirotech in some of the more prosaic environmental-cleanup technologies. In general, Envirotech management didn't consider Bio-Intera much of a business rival. According to this article, it was in financial difficulties.

Alicia had no idea. She'd been so buried in the lab, she'd heard nothing about it.

Suddenly it struck her. The voice on the phone that morning. It had seemed familiar, and Jason had called him Henry. Henry Sondheim, owner of Bio-Intera? *God, no.*

If he was one and the same, that meant Jason was Henry Sondheim's *nephew.* She shuddered, remembering the screaming match she'd endured with Mr.

Sondheim—a man she'd thought of as a gentleman—the day she'd quit.

The facts began to crystalize into a coherent, terrifying whole. Bio-Intera in trouble, owned by Jason's uncle, Henry Sondheim, a man Jason was apparently "working" for . . . Jason's appearance at Envirotech as her work was about to be taken to market, with profits predicted in the multiple millions . . . The mysterious gift Janelle had received, prompting her to quit work . . . Jason taking her place, gaining access to her lab . . .

His seduction of her . . .

"Oh, my God." Alicia rose unsteadily to her feet. Her work. All her years of effort, hours spent alone in the lab, the sacrifice of a social life. Jason Kirkland—*her* Jason Kirkland—was trying to steal the ultimate prize from her. *And he would stop at nothing to get what he wanted, even stoop to seducing her.*

Bile rose in her throat and a hot, angry hand of pain squeezed her chest, making it difficult to breathe. She had to escape, escape from here, get into the fresh air.

She stumbled past the reference desk on her way toward the door. "Did you find everything you needed?" the librarian asked.

"Yes, thank you," she said with a stiff smile. *Thank you for helping me see the awful truth.*

The librarian rose as she passed. "Miss, are you all right? You look a little pale."

"I'm fine." Alicia pasted a smile on her face and continued past the librarian. "Fine. Just fine."

She shoved through the door and onto the stone library steps. The sky was overcast, ominous. Alicia didn't notice cars speeding past on the street, people walking by on the sidewalk. Her eyes flooded with tears and she tripped on her way down the steps.

"Jason, how could you?" she whispered to herself, drawing the curious stares of passersby. "How could you screw me so completely?"

Mechanically, she unlocked her car door and slid behind the wheel. Suddenly, she couldn't hold back anymore. A sob tore through her, then another. She gave herself up to them. She laid her forehead on the steering wheel and wept until her chest ached and her eyes burned.

If he wanted to steal her project, why had he slept with her? Why hurt her so horribly? Did he really think she'd never find out? Or didn't he care if she learned the truth?

Fat drops of rain began to pelt the windshield, encasing her in a gray cocoon of misery. As she tried to work it through, her emotions kept getting in the way, swift, painful flashes of memory, torturing her, keeping her from thinking logically. The tender way he'd taught her to loosen up and dance with him, the murmur of his voice in her ear as they made love, the way he'd smiled at her as if he had deeper feelings for her.

The crushing reality of his deception almost obliterated her logic. Almost. She fought through the haze of crushed hopes, sucked in a ragged breath. She had to do something, she knew that. But what?

At least she could try to stop crying. She wiped her face on her sleeve and looked around the car for her box of tissues. She grabbed a handful and scrubbed her face.

Trying to think clearly, she glanced outside and remembered that she was still sitting in her car down the street from the public library. Rain sheeted down the window, making it hard to tell the time of day. Her digital car clock didn't illuminate when the engine was off, and on her wrist—her wrist!—she still wore the gift he'd given her. A broken watch. Broken. Worth less than nothing.

Wild fury tore through Alicia and she pulled the watch off her wrist. Rolling down the window, she tossed it into the street, heard its face shatter on the blacktop. The sound brought her no satisfaction.

It was time to pull herself together, to scrape up the pieces, figure out what she could salvage. Her project. What had he learned? Was it already too late?

"Oh, my God. I have to—"

Stop him.

Alicia dug her keys from her purse and shoved them into the ignition. A moment later, she was pulling out onto the street, heading toward Bellevue, and Envirotech.

TWELVE

Jason stared at the ceiling, counting the oak boards from the left side of the room to the right and back again.

For the thirty-ninth time, he noticed that the third board from the right was slightly warped. There was a knothole in the sixth board. The tenth board had an extra nail.

And still he had no answers.

He'd been an idiot to think he could fool a woman as smart as Alicia Underwood. He knew she didn't completely understand the situation, but a heavy weight in his gut told him it was merely a matter of time. The jig would soon be up. He'd failed his uncle, hadn't completed the switch. Had decided to save that for after this date. He wasn't even sure why.

The clock was ticking.

Lying in a wrinkled pile of sheets that smelled of their lovemaking was bad enough. But an hour ago, after a plodding trip to the bathroom, he'd found one of her black silk stockings on the floor, sticking out from under the comforter piled on the floor. Now he twisted it around his fist, around and around, then slowly began to unwind it. Straight again, he laid the nylon over his chest and tucked his hands under his head.

It was never supposed to happen like this. Hell, it was never supposed to happen at all. He'd screwed up big time. He should have kept his hands to himself, his urges under control.

He'd always craved risk. But this time he'd pushed it too far, inviting her here. Treating her like he cared about her. Making love to her.

Opening his heart—

All the time he'd romanced her, he'd assumed he could extricate himself—his heart—as easily as casting off and sailing away in his boat. Leaving the same as he arrived, as he'd always done.

But the moment she'd pulled away from him, the pain and confusion in her eyes had stabbed him like a knife in the chest. So he lay here, unable to find the energy to move.

She wanted him when she believed he had virtually nothing. She *loved* him when she thought he was a janitor at Envirotech.

Now . . . Now, he had no idea what she thought of him.

It didn't matter. He couldn't let it matter. He'd been a major screw-off most of his life. Now was his one chance to make it right. He couldn't allow his heart to interfere.

If he didn't get to the lab soon, all the risk—all his pain—would be for nothing. Right before their date, when he knew Alicia was home getting ready, Jason had stayed late and created an exact duplicate of a bacteria sample dish. He'd labeled it with the strain of the strongest bug in storage, then hidden it. All he needed to do now was make the switch and sneak the real bacteria out of the lab. Then he'd be gone from Envirotech and never go back.

Easy. He could do it. He'd finish this right now.

For the first time in his life, he felt no anticipation

at the risks he was about to undertake. Merely a weariness deep in his soul.

He forced himself up on his elbows, then swung his feet to the floor. A lead block seemed to rest on his shoulders, pushing him down and making the smallest movement difficult. Taking a deep breath, he shoved to his feet and headed for the door.

Before he reached it, he realized he was still holding Alicia's black stocking. Infuriated by his weakness, he tossed it to the floor and stalked out.

He'd done an exceptional job. No one would be able to tell that this sample dish was a fake.

Jason stared down at the four-inch-wide dish on the counter, which he'd carefully labeled with the code, GBAV-1462. He'd copied as best he could Helen's distinctive print.

The liquid he'd blended so carefully matched that of the bacteria in the other dishes, nestled neatly in their slots in the liquid nitrogen freezer. He'd watched carefully as Alicia and Helen accessed the freezer, learned the right precautions to take to keep his fingers from freezing off and maintain the integrity of the sample.

Beside the fake sample rested the small cooler that Uncle Henry's scientists had provided. While not an ideal environment, the bacteria would remain frozen, yet viable, for at least two hours, long enough for him to deliver it to Henry.

So what was he waiting for?

A loud click startled him and he spun toward the noise.

The clock on the wall ticking off yet another minute. And still he didn't make the switch.

Do it, Jason. Do it and get out of here.

Why was this so damned difficult? He'd planned so well what he needed to do, but he couldn't bring himself to go through with it. As if mentally prodding him, his uncle's voice filled his mind. *"She's a thief, Jason. She worked for us a few years back and stole her research—research we paid for—I paid for. You have to help me, Jason. You're the rich one, and this company is all I have."*

He traced the curved edge of the lid, his mind feeling as cold and frozen as the bacteria containers in the freezer. Something didn't make sense. It never had, but he'd tried to make it add up, had wanted to believe in Henry.

"This company, and you. We're family, Jason. We stick together."

But Alicia—she was so honest in everything else, the most honest person he'd ever met. How could he sabotage her future without knowing for certain that she was guilty?

His gaze flicked up, his concentration elsewhere. Until a word caught his eye. "Bio-Intera."

The word was on a scrap of newspaper tacked to the bulletin board. Only a few words were visible beneath two other notices that had been posted. Jason pushed them aside, revealing a yellowing newspaper article. A photo of Alicia had been placed beneath the title, "New food irradiation process promises safety."

His gaze glued to the words before him, Jason removed the clipping. According to the article, Alicia had worked at Bio-Intera, just as Henry said. In fact, this article had been published in the Seattle *Times* shortly before she was fired. Which was interesting in light of the fact that she had been heading up a project on food irradiation, which was only peripherally related to her current waste-cleanup project.

Maybe she'd worked on both? His heart began to

pound hard in his chest. How would she have had the time? Common sense told him that she wouldn't. He knew a little about irradiation, a process to kill bacteria in food, enough to know the technology had limited public acceptance. Not a great moneymaker for any company. Especially not Bio-Intera.

He neared the end of the article, still confused, his heart torn in two opposing directions, fighting to puzzle out the ramifications of this information.

Then, in a single instant, everything became crystal clear.

> *Along with her work for Bio-Intera, Dr. Underwood is pursuing private research, trying to develop bacteria that may someday be able to lower radiation levels. Apparently, the highly theoretical nature of her work has made it difficult to find funding sources. "We plan to stick with research that makes good business sense," commented Bio-Intera President Henry Sondheim. For Bio-Intera, that means food irradiation.*

She was innocent. Bio-Intera hadn't even backed her research. Jason suddenly felt sick. His uncle had used him, had lied to him, had completely fooled him. He'd *trusted* him.

It's your own fault. You've had your head in the sand so long, you wouldn't know up from down. Or black from white, for that matter.

There was no longer any gray here. Alicia was completely innocent. And he'd already lost her.

Alicia pressed her hand to the plate by the laboratory door and waited for the light to turn green, then punched in her five-digit code number. The steel lock retracted with a thunk. She shoved through and the door lock snapped closed behind her.

She entered the dim antechamber. Through the double-paned glass in the door beyond, she could see that the far bank of lights had been left on, illuminating a portion of the lab. She would have to talk to the janitor about leaving the lights on.

The janitor?

She would have laughed if it didn't hurt so damn much. She inserted her keycard and shoved through the door into the main part of the lab.

And stopped cold.

Jason turned to face her, surprise and dismay on his far-too-handsome features. He was standing at a counter near the stainless-steel freezer where she kept her bacteria samples. Beside him on the counter was a small cooler of the type scientists used to transport fragile samples. And beside that was one of *her* sample dishes.

He still wore the shorts and T-shirt he'd donned after making love to her that morning. *That morning.* And now he was here, violating her lab, her life's work!

Alicia's pulse thundered in her head, a thousand blood vessels clogging with painful pressure. "You," she whispered, barely able to breathe. She sucked in a breath. "You *thief.*"

Chagrin and guilt crossed his handsome face, and Alicia knew she hadn't misinterpreted the damning situation. Jason stepped toward her, his hands up. "I know what it looks like, but it isn't, Alicia. Listen to me."

"Listen to you? Listen to you? You *bastard!"* Blind fury drove all restraint from her. Having her suspicions proven correct gave her no satisfaction. The pain of his betrayal swept through her anew. Words

were inadequate, talk useless. A deep, primal rage engulfed her, the pain of a mortally wounded animal, and she launched herself at him.

She landed against his hard body, shoved him back several steps, but kept on the attack, pounding at his chest, scratching at his face. With satisfaction, she felt her fingernails sink into the flesh of his cheek and heard him cry out. The still logical part of her brain was appalled at her behavior, but it had lost control.

Like bands of iron, his arms imprisoned hers against her sides, her back to his chest.

"Stop it, Alicia! Stop it and listen to me!"

Still in a blind fury, she bucked in his arms, scratched at his forearms, fought to free herself from this man who only hours ago had used those same arms to cradle her in a lover's embrace.

"Let me go, you bastard! You lying, thieving cheat!"

He lifted her in the air and began dragging her toward the laboratory door. She kicked hard at him and landed a satisfyingly hard blow to his shin that made his step falter. "Damn! Calm down, woman! I'm not going to hurt you."

"Not going to hurt me?" she parroted, knowing she sounded hysterical. "You already did that plenty, Mr. Millionaire. Or is it billionaire? I lost count."

"What in the—" At his surprise, Alicia almost managed to wrench herself free, but he tightened his hold and continued to pull her toward the narrow hall leading to her office. "We have to talk."

"Goddamn you, Jason, let go of me!" She tried kicking him again, but he sidestepped her, and she only managed glancing blows.

He shoved through the door into her small sleeping room and tossed her on the cot. She began scrambling up, but he pushed her back. He straddled her and pressed her wrists into the mattress by her head. She was no match for his strength or size. She wriggled under him, but all it did was make her tired—and painfully aware of how close their hips were.

He stared down at her, breathing almost as heavily as she. "Just—calm—down." His presence seemed to fill the tiny room, which was illuminated only by the light from the hall. She was trapped.

He began to talk, but she didn't want to hear the words. She didn't want to hear her suspicions confirmed.

"Yes, I was going to take a sample of your bacteria, Alicia. But I changed my mind. The one on the counter you saw is a fake. If you doubt me, go check it out."

"Fat lot of good that does. Of *course* you're going to say you changed your mind, since I caught you red-handed! You just waited until I was so delirious over spending all that time in your bed, I wouldn't *feel* like coming to the lab, so you could steal my discovery for your two-bit, floundering Bio-Intera! Bastard! *Bastard!*" She wrenched one of her wrists free and slapped him hard across the face.

"Ouch! Damn it!" He yanked back, then scrambled just as quickly for her hand and anchored it once more in place. "Damn, Alicia, just listen to me." His eyes fastened on hers. "Alicia, I'm sorry. I didn't want to hurt you. I never wanted to hurt you, even when I believed—"

"Don't try to talk your way out of this, Jason. I'm not that much of a fool."

"You aren't any kind of fool, Alicia," he said, his voice alarmingly tender. Alicia tried not to notice the tone he used on her. It was all an act, after all, a ploy to get her to trust him. Tears brimmed in her eyes and she blinked them back, furious at her weakness, not wanting to let him see it.

"How could you? How could you do this to me? I thought you *cared,*" she cried.

"I do, Alicia. I never meant to hurt you. I thought I was doing something for my uncle, to keep his business afloat. He told me you'd stolen the research for your superbug from his company."

"And you believed him, I suppose. Making you innocent? You're engaging in industrial espionage, or didn't that occur to you?"

For a moment, he was painfully silent. "Yes, it occurred to me. I didn't see it that way." His voice escalated with passion. "But I know better now, Alicia. I was wrong. You showed me that, showed me how to care about bigger things, things that matter. Your life's so full of meaning."

"And you're so full of it!" She closed her eyes against his sincere expression and wriggled harder.

He entrapped both her wrists with one hand, above her head, and gently caressed her face, his callused palm amazingly sensuous against her smooth skin. "Listen to me. Look at me, Alicia. Open your eyes."

She couldn't help herself. She did as he wanted, again.

His eyes burned in the dim room. "Alicia, I've never met anyone like you. Don't shut me out now. I've never felt like this about"—his voice broke—actually broke—"any woman."

Alicia fought down a surge of unwarranted pleasure at his words. "Gee, you're so good at this. You almost sound like you mean it. Did you rehearse this in front of a mirror, or do you just make it up as you go along?"

"Alicia, that isn't fair."

"Fair?"

"Christ, you know what I mean."

"How can I know you? You're somebody else! I'm still trying to figure out which part of you is lies and which is the truth."

"Almost nothing I've said to you is a lie, Alicia. Nothing about us is a lie. The way I feel about you—the way we made love—I meant all of it. *All of it.*"He shook her wrists for emphasis. "Alicia—" he whispered harshly, bringing his face so close to her that his breath tingled on her face. "Please. I never thought I'd find you. Don't let me lose you."

His mouth covered hers. Alicia whimpered as he crushed his lips to hers, his tongue taking possession of her mouth. She moaned with shock, with anger and with an unwelcome elation. God, she still *wanted* him, as he was so expertly demonstrating.

His hands softened their hold on her wrists, turned caressing rather than binding. He raised his mouth just enough so he could speak to her through his kiss. "I love you, Alicia Underwood. I swear it's true. I've never loved anyone like this before. You make me feel alive like nothing ever has." He buried his lips on hers once more.

Alicia squeezed her eyes tight as a wave of desire engulfed her. He was smoke. Insubstantial as a dream. Nothing about him was real, except the fantasy she'd created. The heat in her belly—focused on where he sat atop her pelvis—expanded outward as he kissed her, swept up her chest and down her thighs, forbidden now, yet oh, so tempting. It was as if no time had passed since their intimacy on his boat, no secrets had been revealed. She wanted him, even now.

He broke the kiss once more, and she gasped as if her life depended on it. "I don't care. I don't care what you say." She swallowed a quick rush of tears.

"Then let me show you." His eyes filled with poignancy. "Sweet, darling Alicia," he said, "I'm nothing without you. You're everything to me." The words, caressed her heart and soul, words she'd never heard him speak before, words that—until now—she had no idea how badly she wanted to be true. She lay unmoving as his hand shoved her sweatshirt above her breasts, as his fingers snapped open the hook of her bra. He shifted, sliding his bare legs along hers, imprisoning her body with his own.

He pressed his warm lips to a taut nipple and she shivered at the sensation. His tongue swept over it, danced on the tip, sending jolts of pleasure through her body.

Alicia bit back a moan, but she couldn't bring herself to make him stop. She knew she'd hate herself for her weakness later, when she had a cooler head. But now, for once, she cast logic aside and truly lived in the moment. *He'd taught her that.*

He unfastened her shorts—*his* shorts, from his boat—while he made love to her breasts, and yanked them down and off her legs. She didn't fight him. She still wore no underpants.

A moment later, he had freed himself. Alicia allowed him to part her legs, allowed him to claim that part of herself that was already lost to him. She shuddered with forbidden pleasure as he thrust hard and full into her wetness.

"My God, you still want me, as badly as I want you," he cried in her ear. "We belong together. You make me whole."

"Don't say it," she said through gritted teeth. "Don't."

He thrust again, his T-shirt rasping against her swollen nipples, moving harder, faster, his voice in her ear telling her wondrous things, verbally making love to her as no man ever had. "God, I belong with you. I belong here," he said. "You're mine, Alicia. You know it. I'm so goddamned sorry." Words failed him as the passion built between them and he moaned, a deep, guttural, primal sound that brought tears to her eyes.

She dug her fingers into his back, holding on just a little longer to a man and a dream that had never really existed. "Jason—" She choked on a sob as he swept her to forbidden heights of pleasure.

"Yes," he cried. "Say my name. I beg you."

"Jason."

"Darling—" He increased the pace, forcing her above and beyond the final shreds of her control, dissolving her sense of self in an uninhibited blending of pleasure and heartbreak. Alicia cried out as she crested the brink of ecstasy, knew he was right with her, as every perfect fantasy man ought to be.

Their mutual cries of release echoed against the walls of the tiny room, sounding louder, more substantial than they were. Alicia shook, felt her sex tighten hard on his as he thrust once more, spasmodically, into her.

He shuddered in a paroxysm of pleasure, then lowered himself to lie beside her, cradling her in his arms, his head nestled on her chest.

After a moment, with Jason tracing his finger lazily along the globe of her breast, the full reality of what she'd done settled on her. Shame filled her. Appalled at her weakness, she shoved him aside and swung her feet to the floor. Her legs shook as she stood. She picked up the shorts and slipped them on.

Jason sat up and grasped her wrist. "Where are you—"

She twisted out of his hold. "Get dressed and get out, Jason. Out of this building and out of my life."

"Alicia—" He stood and reached for her.

She avoided his touch, shooting him a look filled with fury and pain. "Don't look so worried. I won't tell anyone who you really are. But never show your face around here again."

Jason yanked his fly closed, then zipped and snapped his shorts. Incredulous, he stared hard at her. "So why in the hell did you just let me love you?" He gestured toward the cot.

"Love? That wasn't love," she bit out. "That was casual sex, Jason, what you're best at."

"*Casual* . . . Christ!" He stood before her, and she couldn't avoid his gaze, his emerald eyes sparking with pain. He lifted a hand toward her face, but Alicia knocked his hand away.

At her rebuff, Jason seemed to pull in on himself, his voice taking on an icy edge Alicia had never heard before. "I see. Forgive me for not understanding the rules, Alicia. I've never been in love before."

She couldn't look at his face, couldn't stand to see what seemed to be remorse, anger, even despair. She couldn't stand to feel sorry for him, not after all he'd done. She wouldn't be able to take it. Instead, she turned her back on him and held the door open. "Just get out, before I call security."

He shot her one last glare, filled with torment and pain, before he disappeared.

Another Monday. Another workday, one in an endlessly long series. Alicia checked her E-mail and her inbox, tried to focus on her final research report.

She heard voices raised down the hall, some of the women taking part in an emotional bull session. She heard her name. Then Vana and Helen paraded into her office.

"Do *you* know anything about it, Alicia?" Vana asked, an unmistakable whine in her voice.

"About what?" Alicia's stomach tightened.

"Jason Kirkland resigned! He left a note on the building administrator's desk. He's not coming back." Vana collapsed in one of the chairs before Alicia's desk.

Helen joined her, looking more composed. She watched Alicia carefully. "Any idea why he suddenly took off, Alicia?"

"No. Why would I?" She shot Helen a warning look. No one else knew they'd had a date this weekend. *A date.* Such a casual word for the emotional storm she'd been through—was still trying to get through.

"Alicia, you know *everything,*" Vana said. "Can't you ask somebody? Maybe you could call him and talk to him. He likes you, Alicia. Weren't you friends? Don't you even care what happens to him?"

Alicia's control snapped and she shot to her feet. "Leave me alone, all right? I'm too busy for this right now. Please, just go."

"Well, *excuse us,*" Vana said. She rose and strutted toward the door. "Come on, Helen. At least *you're* willing to listen."

But Helen called out, "I'll be there in a minute, Vana. Shut the door on your way out."

With a grimace, Vana did as requested.

Helen turned back to Alicia. "Okay, toots, what happened? Last I heard, you two had a hot date."

"He . . . It didn't work out," she said, trying hard not to meet Helen's gaze, trying hard to appear as if her world hadn't ended.

"That's painfully obvious. How are you doing?"

"I'm—I'm okay." She smiled wryly and hugged her

arms across her chest. "No, actually, I'm pretty terrible."

Helen rose and circled the desk, leaning against it next to Alicia. "Did he hurt you?" she asked, her voice full of concern.

Alicia didn't know the best way to answer that. She began to nod but then realized Helen might think he'd raped her, or something equally bad. Then again, hadn't he, in a way? "It's just for the best that he's gone, is all."

She wouldn't tell on him. She would take extra measures to protect the security of her work, but she wouldn't hurt Jason. Besides, what damage had been done had already happened. Punishing Jason wouldn't solve anything, except make the entire horrendous incident public knowledge. And Envirotech couldn't take Bio-Intera to court without revealing its trade secrets, putting its intellectual property up for grabs. How could Envirotech claim something was stolen from it, if it couldn't say exactly what it was?

Helen patted Alicia's shoulder. "I guess he was too good to be true, huh?"

Alicia nodded, tears filling her eyes. "Looks that way."

"Alicia, I want you to listen to me and do what I say." Helen passed her a tissue from the box on the credenza. "Go home! You're useless here today. Just go home for a while. Get away from here. The project can wait."

"But—"

"Don't you have a lab at home?"

Alicia wiped her nose and nodded.

"If you get the urge, you can tinker there. But take a break. Lord knows, after four straight years without a vacation, you need one."

* * *

Jason pulled up at the rendezvous in the park to find Henry already waiting, as usual. He swung out of the Jeep and approached the black Lincoln. Henry opened the door for him.

But this time, Jason waved him outside, away from the prying ears of Brian, the chauffeur, and the brutish Ike Tyler, who again was at his post in the front passenger seat.

Henry slid out, clutching a manila envelope in his hand. "Hey, being seen in public together isn't a good idea, Jason, you know that."

Jason stepped back. Without a word, he motioned with his head toward a walking path. Henry fell into step beside him.

Henry spoke first. "I'm assuming you arranged this little meeting to tell me you got the stuff. Even though you refused to give me the code word when you called. So where is it?"

Now that there was enough distance between them and the car, Jason turned to face him. "I'm quitting, Henry."

Henry stared at him for a moment. Then his eyes narrowed and his lips thinned. "Quitting? You can't quit. You owe me this, Jason. Did you forget how desperately I need your help?" He gripped Jason's arm.

Fury surged through Jason. "You lied to me about Alicia. You lied about her stealing from you."

"Lied? What, did she tell you that? And you believe her over me? What kind of family loyalty is that, Jason?"

"She never said a thing. I found out on my own." He took a step closer to Henry, and his uncle backed up defensively. "You never would have told me the truth, would you? That's what galls me the most. You were using me."

He could see the truth in Henry's eyes. "You don't know the full story, Jason. She should have stayed with Bio-Intera. She should have given us her research. She *owed* us."

"For what, hiring her? It doesn't work that way, Henry."

Henry nodded, his lips thinning. "I see . . . I see what's really going on here. You want me to believe you suddenly got a conscience, but I know better. This is all about the doctor lady. Now that you've screwed her, you're ready to screw me." Henry shot him a disparaging look. "It's all about who screws who, Jason. I thought you realized that. I thought you understood that you have to look out for yourself, because no one will do it for you."

"You make me sick."

"Listen to you. Too good for yourself—is that it? You're forgetting everything, Jason. How I bailed you out of prison in Mexico for smuggling pot. I had to pay a hefty bribe to get you out. And the time you stole the police car for a joy ride—if it wasn't for me, you'd be serving time for that one, too!"

Jason felt a flush color his cheeks at the reminders of his past idiocy. This latest was the climax of an entire lifetime of foolish behavior. "I was just a stupid kid," Jason muttered.

His uncle laid a hand on his shoulder and drew him close. "You need me, Jason," he said, his tone tender. "You always have, and you always will."

Jason's insides froze. Uncle Henry had been like a father to him, or so he'd thought. He realized now how dependent his uncle had kept him, teaching him to lean on him instead of standing on his own two feet. Bailing him out of scrapes as a kid had seemed kindhearted. But he'd also encouraged Jason to risk his neck in one escapade after another, expecting nothing from him, laughing along with him. Now that he thought about it, Jason couldn't recall Henry ever expressing more than token worry about his well-being. Had he been used all along? To what purpose?

"It's just you and me, Jase," his uncle continued in a seductive voice. "You and me. We're a *team*. You couldn't handle your businesses alone. You'd have no time to yourself. All that responsibility—you don't want it. You hate business. I worry about the boring stuff so you have time to enjoy yourself. Fast cars, pretty women—that's what matters to you, not some brainy scientist chick."

Jason threw up his hand and knocked Henry's hand off his shoulder. "Not anymore. You no longer have anything to do with my business. Do you hear me? It's *over!* From now on, I call the shots. My first order of business is to keep you as far away from Kirkland Enterprises as I can get you."

His uncle's mouth hardened and his eyes grew wary. "Well, that's just dandy. This is a great time for you to start developing a responsible side, Jason. A great time. Well . . ." He glanced down at his polished shoes, then back up at Jason. He ran his fingers along the edge of the manila envelope he still held. "Since you're not going to get me the superbug, I'll have to approach the problem from a different angle."

A sick feeling curled in Jason's gut. "What in the hell does that mean?"

Henry smiled in an overly friendly manner. "See, kid, I had a hunch when push came to shove, you just might fold. Something about you has changed in the past weeks." His voice hardened. "And I don't particularly like it. You've lost your edge, Jason, your enthusiasm for our little enterprise. So I had Ike arrange insurance for me."

"Insurance." Jason didn't like the sound of that. The hair on the back of his neck stood up. "What in the hell—"

Tucking the envelope under his arm, Henry pulled a cell phone from his inside jacket pocket and tapped in a few numbers. Alarm swelled in Jason, but as yet he didn't know what form the threat would take.

"Give the apple to Snow White," He said into the phone, his voice icy calm. He tucked the phone away and looked at Jason. "Don't blame me, Jason. You made the choice. Here, take a look." Henry slapped the manila envelope against Jason's crossed arms.

Reluctantly, Jason accepted the envelope and tore open the top. He turned it upside down. A dozen photos slipped into his shaking hands, blasting the heart out of him.

Henry's voice came to him as if from a long way off. "Just one set of many, kid. Another's being delivered to her this minute—with a little message letting her know just how she ought to cooperate with us. If she doesn't, her reputation will be trash with her employer—with any employer. No one will ever trust her with research money or secrets again, not the straight-and-narrow corporate types, not research institutes, no one. She'll be a pariah. Oh, and by the way, I'm letting her know you were in on it."

"How—" These photos—they must have been taken with a telephoto lens from another boat. Photo after photo showed them together on the deck of his yacht, laughing together, talking, touching. In a hot embrace, with his lips on hers and his hand under her skirt. His face as well as hers were clearly visible, enough to enable his identification as the owner of Bio-Intera's parent company. And here was Dr. Alicia Underwood, intimately consorting with a business rival.

Henry soon confirmed Jason's questions. "We were on a nearby boat. Notice how your face is showing, along with hers?" he said with obvious pride. "Ike and I picked these special, just to nail her. Did you see the best one?"

Jason knew he was looking at it. Alicia was curled against his chest as they danced together, gazing up at him with heat and wanting and longing. God, she looked so damned trusting! His hand—he'd slid it under her skirt to cup her bare bottom, reveling in her amazingly erotic surprise. The camera had caught a moment when her creamy bottom was partly exposed, showing that she wore no underwear. Showing that she and Jason were or intended to be intimate. As if to emphasize that fact, another photo showed him leading her by the hand to the hatch.

A hot knot of fury swelled in his gut. Henry had done this—his uncle, the man he'd felt closest to in the world. Henry had done this knowing how betrayed, how *violated* he would feel.

And not giving a damn.

"If I could, I would have gotten a shot of you two in bed," Henry said, his harsh voice grating like knives on Jason's nerves. "But I think these will be sufficient to cast doubt on her loyalties."

His awful words faded beneath the pounding in Jason's head. Nausea churned in his stomach, a lead weight crushed his heart. They hadn't been alone on their date. Someone else, some *thing* else, had been there on deck with them, spying on their private moments, among the few he would ever have with the woman he loved.

Jason stuffed the damning photos back in the envelope.

Henry smiled at him, a nasty, victorious smile. Fury surged in Jason's bloodstream, obliterating every trace of loyalty he'd ever felt for his uncle. The risk he'd taken for this man, thinking he *owed* him. He'd considered him a father figure. A *father*—His father's kid brother, who'd taken him under his wing, been his mentor, guided his *life*. To what end? All those years he'd placed his trust in the man—

His hand tightened into a fist. Suddenly he felt filthy. He'd been used, made to whore for Henry. And because of him, Jason had unwittingly dragged Alicia down into the muck.

His control snapped. He slugged Henry hard in the face, felt the satisfying *whump* as his fist impacted. Henry stumbled backward and stared at him in shock, blood running from his nose. "Jase!"

"You bastard!" Jason grabbed him by his expensive designer collar, twisting the fabric until it throttled him. "You sick, conniving bastard!"

In a bizarre twist of fate, he suddenly understood with crystal clarity how badly he'd hurt Alicia. He had betrayed her—someone who loved him—just as his Uncle Henry had betrayed him. The death of that trust was one of the most painful things he'd ever experienced.

Henry grasped Jason's wrist, trying to free his shirt from his grip. "Easy, Jason. The photos were merely intended to be insurance. Smart businessmen plan for every contingency. Now, if you'd finished the job like I told you, they would never have seen the light of day. Unfortunately, I've found it necessary to show her exactly what she's up against."

"You *sicken* me." He tightened his fingers on Henry's shirt collar another notch and yanked the man's face close to his. "I risked my reputation, my safety, *everything* to do you a favor while you were sneaking around behind my back, you with your dirty tricks—"

Henry smiled grimly. "Don't get so worked up. She'll be okay—as long as she cooperates." His eyes hardened into flint. "If not, she gives up everything. Because I don't play to lose." His gaze focused above Jason's right shoulder. "Isn't that so, Ike?"

A strong arm yanked Jason back so suddenly that Henry's collar tore, a hunk of his shirt coming away in Jason's hand. Ike Tyler shoved Jason back and delivered a quick, one-two punch to his jaw.

The blows sent jolts of pain through Jason's cranium. He reeled backward, disoriented for a precious moment. But he forced himself to catch his balance, using skills he'd learned challenging his body and mind over the years in one death-defying sport after another. He could handle Ike Tyler. He moved into a defensive position, crouching low, arms spread.

Tyler was a trained heavy, he realized that now. But he was also big and slow. He leaped toward Jason, but Jason danced sideways and delivered a swift kick to his midsection.

Tyler grunted and fell to his knees, and Jason slammed him across the back with a double-fisted blow. Before either of the men could recover enough to launch a counter offensive, Jason swept up the manila envelope from the grass and sprinted toward his Jeep.

Still dizzy from Tyler's ham-handed blows to his face, he reeled sideways a few steps. But he forced himself to keep the Jeep in the center of his sight, and managed to reclaim his balance. Then he scrambled into his Jeep and gunned the engine out of the parking lot.

He never looked back.

Alicia stared through the microscope at the tissue sample. It remained clean, without the slightest damage. She'd just dosed it with a 7-percent solution. She picked up the Geiger counter on the table and ran it over the petri dish beside the microscope. Background levels only.

The satisfaction she should have felt at this unprecedented breakthrough didn't materialize. She rubbed the bridge of her nose, unable to feel anything but desolation.

Restless, she snapped off the light on the microscope and returned the Geiger counter to its base. She left her basement lab and climbed the steps toward the first floor, dragging one leaden foot in front of the other.

The doorbell rang. Alicia sighed, not wanting to see anyone. Not today. This weekend's fiasco remained a fresh wound deep in her heart.

She peeked through the keyhole. A uniformed man stood there, a package under his arm. She opened the door but kept the key-chain in place. "What is it?"

"Are you Dr. Alicia Underwood?"

"Why?"

"I have a package here for her." He held up a manila envelope.

"Okay. Give it to me." She gestured through the four-inch crack in the door.

"First you have to sign for it." He thrust a clipboard at her. Alicia accepted it and the pen through the crack in the door and signed it, then passed it back. Feeling vulnerable—to men, to the world in general—she was in no mood to open the door to a stranger. She accepted the package and the man left.

Alicia glanced at it. There was no indication where it was from. She slipped a nail under the flap and worked it free, reminded suddenly of how neatly she'd opened the wrapped gift box Jason had given her, and how he'd advised her to "just tear into it."

Well, she was through listening to Jason Kirkland. She'd take all day opening it if she felt like it. What was the rush? There was nowhere she had to be, nothing she had to do but exist.

The phone rang. Alicia stared dolefully at it, irritated at yet another interruption to her misery. But she couldn't keep from answering it. She was too responsible not to.

"Hello?"

"Alicia?" Only one man said her name with that accent, that sexy lilt. The familiar voice thrilled and aggravated her at the same time. "Don't hang up. I have to talk to you."

"No, Jason. I have nothing to say to you."

"Have you opened it yet? It doesn't sound like it, thank God. Well, *don't.*"

Alicia narrowed her eyes and glanced at the forgotten manila envelope in her hand. "What are you talking about?"

"Did someone deliver a package to you, an envelope?"

Propping the phone on her shoulder, Alicia finished working the flap free and began extracting the contents. A cover letter, and some other sheets. "Yes, a few minutes ago. I don't see—"

"Don't open it! Wait right there. I'm coming over. I'll explain everything to you."

It was too late. Alicia had already begun flipping

through the contents. What she saw made her heart stop. "Oh, my God," she breathed, the receiver slipping from her shoulder. Her knees gave way and she sank to the carpet, the implications crystallizing in her mind even without reading the note that spelled it out plainly. Caught consorting with the enemy . . .

She pulled her knees against her chest, tightening herself into a ball. But she couldn't keep her eyes from the photographs. She and Jason, in intimate conversation and even more intimate embrace. The whole time, someone had been watching. Jason obviously knew about the photos *now*. Had he known at the time?

The implication slammed into her. *My God, it had been a setup from the beginning.*

She heard his voice coming from the receiver on the floor. "Alicia! Pick up the phone! Talk to me."

She snatched up the phone. "You romanced me on purpose, to get *these*, didn't you? You heartless, cruel—" She gasped, her lungs aching with unshed tears, with shock and mortification so deep, Alicia thought she would die from it. "Did that make it tolerable to spend time with me, knowing we were being photographed?" she said acidly. "Flaunting your sophistication and wowing the naive egghead scientist? And what a job you did, too, performing for the camera!"

"I didn't—my God, you think I *knew* about this? I swear—"

"Shut up!" she screamed, her heart frozen in rage. "Just shut up and get out of my life!"

"No! You need me, Alicia, whether or not you know it. Don't do anything crazy. Stay right there. I'm on my way. Just . . ." She heard an odd, muffled sound, like the air rushing out of someone's lungs.

Then the line went dead.

THIRTEEN

Two hours later, Alicia started to worry, despite herself. Jason had said he was coming over. And while seeing Jason Kirkland was the *last* thing she wanted, she couldn't help wondering what had happened to him. Nor could she forget the odd way the conversation had ended.

As if she should trust the man! She'd already burned the photos. But the cover letter—the thing that told her the story of how Jason had wooed her in order to blackmail her into working for Bio-Intera—she held on to that, read it again every time she found herself thinking of him. Missing him.

The phone rang. Alicia picked it up tentatively, unsure whether she wanted to speak to anyone. "Hello?"

"Dr. Underwood?"

"Yes?"

"Did you like the photos?"

"Who is this?" Though she recognized the voice. Henry Sondheim.

"I'm your previous employer, Doctor. Surely you haven't forgotten me. And I'm your future employer. That is, unless you want to become a pariah among your peers. The lover of a man who owns a competing firm—one which happens to be carrying out a similar line of research. How do you think President Fielding would look on that, Dr. Underwood? Do you think he'd still trust you? Do you think any research company will ever trust you again? I don't."

Fury tore through Alicia. She counseled herself to at least *sound* calm, even if she felt like screaming. "You think I'm going to work for you because of a handful of photos? You're out of your mind."

The man was silent for a moment. "Your reputation means that little to you?"

"I don't care about the photos. I refuse to be manipulated."

Again, a long silence. Alicia almost hung up the phone. Then that voice came again. "So, that's how you're going to be. Well, I have something you can't ignore quite so easily. You know who I mean. My nephew. I know you have a soft spot for him, despite the way he tricked you. Ike, bring him here."

Alicia heard a muffled background noise; then Jason's voice came over the line, sounding desperate. "Alicia? Whatever he says, don't listen to him. Do you hear me? Don't—ugh!"

"Jason?" It sounded like he'd been slugged in the stomach. Alicia clutched the phone tightly.

Henry's voice again. "He'll be okay. Unless you don't bring me a sample. A healthy, viable sample that my scientists can grow in our own labs. And, of course, you."

Alicia tried to project coldness, but her knees were shaking. Was Jason really in trouble? "He's your nephew. You expect me to believe you'd hurt—"

"Bring the sample to three-two-four-five Lake Shore Drive, by eight o'clock." She found herself glancing at her watch. It was already after six. "And if you call the cops, I'll shoot a bullet into his brain. Got it?"

"Yes," Alicia said, her voice weak. He had to be joking. It was a trick! He would never hurt Jason. They were in on this together. Weren't they?

"And don't be late."

The line went dead.

Alicia slipped through the window of three-two-four-five Lake Shore Drive as silently as humanly possible. She drew it closed behind her, inch by perilous inch.

The streetlight outside provided just enough illumination to enable her to avoid the furniture in the large ranch-style house. She cracked open the bedroom door and heard voices down the hall.

Of all the windows she'd checked, this one was open. Luckily, it connected to a silent, dark room. She knew she was behaving irrationally. She should have called the police. But if Jason was really in danger—No. The threat was too real. The only other option was doing as Henry told her to. But she couldn't stand to let the bully get the better of her.

She'd finally decided to break in, if at all possible, because she had to know the truth. Was Jason in on it? Was everything he'd told her a lie? Or was his life really in danger?

She couldn't admit even to herself why it mattered. Yet, if Henry *had* turned on Jason, there had to be a reason. If he really intended to murder his own nephew—

She shuddered.

Carefully, she slipped through the door and into the hall. The voices were coming through an archway close to the front of the house. She pressed her back against the wall and inched closer to the opening.

She heard Jason's voice. "There are other solutions

to saving your company, Henry. You're committing
all kinds of crimes here. Let me loose and we'll think
this through logically."

So he *was* being held hostage by Henry, if she could
trust what she'd just heard, if it wasn't another act
for her benefit. If they knew she was here—"

But how could they?

Apparently, Jason's uncle had turned on him. The
two rats had gone separate ways, over something. Jason was obviously in trouble. Despite what he'd done
to her, she couldn't fight the fear that swept through
her. Rat that he was, she didn't want him to die.

She wrapped her hand around the butt of the gun
in her coat pocket. It was a tiny thing her ex-husband
had bought her for self-protection because of all her
late nights working alone. She'd had no interest
whatsoever in it. Until now. And she didn't want to
do anything foolish.

She felt so out of her league. She had no experience in anything remotely cloak-and-dagger. Hours
spent in the research lab had done nothing to prepare her for this very real danger. Her pounding
heart echoed in her head, underscoring her own vulnerability.

She heard Henry laughing, and inched closer to
the archway. Peering in, she saw she was at one corner
of the room, and had an excellent view of the interior. It was softly lit, decorated in dark woods and
burgundy accents. A cheerful fire at the far end cast
a cozy atmosphere.

The tension in the room was anything but cozy.
From the side, she could see that Jason was tied to a
massive wooden chair. Thick ropes were wrapped
around his hips, his wrists were bound behind the
chair back, his ankles lashed to the legs. Alicia bit
down a gasp. A bruise colored his left cheek, and a

dried trickle of blood led from the corner of his mouth to his jaw. A huge, brutal-looking man hovered behind Jason.

In front of him paced a silver-haired man in a three-piece suit. She recognized him, all right. Henry Sondheim, CEO and President of Bio-Intera. He'd frightened her before, when she gave notice. First, he'd attempted to sweet-talk her into staying. Failing with that tactic, his words had grown harsh, his demeanor threatening. It had taken her a full day to stop shaking.

At the prospect of taking him on, her heart pounded so loudly that she thought everyone in the room would hear it. But no one noticed her.

"Untie me so we can discuss this, Henry. We don't need her superbug. There are other business opportunities we can explore."

"Name one."

Jason grimaced. Alicia could almost read his mind. He hadn't been paying attention to the business world, so he had no idea what to suggest. He took a different tack. "This situation has gotten way out of hand, Henry. There are other ways to save your company. I'll help you. I'll buy it out. I'll sell off another division if I have to. I can afford it. We don't have to let things go this way. We don't *need* the profits from her research. Hell, I don't even *want* them—not like this."

Henry paced toward the fireplace, his arms crossed over his chest. He seemed to be considering Jason's words.

Jason's voice grew even more conciliatory. "I'm going to be taking more of an interest in the business from now on, Henry, like I said. I'm going to commit myself to making it better, stronger than when my father led the company. I won't let any of our divisions go under—not mine, not yours. I swear it."

Henry's shoulders began to shake, and Alicia thought at first that he was crying. Until he turned around, revealing a wide smile. "Jason, my boy, this is about so much more than Bio-Intera or Kirkland Enterprises. It's high time you realized that." He turned to Tyler, who stood beside the door, his meaty arms crossed. "Ike, leave us."

Alicia stiffened, certain Ike would come through the archway and discover her. But he left the room through a door in the far wall, which probably led to the front hall. Alicia sagged against the wall and tried to steady her heart, praying Ike wouldn't come down the hallway and find her here. He wasn't the sort of man a woman wanted to mess with.

The conversation continued, and Alicia again peered through the archway. Henry had stopped pacing, was now leaning toward Jason, his hands on each arm of the chair. His lips turned up in a half-smile, and when he spoke, the words were almost gentle. "You know what people used to call your dad, Jason? The Golden Boy. Trite and sappy, isn't it?"

He pushed upright again. "Unfortunately, it was also true. Everything he touched he made a success of. His rock-solid business, his gorgeous wife, his bright, handsome son. I was always playing catch-up, every day of my life. 'Oh, and Henry. We'll include him, too,' his friends would say. When his plane went down, I was glad. Glad!" He grinned again, and Alicia shuddered. Her gaze flicked back to Jason, noted how pale he'd grown. "Dad had left him almost everything, and I thought it was my turn. But then I learned your father had left it all to *you*. Do you understand what that did to me, Jason, seeing a kid getting the company? A kid who had no idea what it was even about?"

Jason replied in a steady, calm voice, obviously trying to reason with Henry. "All I understand is that you've gone way over the edge, Henry. You lied about Alicia stealing from you, convinced me I was doing something almost *noble*. That was bad enough." He laughed harshly. "God, I was so naive."

Naive. Alicia would never in a thousand words have applied that word to Jason. She'd been the naive one, hadn't she? But if Jason really had believed his uncle, if he hadn't set out to coldly and calculatedly hurt her—

Her eyes welled with tears she blinked away. A warm glow suffused her. Jason had actually believed he was doing something worthwhile for his family, even righting a wrong. He wasn't the selfish bastard she had cast him as, despite his deception. He was the man she'd opened her heart to, a man who'd opened his heart to her, despite his intentions. The realization washed over her, followed by a flood of fresh emotion toward this man. *He hadn't been out to hurt her.* Despite the confusing mess they'd made of their relationship, she clung fiercely to that one fact.

"But now you've stooped even lower," Jason continued, "to blackmail and kidnapping. And dragging Alicia into this—telling her to *come* here—I swear, if she *does* show up and if you hurt her—"

"Shut up!" Henry snapped, all trace of his smile gone. He ran his hands through his gray hair, then threw them out wide. "I only wanted what I deserved, Jason. That's all. It was my turn, not yours. I'm not a monster. And you—you were my ticket. I ran the businesses through you. You okayed everything I said. Until now."

Jason's eyes had narrowed, and his lips tightened

into a harsh line. "I understand now. As long as I was willing to play by your rules, you put up with me. You probably hoped I'd kill myself at the racetrack, or on the slopes. You *are* my beneficiary." Alicia had never heard such a bitter tone from Jason, hadn't wanted to believe he was capable of feeling such pain. "This Bio-Intera deal—you *wanted* me to get caught, didn't you? You wanted me to get thrown in prison."

Henry chuckled. "Not until after you delivered the superbug to me, Jase. Then of course, it would make sense for them to find out what you'd done. And for me, who had nothing at all to do with such a nasty business, to have full legal control of our family holdings."

Jason shook his head, cursing under his breath. "Damn, I've been so blind."

"What I still can't figure out is why you had to choose this moment to get soft on a woman. You've had models, starlets, heiresses. None of them ever meant anything to you." He crossed his arms and rocked back on his heels. "You know it and I know it. Even that bitch you almost married. She turned on you, or have you forgotten how she devastated you?"

Jason shook his head. "My broken engagement has nothing to do with this."

"Women can't be trusted, Jason. Especially that prissy doctor. She's only getting what's coming to her. She deserted my company when I needed her, and now it's payback time."

"If you dare hurt her, I'll kill you. I swear it!" Jason gritted his teeth, the cords on his neck standing out in stark relief. He yanked against the ropes binding his arms. Alicia stifled a gasp at the angry red welts that had already formed on his wrists. Suddenly, he jerked forward, as if to lunge from the chair.

Startled, Henry jumped back. But he reclaimed his composure soon enough. "Such a weak man after all. I suppose you've convinced yourself that you're actually in love with her."

Jason's impassioned voice filled the room. "Yes, I love her, Henry. That's the way it is and nothing will change it. Got it?"

At his declaration, a rush of tears flooded Alicia's eyes. She fought to remain clearheaded. She couldn't think about what Jason might mean by love. She couldn't allow herself to be vulnerable to him, not anymore.

Henry stared at Jason for several long moments, as if deciding something. He slipped his hand under his coat.

A flash of steel caught the firelight, and Alicia realized Henry had pulled out a handgun. He thrust the muzzle under Jason's chin. "Say good-bye, Jason. It's time."

Without another moment's thought, Alicia burst into the room, pointing her gun at Henry with one shaking hand. She'd never played the tough gal, never even shot the stupid gun in practice. But she had to do her best. "Drop the gun, right now."

Both men's gazes were riveted on her, and Henry's mouth opened in shock. He began to raise his gun toward her. Alicia knew she had to prove she meant business or she'd quickly be disarmed and no better off than Jason. Aiming at the wall behind Henry, she squeezed the trigger. The shot was nowhere near accurate, whizzing much closer to Henry's ear than she'd intended. It shattered the glass of a picture on the wall. Henry tossed the gun away and dropped to the floor amid the shattered glass.

Jason appeared grateful—and devastated. "Alicia!

What are you doing here? Get out of here; it isn't safe."

"And let this bastard shoot you? I don't *think* so." The strength of her voice surprised even Alicia. Keeping the gun on Henry, she knelt and retrieved his gun from the floor. "Now, you," she said, waving the gun at Henry. "Untie him right now or I'll put a bullet through your brain." She hoped Henry couldn't see how her hands were shaking.

As Henry got to his feet, Ike reappeared. Alicia felt the blood drain from her face and her stomach wrenched. He was carrying the biggest, meanest gun she'd ever seen outside of the movies. Her own little pistol was laughable in comparison.

As casually as if he were picking flowers, Ike strode over to Alicia and pulled the gun from her fingers. He tucked it in his waistband, then stood with his legs spread, his gun pointed straight at her heart.

"Lower the piece, Ike. She's not going anywhere. Not so long as I have what she wants." He moved behind Jason and jerked his chin up. "Right, Jase?"

"Fuck off," Jason said.

Henry reacted instantly, slamming his elbow into the side of Jason's head.

"Stop it!" Alicia cried. "Let him go. You want the stupid bacteria, well, I brought it with me."

Henry peered at her. "*Did* you now? That's a good girl. Goodness, Jason, she must really have the hots for you. So, Doctor, where is it?"

"In my car. In the trunk. I parked half a block away. The red Toyota."

"Ike, hold down the fort." Henry strode from the room. Alicia heard the door slam behind him.

Silence descended on the room, punctuated by Jason's harsh breaths. "What in the hell are you doing here?" he asked, his words sharp. "I told you not to come."

"Don't you dare talk to me in that tone," Alicia shot back. She took a step toward him, and Ike raised his gun. She glared at the heavy. A new strength filled her, conviction borne of her love for the man in the chair. "Oh, back off," she said in disgust. "I'm not going to do anything drastic." She lifted Jason's chin and examined his bruise.

"You amaze me," he said, his husky voice playing along her taut nerves. "I can't believe you're here. I'm the one who's supposed to take stupid risks."

His loving gaze met hers and her heart skipped a beat. "I wasn't sure the kidnapping was real," she said softly. "I thought you might be in on it."

"I expected you would," Jason said wryly. "I never thought I'd see you again." He stared at her elfin face, now set with fierce determination. Pride swept through him. She had stuck her adorable neck out for him, after the way he'd hurt her. Risked her life in a foolish—and impossibly brave—rescue attempt. His heart squeezed painfully tight in his chest.

Uncle Henry had resented him from the beginning, resented his father. He should have seen his uncle's real motives. He would have if he'd been more involved in the business instead of off living the high life. He should have pulled his head out of his ass long enough to realize what was going on around him. Because of his foolishness, Alicia would pay the price.

There was no way to predict Henry's next move, and now Alicia was smack in the middle of it. How could he have been so foolish as to put her at such risk? She, this woman who'd awakened his heart, who made him realize he just might have something to live for. She'd revived his conscience. Now he would do everything in his power to protect her from the horror he'd brought on her. "Alicia," he said softly, so only she could hear, "I'm not worth you risking yourself."

"Just—stop it." Her eyes flashed, her lips stiffened. "Just because I'm here doesn't mean I've forgiven you."

Jason's shoulders sagged. He knew he had no right to expect her to forgive him. God knows, she deserved much better than him.

Yet she had come.

If he could have the chance—if he should be so lucky—he would spend his life making it up to her. "I don't expect you to forgive me. I don't deserve—"

"Shut up, Kirkland," she said sharply. She lowered her face to his. "Stop talking so I can kiss you."

Pleasure flowed through Jason at her words, and he snapped his mouth closed.

"Hey!" Ike said sharply.

Alicia ignored him. So did Jason. He lifted his head, closing the inches between them in a deliciously solid kiss that left no doubt how badly he ached to hold her, to make it up to her.

Conscious of Ike's beady eyes on them, Alicia forced herself to break the kiss. She sucked in a deep breath. "Now, listen. I brought what he wants." She gazed at him so lovingly, Jason felt his eyes grow moist. She stroked his sore cheek. "Oh, Jason, I'm so sorry."

"*You're* sorry? *I'm* the one who believed him. I tried to steal from you."

"Don't apologize for trusting your uncle, Jason. Of course you trusted him. You didn't even know me. How else could anyone expect you to feel about your only family?"

Intellectually, he knew why she understood, lacking family of her own. But her willingness to forgive filled Jason with awe. God, he loved her. He opened his mouth to tell her just that, but Ike appeared behind her.

"Back off, lady." He shoved Alicia away with one hand and pressed his gun to Jason's temple.

Alicia lifted her hands and took a step back. "Calm down. We were just talking."

He waved the gun toward Alicia, then at a chair across the room. "Go sit over there."

Alicia did as he ordered, not wanting to put Jason at any more risk. She only hoped his uncle would calm down and let Jason go once he had the bacteria in his hands.

She sat on the couch and found herself gripping her hands together. But she couldn't stop gazing at Jason, unable to deny her strong emotions for this man. She didn't know how—or *if*—they could ever have a future after all the lies between them. Nor could she think about it now, not when they both could very likely end up dead before the night was through. The shocks, the terror of the past hours stripped away all but the most basic emotions—desperate fear for their survival and the fierce, undeniable intensity of her love for Jason, a love that somehow made her feel stronger and more confident than she ever had.

Her gaze caressed him. His wrists appeared raw from the rope, and his fingers almost white. "You've tied his hands too tight," she told Ike. "His hands are going numb."

"How did you—" Jason started.

"Shut up, bitch. We don't want him going anywhere—yet." Ike spread his legs and lifted his gun toward her again.

"Don't talk to her like that," Jason said. His biceps

tensed and bunched as ne tugged them against the ropes, drawing blood from his raw skin.

Ike took a step toward him and raised his fist.

"Don't hit him!" she said. "Henry hasn't said you could, now has he?"

Ike hesitated, then lowered his fist. He backed off, taking a post equidistant between them, his feet braced apart.

Alicia's gaze met Jason's and he smiled gently at her. She knew he didn't want her interfering, but she couldn't help it. Just as he couldn't help trying to defend her. Seeing him like this, knowing he'd ended up this way because he fell in love with her . . . Her eyes met his, and she couldn't hide the love she felt for him. In response, Jason's expression softened still further.

The front door slammed. Seconds later, Henry appeared, a small cooler in his hands. He popped it open and glanced inside. "This is it, hmm? Excellent, Doctor." He cast Alicia a friendly smile. "Just make yourself at home while I put this in the refrigerator."

When he returned, his hands were encased in thick black gloves. He carried a glass of water and a quart-sized cylinder with a handle on top. With shock, Alicia recognized the lead-shielded radioisotope container. Her stomach clenched. She didn't like the looks of this. Henry ought to be letting them go. He had what he wanted.

"Alicia, thank you so much for providing what I need," Henry said. "But there's a small problem. You know too much about me, about how I arranged this little gift from you. You also refused to come work for me, when I just *know* I need a scientist of your caliber to make this marvelous little bacteria marketable. Which leaves me with a dilemma."

He crossed the room as he spoke, and now he was

staring down at her, the heavy container and glass in his hands. He set the glass on the table beside her and lifted the container. "See this? You know what this is, don't you, Alicia? A shielded transport container for a radioactive isotope. Well, let me tell you what we plan to do with this little isotope pellet. Once you take it—I've provided water for you to wash it down with—you're going to die of radiation poisoning in a matter of hours."

Alicia's blood turned to ice and she could almost swear her heart stopped beating. She couldn't image a more painful way to die.

"What!" Jason rasped out.

Henry ignored him. "Once you're dead, we'll take your body to your house and dump it there. The police, when they find out your occupation, will understand that this was, indeed, an accident. And you'll never be able to tell anyone about our little arrangement."

"You're insane, Alicia whispered, fighting desperately to hide the shivers that had taken over her body.

"No, no, not insane. I merely understand what I need to do to get ahead—unlike some men." He glowered at Jason. "Of course, there *is* an alternative."

"Let me guess," she said through stiff lips. "You want me to work for you."

Henry smiled a winning smile. "Exactly. You should never have left me, Alicia. I want you back. You, and all of your work. Now, that's not such a hard decision to make, is it?"

"No, it isn't," Alicia said, unable to tear her eyes from the lead container Henry cradled in his hands. Cold, stark, a vessel carrying certain, painful death. She lifted her eyes to his flintlike gaze. "Okay. I'll work for you, Henry. But you have to let Jason go, right now."

"Alicia, don't worry about—" Jason started.

Henry cut off his protest, his face hardening. "Oh, *Jason*, is it?" he said sarcastically. "That's what you're concerned about, *Jason*? You fancy you *love* Jason, don't you? You make me sick."

He paced back toward Jason, the isotope container still in his hands. "Ike, put your gun to the good doctor's head, please."

Alicia froze as the metal touched her temple. Her eyes wide, she met Jason's panicked gaze.

"Henry, let her go right now," Jason rasped. "You can *have* my dad's company, or whatever you want."

"You read my mind, Jason," Henry said, his voice silky smooth. "As you said, I am your beneficiary." He set the isotope container by Jason's feet. "Now, unless you want to see the good doctor's brains spread all over the room, you'll take the pellet in this container."

"No!" Alicia started up off the couch, but Ike shoved her back. She landed on the cushions. "Jason—"

"If I take it, how do I know you won't kill her anyway?" Jason asked.

Henry shrugged. "It's a risk, admittedly. But you won't die right away. You can even kiss her goodbye—after you swallow the pellet."

Alicia met Jason's gaze. His face appeared white, but his jaw was locked with determination. "I'll do it, on one condition. Those photos of Alicia and me. And the negatives. I want to see them burn."

Henry nodded his head. He retreated to his desk in the corner and unlocked a drawer. Alicia watched in horror as he extracted an envelope. He was going to meet Jason's requirement. "Here they are. Are you certain you want them destroyed? Ike did such a fine job taking them."

"Let me see them, so I know that's all of them." Henry held the negatives up to the light, and Jason studied him, one by one, his expression grim. Then he nodded. "Throw them in the fireplace. I won't have you threatening her with them."

"They won't even matter after Alicia joins my staff and everyone learns she's been working for me all along. Of course, she might have to go to prison for violating her agreement with Envirotech—"

Jason gritted his teeth. *"Burn them."*

Henry threw the photos on the fire, along with the negatives. The acrid smell of burning film filled Alicia's nostrils.

While they burned, Henry returned to Jason's feet and began unscrewing the top of the isotope container.

Panic spread through Alicia. Forgetting about the gun at her temple, she jumped to her feet. "Don't do it, Jason. There's no cure for it—you *know* that."

Ike rammed the gun on her shoulder and she fell back into the couch once more.

Tears welled in Alicia's eyes as Henry used a pair of tweezers to extract the hard black pellet, about the size of a marble. He lifted it toward Jason's face.

Alicia didn't care about Ike and his gun—she shoved past him and ran toward Jason. Ike caught her when she was two feet away. The steel bands of his arms locked around her, freezing her in place. She struggled futilely against the massive man. Ike shoved the barrel of his gun under her chin.

"Should he blow off her head, Jason?" Henry asked, holding the pellet toward Jason's mouth. "Or are you going to swallow this? It's convenient that you work at Envirotech, around all that radiation.

We'll simply dump your body on your boat and let the authorities figure it out."

"It won't work," Alicia burst out, desperate. "I'll know the truth."

"But you won't say anything, will you? Because if you betray me, the same thing will happen to you, and Jason's death will have been in vain."

Alicia gaped at him. "You're crazy!"

"No, dear, only desperate. *Now,* Jason. Take it now, or Ike shoots her."

Alicia talked fast, dread pounding through her. "Jason, there's no guarantee he won't shoot me anyway! Don't take it, I beg you—"

"Alicia," Jason said, his voice unnaturally steady. "I don't have a choice. If there's a chance he'll free you—"

"Jason, no!"

He smiled, his eyes reflecting tenderness and a deep poignancy. "It doesn't take a nuclear scientist to figure out which one of us the world will miss more."

Alicia cried out, struggled harder, but Ike clamped a hand over her mouth, nearly suffocating her.

"I didn't want to have to do this, Jason," Henry said. "But you've driven me to it." He yanked Jason's head back and shoved the pellet down his throat. Jason gagged, then swallowed, and the deed was done.

Tears burst in Alicia's eyes, trickled down her face. She blinked rapidly, wanting to see Jason, let him know she was with him.

"Let her go, Ike," Henry said.

Ike complied. Alicia's legs gave way and she fell to her knees. She crawled toward Jason. When she reached him, she pressed her head into his lap. She knew he'd ingested hundreds of rads. He would be dead in a matter of hours. She shot a bitter look at Henry. "Untie him. He can't hurt you anymore."

Henry nodded. "Go ahead and free him, Ike, but keep the gun on them both."

Ike did as Henry said.

Jason rubbed at his raw, bleeding wrists. Alicia's heart twisted in agony. She pulled his face into her hands. "You shouldn't have, Jason. You shouldn't have."

He tore his eyes from hers and looked at Henry. "Let her go, Henry."

Henry shrugged his shoulders. "I thought she would want to stay around and watch you die. It isn't every day a nuclear scientist gets to witness a case of lethal radiation poisoning. Tell me, Alicia, what's the first symptom we can expect?"

Alicia turned on Henry. "You *monster.*"

"Don't—" Jason warned, his eyes on Ike's gun.

"Don't worry, Jason. We'll take care of her, in time. Once my scientists are certain the bacteria is healthy."

"What—" Jason began.

He crossed his arms, a wicked smile curling his lips. "Oh, I wasn't planning on killing her *that* soon, Jason. Do you honestly think I'd be fool enough to trust her a second time? She deserted me once as it is." He must have forgotten Jason was no longer bound to the chair, for he turned his back on him.

The next moments happened so fast, Alicia fought to follow them. One minute she was kneeling before Jason, the next he'd launched himself out of the chair and toward Ike. He shoved the large man down and rolled with him on the floor, the gun between them. Alicia cried out.

Henry scrambled toward them, but before he could reach them, Jason tore the gun from Ike's hands and slammed the butt against the thug's huge head. The man folded like a paper doll.

Jason jumped to his feet and grasped Henry around the throat, holding the gun to his head. "Okay, Uncle, let's play this my way. Alicia, get behind me and go out the door to your car. Go straight to the police."

Alicia ran to the isotope container and picked it up, screwing the lid on. She hurried back to his side, but not before snatching up a throw from the back of a sofa.

Jason appeared mystified by her actions. "Alicia?"

"No, Jason. I'm not going alone."

Jason looked at her in confusion. "Now's not the time to argue!"

"I won't leave you."

"Does it honestly matter anymore?"

"Yes! You're coming with me, and that's final!"

"All right!" Jason shoved Henry away. The man stumbled to his knees, joining Ike on the floor. Jason covered both Henry and the prone Ike with the gun and began backing toward the door. "Don't move," he said. "Alicia, get out now."

The container and throw in her arms, Alicia stepped out of the room first, but Jason didn't follow. He stared down at his uncle, then lifted the gun, aiming it at Henry's head. "I *trusted* you," Jason said, his voice shaking. "I was a lonely, lost kid, needing guidance. But you *used* me." He cocked the hammer, his arm tensing. "You're nothing but a crook and a murderer."

Alicia had never seen such a terrible look on a man's face. Jason had absolutely nothing to lose. "Jason, *no*," Alicia said. "Don't make it worse. You're above that."

He cast her a sideways glance, must have seen the

pleading in her eyes. After an endless moment, he released the hammer and stepped away from his uncle, then followed her out of the house.

"We have to get out of here, Jason," Alicia said. "Fast."

"This way." Jason led her in a dead run toward a sleek Maseratti parked in the circular drive. He yanked open the door and slipped in. "I left a spare key—here." He pulled it from its hiding place under the floor mat.

Alicia followed him to the driver's side. She tossed the container and throw in the backseat. "Get in the back and let me drive, Jason! You need to lie down and rest."

Jason glanced at her. "What are you talking about? Get in!" He jammed the key in the ignition and gunned the engine. Just then the door of the house flew open and Ike lumbered out at a dead run.

Alicia knew when to give up. She scrambled around the car and hurled herself in the passenger side. Jason was backing the car out of the driveway before she closed the door. The car screamed down the incline into the street. Jason shifted into drive and the car shot forward.

Alicia pressed herself back against the seat as Jason pressed the powerful engine into performing for him. They were already doing fifty in this residential area.

Several blocks later, Alicia told him to pull over. "Why?"

"Just do it, Jason."

He squealed the car to a stop at the curb.

"Now, throw up."

"On demand?"

"Do it! If you don't make yourself get that thing

up, I'll do it for you, and I warn you, I can be real rough if I have to be."

She peered closely at him as he attempted to gag himself. Shoulders hunched, he jammed his fingers down his throat. It worked. He fell to his knees, retching. Alicia held his head, but her eyes were on the contents of his stomach. She made certain he'd expelled the nasty pellet. Then, using the throw she'd grabbed from Henry's house, she quickly lifted it and replaced it in the receptacle. She stashed both in the trunk, knowing the car would have to be decontaminated—and so would she.

But Jason . . . Her gaze fell to where he still knelt by the curb. "Jason, get back in the car. We have to get to my place. There's a chance. It's slim but we have to try."

He rose, his face ashen, and wiped his face on his torn shirt. "You'd be safer with the cops, Alicia."

"We don't have time for that."

She began to slip behind the wheel, but Jason pulled her out. "If we're moving fast, I'm driving."

"Do you feel well enough?"

"Get in, Alicia.

She sighed and reclaimed her passenger seat. This time, she managed to get her seat belt fastened before Jason slammed his foot on the accelerator.

If Alicia had thought they were moving fast before, she'd been dreaming. At every reckless pass between and around other vehicles, at every squealing tight turn, she thought she'd pass out. Jason took each corner without even braking, moving in a wide arc that barely missed the sidewalks. He all but ignored the stop signs and signals. Center medians meant nothing to him. But he was driving a hell of a lot faster than she would have dared.

"Let me guess—you race cars for fun, right?"

"Mm-hmm," Jason grunted. "You said you wanted fast, Alicia. Just hope I don't run into any cops."

"If you do, outrun them. We *have* to get to my place."

"Why?" He shot her a wry smile. "Because you want me to die in your bed?"

"That doesn't even begin to be funny, Jason Kirkland."

He grew somber. "Yeah. I know."

"You did an incredibly stupid thing, swallowing that pellet," she said. She blinked furiously to keep the tears at bay. "Stupid, and extremely brave."

"Hey," Jason said tenderly. He glanced at her, reached out and brushed a tear from her cheek. "It's like I said—I'm not worth much. You're what's important here."

"Don't say that, Jason," Alicia said hotly. "Talk like that really infuriates me."

"All right. Think of it this way: I'm the original risk-taker. What's one more?" He tried to sound humorous, but Alicia heard his underlying despair.

"Well, you just took a whopper of one. I don't know if I can save you."

Jason snapped his head toward her. "*Save* me? You can do that?"

"I don't know. Just—just don't let your body metabolize too fast."

Jason exhaled. "Yeah, right." He skidded the car around a corner. Alicia could almost feel his adrenaline surging as he concentrated on getting maximum speed from the high-performance car. "Just being around you gets my blood pumping, Alicia."

"Well, stop it."

He flashed her a smile. "Yes, Doctor."

Alicia found herself smiling in response. Just being with him again made her feel good—

What was she thinking? She was about to lose him. She bit her lip; her stomach twisting with fear, in panic. Never in her life had she felt such desperation, as if all her brain power had to matter—*now*—or nothing would ever matter again. "Damn oh damn oh damn," she cursed under her breath. "Just hurry. But don't crash."

Jason hit the highway and accelerated to ninety, dodging in and out of other cars from one lane to the other. The speedometer slipped up to one hundred. Then one fifteen. The scene flashing outside the windshield reminded Alicia of racecar arcade games—except when she played them, she always crashed and burned.

She forced her gaze from the frenetic scene before her and pinned it on Jason. If they crashed—if she died—they'd die together. She could accept that. Any chance to save him was worth the risk.

She didn't speak the rest of the way, didn't want to distract him. His handsome face was set in grim determination, his grip on the steering wheel turning his knuckles white. Beads of perspiration sprang out on his forehead, whether from concentration or from the ill effects of the pellet, she didn't know.

Finally, he turned onto her street, the tires skidding on the pavement. After two more blocks, Jason slammed on the brakes, yanking the car into her driveway.

"Follow me," she commanded, jumping out of the car.

Jason didn't come as quickly as she hoped. He looked whiter than before. But he pried himself out of the narrow seat and followed her to the door.

Once inside, Alicia made him lie down on the couch. He looked deathly pale. He curled up on his side and started to shiver. Alicia pulled a blanket over him. "Just stay put. I'll be right back."

She ran down the basement steps into her lab and snapped on the light, then pulled two flasks from the refrigerator. On her way up the stairs, she worked the stopper open on one.

She knelt beside Jason and held the open flask out to him. "Here. Drink this. All of it."

Jason sat up and took it. "Magic potion?"

"Drink it, Jason."

He up-ended the flask and drained it. Then he shuddered and handed it back to her. "That was noxious, Alicia. What'd you give—aah!" He crumpled, his hands pressing to his stomach, his face twisted in pain.

"Jason!" Alicia sat beside him and pulled him into her arms. "It hurts, doesn't it?"

He nodded, his head pressed to her chest. "A cramp," he gasped out. "But it's fading."

It didn't look like it was fading. Jason was alarmingly pale. He was already exhibiting the first sign of an intense internal radiation dose—nausea as the stomach began to disintegrate. Her solution was no doubt pointless. But she'd had to try.

It had done so well in controlled laboratory tests here at her home. She had been about to request funding from Envirotech to move on to small mammal testing. Instead, she was jumping straight to a human test subject. To the man she loved.

She opened the second flask and drained it, trying hard not to gag at the rotten-egg taste. She had to take it, too. Just being around Jason right now put her in danger of exposure. He himself had become a radiation source.

She set the empty flask aside and cradled him in her arms. "I really hate that uncle of yours."

"I'm not too fond of him myself right now," Jason said, his voice strained. He nestled his head on her lap, his knees curled tight against his chest. He groaned, another spasm wracking his body.

Alicia stroked his forehead. "I'm sorry, Jason. I haven't had a chance to develop the treatment. It's completely experimental. All I know is it that absorbs radiation exposure to tissue samples in petri dishes, seems to repair damaged cells, even at the chromosomal level. The chance that it will do any good at all for you is slim to none. But if I'd taken you to a hospital . . . They couldn't do anything for you either but watch you die." Tears clogged her throat. "I—I wish I were smarter. I wish I'd spent more *time* on it! I've been working on my own to develop it. If I hadn't spent so many hours at Envirotech—"

Jason grasped her hand and pressed it to his lips. His eyes met hers, bright and tender. "I love you, Alicia."

She swallowed past a lump in her throat. "I know."

He pressed her hand to his chest. "You came to rescue me."

"I came to find out if you were in on it," she said. "I—I didn't want to think you would be, but—"

"But I didn't give you much reason to trust me. I'm amazed you can stand the sight of me."

She forced a weak laugh through her tight throat. "Yeah, well, when a man sacrifices himself for a woman, that tends to mean something." Her heart filled with tenderness, and she knew that, if by some miracle he survived, she would give him every chance in the world to prove his words. She tenderly pushed a sweat-soaked tendril of hair off his forehead. "Why did you go along with his plan, Jason? You're such a sweet guy."

Jason's lips turned up at the corner. "Right. When

I'm not cheating, stealing or otherwise causing trouble for beautiful lady scientists." He sighed, and his eyes grew distant. "Would you believe I actually thought I owed it to my uncle? He told me he needed me. I guess I liked being needed by someone."

Alicia pressed her lips to his forehead, which felt unnaturally hot. "Hey, you don't have to worry about that anymore. I'm quite happy to take on that job."

His eyes darkened. "Well, I need you right now, darling. I'm—I'm going to be sick here—"

Alicia jumped up and helped him to the bathroom, helped him through the worst of the nausea. After the ordeal, she couldn't help but notice that deep circles had imprinted themselves under his eyes, and his skin had taken on an ashy pallor.

Once she'd settled Jason on the couch again, Alicia ran to her lab. She pulled out another flask of the bacterial solution and grabbed the Geiger counter on the way out the door.

She made Jason drink the second flask. When she ran the Geiger counter over him, the needle shot up to one thousand millirems.

Jason looked dolefully at the device, which emitted a rapid clicking the closer she moved it to his stomach. "That's bad, isn't it?"

"Well, it's not good."

"Hold me, Alicia. I'm getting a little scared here."

Alicia cradled his head on her lap again. *A little scared.* Quite an admission from the original risk-taker. And he had every right to be. In a matter of hours, he'd start to bleed out, his hair would fall out, and his vital organs would cease to function. She'd seen it all before, seen it happen to her own mother, only over a period of months. The horror of it haunted her still. And now she would relive it again.

Alicia bit back a sob, not wanting to cry in front

of Jason. But nothing equaled the pain Jason was about to endure, the gut-wrenching agony of massive exposure.

Alicia knew she was violating all the rules of science. And she was breaking the protocol for working with radiation. Jason should be handled with plastic gloves. She was probably exposing herself just letting him rest his head in her lap.

And she didn't give a damn.

Jason fell into a restless sleep. Most likely, he would never wake up.

Several hundred rads . . . Enough radiation to kill a man a hundred times over. His uncle was evil, pure and simple. And he'd acted out of pure, unadulterated greed. His nephew had meant nothing to him but a means to an end, a way to claim the family fortune he thought was owed to him.

Alicia pulled the phone over and dialed 9-1-1. She began to make a report, knowing that in a few hours a murder would have been committed. The victim was even now lying in her lap, the life seeping out of him. She didn't give her name, not yet. She couldn't risk the cops sending an ambulance, taking Jason away and putting him in isolation somewhere, to die alone.

Her voice sounded remarkably cool as she spoke to the detective on the line. She drew on strength she never knew she had. If it was the last thing she did, she'd see Henry Sondheim punished.

"Alicia?"

She started awake. Sunlight cascaded through the living room window.

Alicia rubbed her eyes. She must have nodded off some time toward morning.

The police had called her back once, around 2 A.M., to tell her that Henry Sondheim had been found dead at the house he'd been renting. All the signs pointed to suicide. Her small silver pistol had been found clutched in his hand, and the back of his head was blown off as if he'd shot himself in the mouth. Alicia wondered if he'd really killed himself, or if Ike Tyler had had something to do with it. The police were looking for him, but Tyler had disappeared back into the gutter he'd crawled out of.

"Alicia?"

She glanced down, surprised to see Jason calmly gazing up at her. His head was still nestled in her lap.

It was morning. Hours had passed—far too much time for Jason to be alive. "Jason? How do you feel?"

He yawned, with a healthy full-body stretch. "I must've drifted off."

"Yes, you did," Alicia said, staring at him in shock. "But now—"

Jason resettled his head on her lap and ran his hand over his flat stomach. "It doesn't hurt anymore. My stomach, I mean. Is that what usually happens?"

"Usually?" Her eyes grew wide. "Jason, are you telling me you feel *better?*"

"Yeah, that's the gist of it." He sat up. He still looked pale, but his eyes sparkled. "The cramping's stopped. What other symptoms are there?"

"Diarrhea, vomiting, bleeding—"

Jason grimaced. "Nope, I don't feel inclined, thank you very much." He stood up and headed to the bathroom.

"Where are you going?"

"To clean up. I feel kind of . . . grimy."

Alicia followed him, shocked to the core. She stared as he turned on the water, then stripped out of his clothes. He glanced at her. "Are you here to join me, or what?"

Alicia lifted her hand, as if afraid he'd vanish. "Just hold it right there. Hold it—" She ran into the living room and grabbed the Geiger counter, then rushed back into the bathroom.

The device was clicking at background levels. When she brought it to Jason's stomach, it continued to click at the same level.

"My God, Jason. My God, you're not hot anymore."

Jason arched an eyebrow. "Oh, really?" He took the Geiger counter from her hands and set it down, then narrowed the distance between them to a matter of inches. He ran his knuckles along her cheek, his voice dropping seductively. "If you don't think I'm hot, it just may ruin my plans."

Alicia's heart pounded. "Plans?"

"To convince you to marry me." He winked. Then he slipped into the shower and closed the door behind him.

Alicia stared at his silhouette behind the door, numb with shock—and a growing elation. "Jason Kirkland Sondheim," she called out. "What do you think you're doing? Don't you realize what this means?"

Without warning, Jason popped open the shower door, reached out a hand and yanked her under the water with him. The warm spray pasted her clothes to her body, plastered her hair to her head and washed away all the fear and pain of the past few hours.

Jason slipped his arms around her and pulled her hard against his amazingly healthy body. She gazed up at the brightest emerald eyes she'd ever seen. "For your information, I know exactly what this means.

You just saved my life. And I'm going to make sure you never live it down." He kissed her gently. "With you in my life, I have a hell of a lot to live for, Alicia. No more pointless risks. You will marry me, won't you?"

Alicia nodded, joy filling her. "Yes." She smiled coyly and looped her arms around his neck. "After all, I *have* to stick around, just to make sure there aren't any strange side effects from my treatment. It's the scientific thing to do."

Jason's hands swept down her back and he cupped her bottom firmly. "Oh, so *that's* the reason?"

"Well, maybe there's another."

He arched an eyebrow. "And that is?"

She bit her lip and smiled. "I'm not quite done conducting experiments with the office janitor."

Jason chuckled. "Ex-office janitor," he corrected, just before he buried his mouth on hers.

ABOUT THE AUTHOR

As a corporate communicator, Tracy Cozzens spent much of her career writing about the decidedly unromantic topic of nuclear waste cleanup. Not finding the subject quite as compelling as Dr. Alicia Underwood does, she turned to romance writing to stretch her creative wings. After years in the Pacific Northwest, Tracy Cozzens now lives in New York State with her husband and son. *Seducing Alicia* is her second Bouquet romance.

Tracy loves to hear from readers. You can contact her via E-mail:

Tracy Cozzens@aol.com

Or in care of the publisher:

Kensington Publishing Corporation
850 Third Avenue
New York, NY 10022

BOOK YOUR PLACE ON OUR WEBSITE AND MAKE THE READING CONNECTION!

We've created a customized website just for our very special readers, where you can get the inside scoop on everything that's going on with Zebra, Pinnacle and Kensington books.

When you come online, you'll have the exciting opportunity to:

- View covers of upcoming books
- Read sample chapters
- Learn about our future publishing schedule (listed by publication month *and author*)
- Find out when your favorite authors will be visiting a city near you
- Search for and order backlist books from our online catalog
- Check out author bios and background information
- Send e-mail to your favorite authors
- Meet the Kensington staff online
- Join us in weekly chats with authors, readers and other guests
- Get writing guidelines
- AND MUCH MORE!

**Visit our website at
http://www.zebrabooks.com**

COMING IN JUNE FROM
ZEBRA BOUQUET ROMANCES

#49 THE MEN OF SUGAR MOUNTAIN: TWO HEARTS
by Vivian Leiber
__(0-8217-6623-6, $3.99) Kate left home in search of Mr. Right, and thought she'd found him in the big city. Now, broke and rejected by her blueblood husband, Kate is back home. She's determined to salvage her marriage, with some help from an unexpected ally—Sheriff Matt Skylar. Little does she know, the hunky lawman is planning to make her *his* wife!

__**#50 THE RIGHT CHOICE** by Karen Drogin
(0-8217-6624-4, $3.99) Carly Wexler is planning her wedding the same way she has planned her life—perfectly, with no loose ends or real passion. Though her heart doesn't leap when she thinks of her fiancé, she's certain this union is for the best. Until she meets sexy Mike Novack, who is everything she's trying to avoid . . . hot, passionate, and forbidden.

__**#51 LOVE IN BLOOM** by Michaila Callan
(0-8217-6625-2 $3.99) Seventeen years ago, model Eva Channing ran from the glamorous world of New York fashion to small town Texas where she could forget her passionate, doomed affair with photographer Carson Brandt. Today, Eva is content . . . until a magazine piece on former models brings Carson tumbling back into her life . . .

__**#52 WORTH THE WAIT** by Kathryn Attalla
(0-8217-6626-0, $3.99) Abandoned to foster homes as a child, beautiful Charlie Lawson is steel and velvet on the outside but, on the inside, she's vulnerable and lonely. Even though she longs for romance, Charlie decided never to give anyone the chance to hurt her . . . until sexy, compassionate Damian Westfield makes her believe in love again.

Call toll free **1-888-345-BOOK** to order by phone or use this coupon to order by mail.

Name_____
Address_____
City _____ State _____ Zip _____
Please send me the books I have checked above.
I am enclosing $_____
Plus postage and handling* $_____
Sales tax (in NY and TN) $_____
Total amount enclosed $_____
*Add $2.50 for the first book and $.50 for each additional book.
Send check or money order (no cash or CODs) to: **Kensington Publishing Corp. Dept. C.O., 850 Third Avenue, New York, NY 10022**
Prices and numbers subject to change without notice. Valid only in the U.S.
All books will be available 6/1/00. All orders subject to availability.
Visit our website at www.kensingtonbooks.com.